## Advance Praise for *When the Stars Go Blue*

"A fresh, new spin on a classic tale; Caridad Ferrer delivers a dreamy romance with all the necessary ingredients: a feisty heroine, an irresistible hero, and an ending that will make you swoon. Delicious from beginning to end—I devoured it in one sitting!"

—Alyson Noël, number-one *New York Times* bestselling author of The Immortals series

"With the grace of a ballerina and the fiery moves of a salsa dancer, Caridad Ferrer's *When the Stars Go Blue jetés* into the reader's heart in a story as romantic, funny, dramatic, and moving as the best of *So You Think You Can Dance.*"

—Lauren Baratzé-Logsted, author of *Crazy Beautiful* and *The Education of Bet*

"For fans of drum corps or marching band, this novel is your automatic read of the year. For everyone else . . . Come for two hot guys in love with one driven dancer. Stay for the lyrical prose that captures spicy Miami and entices you on a young woman's cross-country tour as she comes of age among a hundred and fifty men! Don't miss this adrenaline-filled performance of a lifetime."

—Jennifer Echols, author of *Going Too Far*

"*When the Stars Go Blue* captures the best of YA romance, and much like *Adiós to My Old Life,* it allows unique characters with incredible talents to reach out to the reader and sweep them away. The pace is fast, the writing is lyrical, and the characters are graceful and real. Soledad allows the reader to experience again the painful clarity and confusion of love through the complexity of her own perspective. Books like this are why I love YA romance."

—Sarah Wendell, Smart Bitches, Trashy Books blog and coauthor of *Beyond Heaving Bosoms: The Smart Bitches' Guide to Romance Novels*

## also by caridad ferrer

*it's not about the accent*

*adiós to my old life*

# when
# the stars
# go blue

## caridad ferrer

Thomas Dunne Books
St. Martin's Griffin
New York

THOMAS DUNNE BOOKS.
An imprint of St. Martin's Press.

WHEN THE STARS GO BLUE. Copyright © 2010 by Barbara Ferrer. All rights reserved. Printed in the United States of America. For information, address St. Martin's Press, 175 Fifth Avenue, New York, N.Y. 10010.

www.thomasdunnebooks.com
www.stmartins.com

ISBN 978-0-312-65004-9

First Edition: December 2010

10  9  8  7  6  5  4  3  2  1

For Lewis, who always believes
And for Torrie, through thick and thin, my sister

# acknowledgments

This book has had such a long road and there are so many thanks I have to offer. First off, to my fabulous agent, Adrienne, who totally "got" this story from the get-go. Thank you for the roosters and talking-me-off-the-ledge conversations. To my lovely editor, Toni, I'm so glad we finally found the perfect project on which to work together. It's been absolutely fantastic.

Thanks also to Shelley, who provided me with the seed of an idea and encouraged me to run with it and make it my own. In that vein, I must absolutely also acknowledge Prosper Mérimée and Georges Bizet, for providing me with tremendous source material. I can only hope I've done it justice.

Thanks to my girls, the Werearmadillos, who offer cheerleading, kicks in the pants, and wine to go with my whines. You guys make this traversing this very bumpy road a lot more enjoyable.

To the Buffistas, you guys are my sanity, which is kind of scary, when you think about it. But I defy anyone to find such a smart, sexy, gorgeous group with answers for absolutely everything. I love us!

Normally, I'd mention musicians who were particularly inspirational in the creation of the manuscript, but this one had so, so many. From Bizet to Sting to Vince Guaraldi to Alejandro Fernández, the list runs the gamut and just goes on and on. Let's just say there were a lot.

For all the members, past and present, of the North Miami Pioneer Regiment, the Florida State University Marching Chiefs and especially, the late, great, Florida Wave Drum and Bugle Corps. Thank you for being such a huge part of my life for so many years.

And finally, for Nate and Abby, who inspire and infuriate in equal measure. You are *so* my children. I love you.

# author's note

The tarot deck Mamacita uses for Soledad's readings is a real and very beautiful deck: *The Lover's Tarot,* by Kris Waldherr.

The poem Taz quotes is the "Romance sonámbulo" from *Primer Romancero Gitano* (*The Gypsy Ballads*) by one of Spain's finest poets, Federico García Lorca (1898–1936), translated by William Logan.

# so she dances

Turning, soaring, feeling the hum of the strings like a caress along my skin, the notes from the brass and woodwinds swirling around my body like a cape. The percussion throbbing beneath my feet, urging me to turn faster, leap higher and farther, to push my body to its absolute limits—to reach for the heavens.

The beautiful movements set to music—swathed in graceful tulle and flowing satin, the stories played out on the stage for an audience held under a spell.

The pretty façade.

What was real was the stink and clamminess of gallons of sweat. Of blisters, oozing and raw, skin sticking to leather slippers. Of joints and muscles burning with such a deep pain I couldn't imagine ever being able to move again. My feet numb and entire body so exhausted, it took monumental effort just to draw another breath.

It was knowing that for every four perfect minutes of a solo, there were hours of repetition and tears, my throat aching and tight from screaming because it just wasn't right and it had to be done again. And again. And again.

The applause—that was a bonus, Approval acknowledged with a deep, graceful curtsy and a grateful smile. But I didn't need it. When it was right, I could *feel* it. The audience—they didn't even exist in those moments. I wish I could describe it, but it was . . . gossamer. A fleeting sensation that coursed through my system like a drug. Lasting just long enough to block out all the pain and sweat and entice me to do it again. And again.

People always asked why I danced. Why I'd devoted so much of my life to something that seemed to offer so little in return. But good as I was with words, in this they kind of deserted me. Every once in a while, I wished I *could* talk about it. How dancing created this huge, chaotic jumble of emotion and adrenaline rushing through my bloodstream—the freedom and power that came from the ability to command my body so completely. But when I tried, the words just came out a mess and sounding completely lame. I don't know—somewhere along the line it had just gotten easier to keep quiet.

Maybe, too, it was because I knew that in the end, the words, they'd find a home on the pages of my journal, the only other place I felt the same freedom as with dancing.

And if I was being completely honest, I *liked* being able to keep the actual emotions to myself. Kept it . . . special.

may

# first impressions

"Hey, Soledad, have you ever done Carmen?"

With the static buzz and ringing going on in my head, it took a few seconds for the words to penetrate. Not that they made any more sense once they did.

"What?"

"Have you ever done Carmen?"

I continued staring at the reflection in the dressing room mirror, rational thought kind of . . . starting to return. So I'd start with the most rational question.

"Jonathan, what are you doing in here?"

The reflection's startlingly pale eyes widened. "There you are. I was wondering if you were *ever* going to hear me. I've been trying to talk to you since you came offstage."

"You were?"

"I was."

"Huh." I took a sip of water, trying to clear out more of the post-performance adrenaline haze. "You know, Jonathan, I'd think you'd know better. I mean, it's just a rehearsal, but still."

The reflection cringed. "Sorry."

I knew he was. Even though he was a musician and I was a dancer, and generally never the twain shall meet, four years as classmates meant I at least knew him well enough to know that normally, he'd be all about respecting the boundaries. But for whatever reason, the boundaries seemed to have gone AWOL, prompting him to barge into the dancers' dressing room and pepper me with bizarre questions. The temptation to smack him upside the head was definitely strong, but so was the adrenaline high of a performance well done. Lucky for him.

"Okay, now that I'm marginally more with it, let's try again— what are you talking about and why are you back here anyway, instead of down in the pit, where you belong?"

And regardless of what he was going on about, I still needed to get ready for my next number, so I went ahead and peeled down the sleeves of the formfitting Firebird costume, holding it to my chest as I bent over to untie my pointe shoes. Not that he was actually checking anything out. His entire focus—laser-beam intense—was centered right on my face. Okay, strike that. *Mostly* centered on my face. Because just as I finished wiggling out of the costume, I saw his gaze drop—just for a second—before it returned to my face, like it was determined to stay there.

"I'm back here because I'm off for the next few numbers and I needed to find out if you've ever done Carmen."

"Uh-huh."

Yeah . . . Still not making much sense. I shook out the bodysuit and draped it over the chair next to mine. As I moved, I saw his gaze do its thing again, with an added small shake of his head like he was scolding himself. You know, I almost felt sorry for him, but this *was* the dancers' communal dressing room. It's not like our rep as a notoriously immodest bunch—girls and guys alike—should come as any big surprise. Honestly, in tights and the flesh-colored pasties that played defense against clinging Lycra, arctic air conditioners, or any potential wardrobe malfunctions, I was *almost* fully clothed.

Chilled from the air conditioner blasting through the theater—and taking a tiny bit of pity on him and the wandering eyes he couldn't seem to help—I grabbed my heavy terry cloth robe from the back of the chair and pulled it on, sneaking my share of looks in the mirror, trying to figure out what his deal was. And *why* did I care? For God's sake, I had another performance to get ready for. Just as I was getting ready to tell him to get lost, that whatever it was could damn well wait, he shoved his hands through his hair and huffed out a massive breath that blew loose wisps of air against the back of my neck.

Closing his eyes, he took another breath, this one deep enough to pull his ratty gray T-shirt tight across his chest. Fascinated, I watched as his mouth went visibly firm and he released the breath in a slow, controlled stream though a small opening between his lips. Opening his eyes, he tried again.

"Have you ever *portrayed* Carmen?"

As our gazes met again in the big mirror the last of the woolies cleared away and everything clicked into place. "'Carmen' as in gypsy, opera, ballet, exceptionally misguided role for Beyoncé to play in a really cheesy and unimaginative reworking of a classic. Right?"

Thick sandy brows drew together in a line as straight as a practice barre. "You lost me on the last part, but otherwise yeah, *that* Carmen."

"No, but I have studied the role." I shrugged and stood from the chair, blinking as we came face to neck. Had he always been this tall? Or had we just never stood quite this close to each other? I mean, given that I stood five-ten and most danseurs tended to have maybe only a couple of inches on me, this was definitely . . . novel. Edging past him I said, "It's one of my favorites." Carmen. The Firebird. Those were my kinds of roles. Not every ballerina aspired to be the wee, dainty Sugar Plum Fairy.

Ducking behind the garment rack, I pulled my black-and-burgundy dress off the hanger. Half hidden by a forest of spandex and chiffon and ribbons, I stepped into the costume and slipped the thin straps over my shoulders, yanking the zipper up myself rather than flag down one of the poor freshmen running around doing minion duty.

I dropped back into my chair and ducked under the vanity, rummaging around in my bag for my ballroom shoes. "So what about it?"

"Would you like to portray Carmen?"

"Sure. Who wouldn't?" Yanking on the black leather heels, I stood and shouldered my way past him again and out of the dressing room. Threading my way through the mad backstage chaos, I headed for the wings, fighting the nervous urge to bounce up and down and pump my arms. No reason to waste energy that would be more valuable channeled onto the dance floor.

"I'm serious. If you're interested, you can *be* Carmen."

The words, I understood them, but they didn't make a damned bit of sense. And right this second, I really didn't have the time to try to dissect Jonathan's cryptic statements.

"Look, the only thing I'm interested in right now is my performance. Period." I paused by the rosin box, rapidly grinding the ball of one foot, then the other, in the yellow-white powder, knocking the excess off against the edges before resuming my path toward the wings. The closer I got, the more I made a point to walk slower, consciously matching my breathing to each step, the chaos, the bodies, the extraneous chatter all falling away as I dropped into my zone.

"I know . . . I know . . . I'm really sorry, I know my timing blows."

Each word sounded as if it was coming from farther and farther away. "Yeah, it really does. Seriously, whatever this is about, it's just going to have to wait."

"I know. I got impatient, I'm sorry. I can wait."

I risked a glance over my shoulder, looking straight into those pale eyes and catching my breath again at the intensity. Feeling myself wrapped—for just a split second—in a surprising sense of familiarity. Strong enough and shocking enough that those little hairs on the back of my neck went straight to red alert.

"You're on in sixty," the stage manager whispered beside me.

"Thanks," I replied absently, still staring over my shoulder.

I took a deep breath, glanced out toward the empty expanse of stage that beckoned, then back into that steady, *simpático* gray gaze. "Meet me after rehearsal's called."

"Where?"

"Mack and Mabel's."

"Okay." He smiled, full out for the first time, revealing ever-so-slightly-crooked front teeth. "You know, don't know if I've ever mentioned it before, but you're a seriously kick-ass dancer."

It came so out of nowhere that even as the disciplined dancer was urging me toward the stage, the other part of me, the girl, couldn't help but do a double take, an answering smile tugging at the corners of my mouth.

With the unexpected compliment echoing in my mind, I strode out onto the worn floorboards of the stage and assumed my opening pose. Breathing deep, I waited for the strum of the guitar, for the dark insistent rhythms of the percussion to sink into my skin and work their magic, transforming me into an enchantress, a siren. With each note, the minutiae of dress rehearsal, of intense boys with pretty eyes, of the petty annoyances of life, of school, of everything—

All faded into insignificance as once again the dancer took over.

# consider this

I slammed the door on the faded blue Corolla I shared with Mamacita and made a beeline for the air-conditioned interior of Mack and Mabel's, feeling like I was swimming through the muggy air. Eighty-five degrees at ten at night, and it was only mid-May. Keep going this way, and summer was going to suck big hairy ones. Okay, it was Miami—summer always sucked big hairy ones, but at least I wouldn't have to be out in it. Let's hear it for air-conditioned studios.

As blessedly cool air washed over me, a loud "Soledad!" sounded from the back of the narrow diner.

"Hey, girl, come over, we got room."

I grinned and waved at the posse of dancers from school as I scanned the counter and vinyl booths of the vintage diner. Nope. Not here yet. Kind of a surprise, considering I was the one who was running late. "Thanks, but I can't. Meeting someone." *We'd said Mack and Mabel's, right?* I mean, where else was there? It *was* the de facto school hangout, but in retrospect everything was so fuzzy and surreal about that whole encounter—like it had happened to someone else and I'd heard about it secondhand.

A good-natured chorus of *ooooohs* had my wave turning into a one-fingered salute, prompting laughter. "You guys seriously need to get out more." Even though they kind of had a point. Not like I was Miss Social. With a sigh, I tossed my backpack into a booth and dropped down beside it, reaching inside for my favorite time killer. Might as well just chill—order a shake and see if he showed. I took another look around, as if expecting him to maybe pop out from behind the brightly lit jukebox or one of the many towers of Miami kitsch souvenirs. Nope. Still nowhere to be seen. He probably got hung up, too. What with everyone flipping out about performance finals and trying to squeeze in that last little bit of practice, even if lips, feet, and/or fingers were on the verge of falling off from overuse. Opening my book to where I'd left off, I immediately got sucked into the story, pausing only long enough to order a double chocolate shake.

"I'm glad you didn't blow me off."

I glanced up to find Jonathan standing beside the booth. "I was starting to wonder if it was the other way around."

He laughed as he slid in across from me. "And cue the image of the snake eating its tail."

I draped my beaded bookmark between the pages and set the book aside. "Come again?"

"You know . . . from the mythology unit we did in Lit?"

"Right—the Ouroboros. What does that have to do with anything?"

He grinned as he pulled a couple of menus from behind the napkin dispenser, handing me one. "I waited for you after we broke

12

rehearsal, but you kept going . . . rehearsing that flamenco number over and over. I watched you work for a while, then assumed you'd totally forgotten, or at least weren't going to remember until you were satisfied with your work and the rest of the world made a reappearance. I figured you were good for at least an hour, so I went and did some practicing of my own."

"Oh."

"I checked every few minutes and when I saw that you'd finally left the auditorium, I packed it up and came over. Hoping *you* hadn't totally blown me off."

"Oh." So it had been what I assumed. Sort of. Except *I* was the one who'd been flipping out and trying to squeeze in that last little bit of practice.

*And Miss All Dance, All the Time strikes again.*

"Shut *up*," I muttered to that pesky inner voice that had a habit of popping up at really inconvenient times. And Mamacita kept insisting I should listen to it more often. As if.

"'Scuse me?"

"Tell you what, whatever you want to talk about must be pretty important. Hanging around and waiting on top of that whole backstage stalking and barging into the dressing room thing." When in doubt, go on the offensive. Beat trying to explain about stupid inner voices.

But the way he ducked his head and mumbled "Yeah, um, sorry about that—" made me feel like a total worm for even bringing it up. He didn't need to apologize. I understood he really had been more focused on whatever his mission was and not so much on what I was—or wasn't—wearing.

*Hey, he did cop a look at the boobs. Twice.*

*So he looked,* I silently argued back. *Proves he's human and probably straight.*

13

*Yeah . . .*

Oh, for God's sake. I'd known the guy for four years. He was *just* a guy. A good musician. Tall. With pretty eyes. Really pretty eyes, practically glowing silver in the light from the vintage pendant hanging over the table.

*Glowing?* Oh, *brother.* I had to be wicked tired.

"Hey, Soledad, you all right?"

"Yeah, just tired. Hungry, too—"

And like he was some blessed, patchouli-scented angel sent from on high, Mack showed up, in all his Birkenstocked glory, ready to take our orders—or rather, to tell us what we should eat in order to keep our strength up. Not that anyone ever argued with him or Mabel. They were like the cool hippy aunt and uncle everyone wished they had. Their house was open 24/7, they were mellow about how long you hung out, and the munchies were always awesome. One of the things I was seriously going to miss about Miami after I left.

After Mack cruised back toward the kitchen, Jonathan reached across the table and touched the battered cover of the book I'd been lost in when he showed.

"*Heartbreak Hotel.* Not exactly required reading for our final."

I shrugged. "An old favorite."

"Why?" He was rolling his wrapped-up silverware back and forth, an even, steady rhythm, perfectly in sync with the music coming from the juke.

Whoa. Surprise. Usually, if anyone ever asked what I was reading, they'd nod and say, "That's nice," and move on to a more interesting topic. Like the weather. I stared at him, trying to read his expression, but couldn't see anything in there beyond honest curiosity. Which was the only reason I could figure that instead of just coming up with something pallid and boring and acceptable like, "Just because," I found myself actually giving him a real answer.

"Um . . . because I really love how Maggie, the lead character, defies logic. She fights her upbringing and her surroundings and her self-imposed expectations of being a woman in the South in the fifties to become something"—I floundered around, trying to find the right word and finally settling on—"more. Becoming who she's meant to be."

What can I say? It resonated. But that part wasn't for sharing. No matter how pretty and compelling his eyes were, making him look like he was ready to hear any and everything—and *damn*, I must be more tired and hungry than I thought, because my brain was going to all sorts of weird places tonight.

Thankfully, our food showed up just then, preempting any other questions followed by way-too-revealing answers on my part. No one needed to know that much about me.

He stared at my plate as he squeezed a huge glob of ketchup on his own. "A hamburger and an order of fries."

I returned the book to my backpack. "Root veggie fries. Air baked."

"And you already have a shake."

Heat prickled along the back of my neck. "Yeah, what of it?"

"I thought most dancers didn't eat."

The sound I made was somewhere between a choke, a laugh, and a snort, and made his eyes go wide. "Dude, do I *look* like most dancers?"

I made myself sit perfectly still as his eyes narrowed and he looked me up and down—leaving me with the distinct feeling he was seeing more of me than he had back in the dressing room. A lot more. Finally he said, "No, you don't. You don't have that stick insect look." He nodded at the nearby table where the dancers still congregated, a single plate of fries sitting in the middle of the table, still half full.

"Yeah, I know, and thanks for saying it so politely."

"What do you mean?"

I began yanking bobby pins from my hair. "Most people just say *fat*."

The ketchup bottle hit the table with a thump. "That's crap."

"Not in the dance world. It's problematic."

"Why? You're a great dancer. You look so—" He stopped, his gaze following the movement of my hands as I pulled pin after pin from my hair. "I don't know . . . So alive and *real* up on the stage."

Wow. Just . . . *wow*. Slower now, I pulled the last few pins from my hair and shook the heavy length of it free from the bun it'd been in for the last eight hours, rolling my head around on my neck. I savored the prickling sensation rippling along my scalp for a few seconds before occupying myself with gathering the pins into a pile and dropping them into a side pocket of my backpack.

"That's a really nice thing for you to say," I finally managed. "But in classical dance, especially, they tend to prefer ethereal. Dainty. Kind of tough to accomplish when you're built like me." Tall and not an ounce of fat, but I had broad linebacker shoulders and genuine B-cups instead of mosquito bites on my chest. Although my *tías* claimed I had no hips (compared to *them*), they were definitely there, leading into heavy, muscled thighs, the curves offset some by the sheer length of my legs. Overall, the impression I gave on the stage was of power, but light and delicate? Not in this lifetime. And it was okay. I'd made my peace with it a long time ago—mostly.

But couldn't deny that every time I heard some variation on "Your dancing is superb, but you're really not . . . *right* for the part," I'd find myself wondering, *What more?* The dancers who got those roles—I could speculate all I wanted about their ability or experience or discipline, but the one thing that was always fact was the one thing I couldn't change. Those dancers—they were always, *always* smaller. Something I couldn't physically do anything about unless I went on the dancer's diet of surviving on coffee and cigarettes or sticking my finger down my throat. Both options were completely gross, not to mention I'd seen up close what it did to some of my classmates. No, thanks. So all I could do was put my faith in talent and even more hours of practice. And hope that I could somehow defy expectations.

Story of my life.

Underneath the high-pitched whirr of the shake machine and the clatter of silverware and plates and a new song drifting from the jukebox, I still managed to pick up, "God, what morons."

"Jonathan?"

He glanced up from tearing the wrapper off a straw. "Yeah?"

"I—" My hand moved, stopped—then moved again, until my fingertips brushed his arm. "Thank you. That means a lot." Even more than his unexpected compliment from earlier.

He fidgeted with the wrapper, twisting it between his fingers. "Well, I'm just telling the truth."

"So am I."

# getting into something

After I inhaled half my burger, I took a long drink of water and looked across the table. "Okay, so let's get down to it. Carmen?"

Looking up from dunking fries in ketchup, he answered my question with one of his own. "What do you know about competitive drum and bugle corps?"

"Um . . . nothing?"

"That's okay. Let me explain—" He stopped, cocked his head to the side, then with a sly grin added, "No, there's too much, lemme sum up."

I choked down the sip of chocolate shake I'd just taken, fighting to keep a straight face. "'My name is Inigo Montoya, you killed my father, prepare to die.'"

He *tried* to keep his face stern as he spluttered, "'Inconceivable!'"

"'You keep using that word. I do not think it means what you think it means.'"

We both sagged against the high backs of our booth seats, laughing like loons. Still chuckling, he handed me a napkin. "A *Princess Bride* fan—that's awesome."

"Oh yeah. I mean, how can anyone not like *The Princess Bride*?" I wiped beneath my eyes and took another sip of water.

"There are rumors such sad creatures exist." Jonathan shook his head and let loose with a big huff of breath like back in the dressing room, reminding me we were actually here for a specific reason.

Shoving my hair behind my ears, I pushed my plate away and pulled my shake closer. "So—drum and bugle corps."

"Right." He nodded, then looked at my abandoned plate. At my wave, he pulled it close and started working on the fries I hadn't been able to finish. Between bites he explained, "It's sort of like a marching band—we play instruments and march in formations on a football field, but that's about as close as the comparisons are allowed to get. Don't *ever* let anyone in corps hear you refer to it as band."

I blinked over the rim of my tall shake glass. "Hardcore?"

"You have no idea."

"Um, dancer," I reminded him. "Those stick insects can be hella bitchy if you mess with the natural order of their world."

"Point made." With a grin, he slid his shake glass across the table until it clinked against mine, a dull, completely unmusical noise but no less sweet for it. "Anyhow, corps is precision and discipline and musicianship and artistry, and it's amazing, Soledad. Everything, down to your heartbeat it seems like, is so completely in sync with all the other people performing with you, it's like you're one person. And before you've even finished, the crowd's going insane and then you hit that final note and all the sound is washing over you, breaking into this self-contained bubble you've existed in for eleven minutes."

He leaned forward, propping his arms on the table, the air around him practically vibrating. I still didn't really have a clue what he was talking about, but my *God*, the way he was describing the experience—it was *so* intense. So . . . familiar.

"Anyhow, the corps I'm part of, the Florida Raiders, is performing *Carmen* this year."

"Okay."

"And we need a Carmen for the color guard."

"The what?"

"Flags, rifles," he clarified. "Props for visual effect. A precision dance auxiliary, essentially."

"Okay," I said slowly. "And—?"

"You're a woman."

"Uh . . . yeah, last time I checked."

And *he* checked. Again. Clearing his throat, he finally said, "Um, CliffsNotes version is, once upon a time a lot of corps were male only, but these days most of them are coed, only a few old-school left. We're old-school."

Okay, starting to get the picture. Sort of. "But it's not like you're actually going to perform the actual story, right? Just play the music? And"—I waved my hand—"move around?"

"March. Execute drill formations. Like choreography, but on a monster scale."

"Uh-huh." The picture began sharpening. Envisioning little bits and pieces of the few halftime shows I'd caught when my uncles and cousins would have their New Year's bowl game orgies.

A thump sounded as Jonathan slouched against the back of the booth. "But thing is—" He ran a hand through his hair and sighed. "Originally, the show as a whole was envisioned as this abstract creation, based on twentieth-century Spanish art masterpieces, blah, blah, blah. But it's not working."

"Uh-*huh*."

Jonathan must have understood how bizarre that sounded because he shook his head and said, "Sorry, geek alert—corps is all about the overall concept and vision and—" Again, he stopped himself with another sharp head shake. "Never mind. It's just easier for a newbie to see it in person."

My head was starting to hurt. "Jonathan—"

"I know, I know . . . Sorry. Again." He took a deep breath. "Anyhow, the idea is great, but like I said, it's just not working. It's missing something. Then our director suggested that maybe what we needed was an actual, flesh-and-blood Carmen, and that's when I said I knew the perfect one."

"Me?"

He nodded. "You."

"But how could you be so sure—"

"Flamenco number? Showcase? We've been rehearsing how long now?"

Just as I started to point out that that wasn't really an answer, his gaze met mine, that laser focus back up to full strength. "It's not just that you're a great dancer—you're different. I know you have tremendous discipline. And like I said—" His thumb rubbed at a spot on the table's surface. "You're real and . . . I don't know—" Two bright spots of color appeared high on his cheeks. "Alive, I guess. You're larger than life when you're on the stage."

Another snort escaped. "That's just because I'm so much bigger."

"It's *not* a bad thing."

I reared back against the bench—him, too, eyes widening like he was just as blown away as me by how fierce he'd just sounded.

After a few seconds of just staring at each other he went on, his voice softer. "All I'm saying is it'll work to your advantage on the

field. Those little stick insect chicks would totally get lost. You—"
A small smile pulled at the corners of his mouth. "You'll *own* it."

Not often I was caught utterly speechless. But seriously, what *could* I say to something like that?

*"Thanks" might be a good start.*

*Bite me.*

We sat quietly for another few minutes, me trying to finish my shake and gathering my thoughts while, amazingly, he seemed willing to just be still and let me think without all that fierce intensity pushing at me from all sides.

"Okay, if I agree to check this out. *If*—" I repeated, as his eyes lit up and he leaned forward again. "What would I be agreeing to?"

"Well, you come audition and if the director likes you, you dive into rehearsal, then tour starts mid-June and goes for eight weeks and—"

"Whoa, whoa, *whoa*. Tour? Where? And eight weeks? Jonathan, that's the whole summer."

"Oh yeah—I guess I skipped the part where we spend the summer traveling across the country, competing against other corps, huh?" At least he looked apologetic.

"Yeah, you sort of did, and seriously, I can't afford to lose those two months."

"Why is it losing?" He looked genuinely blank, like he couldn't fathom anyone doing anything else for the entire summer. Or wanting to. "College doesn't start until September—at least Indiana, where I'm going, doesn't. I guess I just assumed most schools didn't start until then."

"It has nothing to do with college. I'm not going."

"Not even an arts school?"

I shook my head.

"Why not?"

"Why would I want to spend four years going into massive debt for something I can already do? Especially when most dance companies have their own schools where members can take classes." I sat up straighter, tucking one leg beneath myself on the seat. "A ton of the ballet companies, including a lot of the international ones, hold these huge auditions in New York a couple times a year. I'm gonna go up there, sublet an apartment for a few months, and make the rounds. With all those companies—someone's going to be willing to take a chance on me, I just *know* it."

My voice was rising, the words chasing after each other in a giddy rush. Sounding just like Jonathan, actually.

"When?"

I blinked my way back from fantasies of the capitals of the world and wildly applauding audiences. "When what?"

"When are you going to New York?"

"January."

"So why would doing corps be a problem?"

"Because—" I poked my straw at the soupy brown remains of my shake. "I've got a job at my ballet teacher's studio—classes at my disposal, unlimited free studio time to practice, and a welcome paycheck."

"What if I told you we had scholarships that would give you a stipend?"

"Excuse me?"

"We've got scholarships. You audition and blow them away, then explain your situation—I can't imagine them not wanting to give you one. Practice time won't be any big deal and meals are all taken care of, so you don't have to spend money on food."

My hands curled around the bench seat on either side of my legs, so hard, I felt my fingers start to cramp, the vinyl slippery beneath my palms. The longer I sat there, the more I could almost *see* an aura hovering around Jonathan tinted the same shades of red and orange as my Firebird costume. "Jesus Christ, I cannot believe you."

His jaw dropped. "What?"

Groping in my backpack I found a ten and tossed it down for my half of the meal. Sliding from the booth I glared at him. "It's not *just* the money, you spoiled little twerp. Haven't you heard a damned thing I've said? I know I'm going in with some pretty massive strikes against me. The one thing I can control is my technique, and I have to be absolutely certain it's impeccable. This is probably the best shot I'll ever have."

"Wait—" He grabbed my wrist before I could make my escape. "Look, I'm on the scholarship, too."

I looked him over in his gray Abercrombie tee with the fake-raggedy edges, the glint of a gold chain peeking out from the neck, the expensive-looking sports watch, the Pumas, beat up and scuffed but undeniably high-end.

"*Please*. You're not hurting for cash." I tried to yank my arm loose, but his hold tightened.

"It's not *just* the money." He threw my own words back, the sharp edges making me flinch. "You think I didn't hear you? I did. I get it. More than you'll ever know. How looks are deceiving. How your entire life hinges on ability. How sometimes, no matter how hard you work, it's never enough—" His hand dropped away as he let loose with a short, hard laugh.

Now that he'd let go, I could've left. Meant to. Instead I found myself asking, "What do you mean?"

Nice trick, avoiding answering by taking a long drink of his water, all the way down to the ice cubes, before sucking one into his mouth and crunching into it, the sound oddly loud in the space between us. "Never mind," he finally said in a flat, cold tone that made it clear I wasn't getting more. Not about this, at any rate.

Not that it was any of my business.

He stood and tossed another ten onto the table, then shoved his hands into his shorts' pockets. "Look, what I said—it came out wrong. It's not the money or that your practice time's not important." His eyes narrowed in that intense gaze. "What I meant was that maybe you could think of corps *as* a job—being part of a company. Maybe it's not ballet, but it is a medium where you're going to practice until you're ready to drop, your skills are going to be polished into something you can't even begin to imagine, *and* you'll be performing almost every night in front of crowds that will totally get you and love you for all your strengths and abilities. Isn't that exactly what you want?"

I heard him talking in this way, like in his mind it was a done deal. Like he *knew* there just wasn't any other choice. Maybe it should've felt a little scary and I guess, truthfully, it was, but more than that, it was . . . well, thrilling, really. How was it that this boy that I knew, but not really, had zeroed in on my desires and what made me tick, so easily? I all of a sudden wanted to find out.

And all of it left me breathless in a way I'd never experienced before. I pondered that as we silently walked out to our cars.

"Okay, so again with the *if*—and trust me, it's still a pretty big one—*if* I decide to give this a shot, what do you need from me?" Because if anything, it was good practice—auditioning in a new environment.

*Shyeah, right.*

I clamped my lips tight against the automatic "shut up" I wanted to hiss, instead focusing my attention on Jonathan.

"Are you available on Sunday?"

"Yeah, as a matter of fact, I am."

"We have a rehearsal. All day, but you probably wouldn't have to stay for the whole thing."

I pulled my hair forward over my shoulder and twisted it around my hand as I considered that. "I think if I go, I'd like to stay— probably best way to get a feel for the whole thing."

A slow smile crossed his face as he nodded. "I could give you directions or . . . well . . . you could ride with me." Then he bit his lip, like he was nervous. After everything tonight, of all things to be nervous about.

Maybe that's why I made a point to make my voice gentle as I answered. "Yeah, I'd like a ride. But remember, I'm not making any guarantees, okay?"

His smile got bigger. "I can live with that."

# all good things

I dropped the keys in the bowl sitting on the table by the kitchen door, the clatter of metal against china almost drowning out the deep breath I released as soon as the door closed behind me.

"*¿Qué pasa, angelita?*" The soft voice drifted through the heavy, late-night quiet—a mere whisper above the hum of the air conditioner.

"I'm okay, Mamacita," I responded in Spanish. "Just thinking."

"You'll know what to do."

You know, I'd given up, long, long time ago, trying to figure out how she knew. She just did. She knew without a word from me or even so much as a look at my face, whenever I felt lonely or mad or just had something on my mind. Like now.

"You think so?" Unzipping my dance bag, I pulled out my tights, leotard, and cardigan, dropping them in the basket sitting by the laundry room door before passing through to the converted carport where Mamacita had her space. With its terra cotta tile floors and pale aqua and sea green walls, it was the coolest room in our small house—literally and metaphorically.

This was where she had her nail salon during the day, giving the ladies (and occasional guy) their manis and pedis, but more than that, it was just *her* space. There were family pictures and baskets of her favorite celebrity magazines, and along one wall, the huge, tropical green leather sofa my godmother, Tía Gracy, had given us when she got another, even more hideous, definitely more expensive sofa, courtesy of one of her boyfriends. At least the thing was comfortable.

"You really think I'll know the right thing to do?" I dropped onto the sofa beside her.

Rather than answer, she took both my hands and fixed my ragged nails and cuticles with the Evil Eye. "You need a manicure in the worst way," she finally said, switching back to English. "Your hands are too beautiful for this." She flicked a fingertip across my thumb, making a show of flinching at the rough, bitten edges of the nail.

"I'll let you have your way with me before the showcase."

"Tomorrow," she retorted. "Then again, before the showcase. How can I allow you out of the house like this? I'd like to keep my good reputation intact."

"Just say I'm a rebellious teenager. Or neurotic artist—either one works, really." I tried to pull my hands free, but her grip tightened. Lot of that going on tonight. But then I relaxed as she released one to reach for the tub of coconut hand cream. I closed my eyes as she began the massage in the middle of my palm before she worked her way out, tugging each finger. Moving to my wrist, she pressed down on the pulse point, the throb of my heartbeat reverberating back through my whole body and making me shiver. Then she did it all over again with the other hand, leaving me just this side of limp noodle.

Like I didn't know what she was up to.

"*Deja los ojos cerrados,*" she ordered as my fingers automatically curled around the deck. "Shuffle and when you're ready, cut."

Keeping my eyes closed and breathing deep, I shuffled the cards until I felt the familiar, odd tingling running along my arms and down my spine. "How many?"

"*Tres.*"

I opened my eyes and carefully placed three cards facedown on the cushion between us, then set the deck to one side. I watched as Mamacita slowly flipped each one—the Queen of Cups, Death, and the Hanged Man.

"Hm."

"That's illuminating." But I knew better than to push for an answer. She was good at this, her side business—her real business, in a lot of ways—but the one thing you couldn't ever do was push her for answers. I'd seen her kick people out of the house and throw their money out after them for trying to get an answer out of her before she was ready.

"Many changes on the horizon, *mi angelita.*"

"I could've told you *that* without the cards." Graduation was in ten days, and that qualified as a big life change, right? At least that was the line our counselors and teachers kept feeding us.

Her lips pursed, she fixed me with another Evil Eye, but really—

"Hey, I didn't exactly *ask* for a reading."

"You go ahead and think that."

"Fine." I sighed and sank back against the cushions. There just wasn't any point in arguing when the woman had an idea in her head.

Her mouth relaxed and she hit me with another stare, less with the evil, then looked back down at the cards. Reaching again for my right hand, her thumb rubbed gentle circles on the palm.

Now don't get me wrong—I didn't disrespect the tarot and I seriously appreciated that Mamacita knew what she was about, to the point it gave us enough extra income that while things were occasionally on the lean side, we'd never once needed public assistance. But really, sometimes her timing left something to be desired.

"Trust yourself, *m'ija*," she finally said. "You're going to know the right thing to do with the opportunities you're presented with. Which ones to take. And most of all, don't be afraid to look at things with new eyes." Releasing my hand, she rose and crossed the room to the small counter where she had the electric kettle set up.

I watched as she went through the ritual of preparing tea. "Do you really think I'll know what to do?" I asked *again*, hoping she'd finally give me a straight answer.

Returning to the sofa, she handed me a steaming mug. "You always have before."

I sipped the hot Darjeeling. "Not like there's really been a whole lot of earth-shattering decision-making in my past."

"*Bueno*, it's true you've been a focused soul since the age of four." She smiled and lifted her mug to her lips. "And it's earth-shattering, hm?" She blinked over the mug's rim.

"'Innocent' and you don't really mix, Mamacita." Sighing, I kicked off my flip-flops and tucked my left leg up under me, stretching my achy right leg out on the nearby ottoman. Too late to ice it now.

"And no, not exactly earth-shattering."

Delicate black brows rose. "Is it illegal?"

You know, other people got normal Cuban grandmothers—white-haired and demanding you eat more; yelling at you to make sure you were decently covered, *m'ija*, even if it was ninety-five degrees outside. Me? I got a comedian with OPI Kangarooby red nails.

"No," I grumbled. "I'm just trying to decide if I want to change my summer plans."

"*Now?*" The brows went higher. If I hadn't been so sunk into trying to figure things out, I might've been amused by the fact that I'd finally shocked the unshockable Mamacita.

"I don't know, *niña*—for you, this *might* qualify as earth-shattering."

I shifted my position, wincing as I readjusted my leg on the ottoman. "Well, it's a chance to perform for the entire summer that came kind of out of nowhere, but you know . . . I hate to disappoint Madame Allard. . . ."

"*M'ijita*, the *last* person in the world who would stand in the way of any opportunity to expand your artistic horizons is Madame."

"I don't know . . ." I picked at a loose thread on my skirt. "This is pretty out there. And it's not ballet."

Her gaze was steady and not in the least bit perturbed. "So?"

Damn her for being right. Because if there was anyone who'd understand . . . who, along with Mamacita, encouraged me to embrace my physical quirks and develop them into strengths. She'd probably even say that it would be an asset to my ballet.

"*Yes muchacho chévere.*"

My entire body jerked at her quiet words. "*Oye*, talk about out of left field, Mamacita! What makes you so sure there's a boy involved?"

All she did was tap the cards spread on the sofa cushion. "Something drew me to choose this deck, *verdad?*"

I studied the cards, stunning even against the violent green leather with their illustrations of famous lovers throughout the ages; slowly traced a finger around the image of the hauntingly beautiful Isolde, representing the Queen of Cups. As a familiar growling engine drew closer then abruptly stopped, I grinned and gathered up the cards. "Nooo, I can't imagine *why* on earth you might have chosen these," I said as a dark head appeared in the glass window of the outside door.

*"No seas fresca."* Fluffing her ink dark curls, she walked across the room, arranging her shawl so it draped in a casually sexy way over her shoulders—the perfect vision as she opened the door for her obviously expected guest. "And at least stay long enough to say hello."

"Hello, Domenic," I dutifully intoned with only minimal snark as her latest conquest came through the door. Like he even heard me, the way he was staring at my grandmother.

*"Ciao,* Soledad," he said with a quick glance my way. Okay, so he heard me. Barely. I smiled and fluttered my fingers as he tossed his bike helmet onto a nearby chair, followed by his leather jacket, before he went back to ogling. And she was ogling back just as hard, and who could blame her? Dom was six feet of sleek Italian goodness who Mamacita *swore* was past forty. She'd met him while he was bartending at one of the hot new SoBe clubs, the one that Tía Gracy had dragged her to last month, and I was seriously going to have to have a talk with my godmother. Dragging Mamacita into such a total cliché.

Then again, cliché or not, Dom was clearly hot for Mamacita, and if she was busy with him, she'd appreciate the space, whether I was busy working or . . . well . . .

Right. Choices.

After taking a quick shower, I flopped down onto my bed with my cell. With a napkin from Mack and Mabel's balanced on my knees, I carefully typed the number written on it, storing it, before starting a new text entry.

**I need to think on this some more.**
**I'll let you know for sure tomorrow.**

I set the phone and napkin on the bedside table, then turned out the light and settled myself against my pillows. Just as I was almost completely gone, my phone chimed. Without turning on the light, I groped for the phone and hit the message key, making the screen glow.

Struggling to focus around a huge yawn, I finally made out the message:

**Didn't figure you for a coward.**

"Ass." Typed it in, then figured I was just better off ignoring his arrogant ass. Although now I could forget sleep, no matter how tired I was. I stared up at the ceiling, closed my eyes, concentrated on the rhythmic clink of the chain against the light globes of my ceiling fan, tried mentally going through my *Firebird* routine, then my flamenco routine, but *nada.* I just lay in bed, every muscle rigid and tense and aching more than usual.

*Finally,* sheer exhaustion took over and I started drifting off again. Until the chime of the phone. Bleary, I reached out and grabbed it, squinting at the screen.

**Sorry. Uncalled for. Just let me know what you decide.**

Okay, then. Maybe not a *total* ass.

# it's amazing

Now *why* was I clutching my phone instead of my favorite stuffed Opus? In the watery early-morning light, I blinked up at my ceiling, watching the blades on the fan turn until little by little the weirdness that had been the night before came back.

Utter weirdness, this boy I didn't really know approaching me with an outrageous offer. And more outrageous still, that I was *considering* it. It was all so off the charts. However, after dwelling on it through a shower and the first coffee of the day, I shoved it straight out of my mind because seriously, I had *things* to do. Had to teach the Saturday morning classes to the Tiny Tots and take advantage of the time between to rehearse my showcase numbers. *Not* stress over weirdness.

Chalk it up to a lifetime of discipline giving me the ability to dismiss it—at least from my conscious mind. My subconscious, on the other hand, had different ideas, the traitor. Partway through my last class, right between the *battement frappés* and *rond de jambes,* "let me know what you decide" jumped front and center and started scrolling through my mind, just like on those big screens in Times Square.

I was tempted to bring it up with Madame. If only to get her take on it. But more weirdness—for the first time *ever,* I found myself reluctant to discuss something career-related. Especially after I caught her watching from the doorway of the studio as I spun through the finale of *Firebird,* smiling and nodding in that utterly French way of hers that said she was pleased more than any words could.

You know, if I didn't say anything at all—if I didn't call back—it was as good as letting Jonathan know what my decision was, right? Tacitly and all? I wasn't good at dealing with disappointment.

*Coward, coward, coward.*

Like an evil mantra, the whole drive home. And why was I worrying about disappointing him?

*Cow-waaaard.*

"Fine—so I'll call and tell him to forget it and be done with it. Happy?"

Great—I'd progressed to out-loud arguing with the inside voice. With the windows down where anyone and their mother in the neighborhood could hear as I pulled into my driveway. Like— Oh, *no.* The wicked cute guy leaning against the hood of the shiny pickup truck parked on the street in front of my house.

*God, I hope he didn't hear.*

Whether he heard or not, probably best to go on the offensive. Stepping out of the car and leaning on the open door, I commented, "We're flirting with stalker behavior again, Jonathan."

"That's such an ugly way to think of it, Soledad." He pushed off the truck and walked toward me, iPod stuck in his shirt pocket, earbuds draped around his neck. And there went that full-out smile again—and who knew that slightly crooked teeth could make a grin so charming? "I prefer persistent. Besides, I wanted a chance to argue my case in person."

Reaching behind the front seat, I pulled out my dance bag and dropped it by my feet. "Why?"

"Because my guess is, you're this close"—he held thumb and forefinger close together—"to saying no. But before you do, I have something I want you to see."

"What is it?"

"I want you to *see* it, Soledad, not tell you about it. Then afterwards, if you still say no, at least you know exactly what you're saying no to, and we're cool. I won't bug you again." His eyes narrowed as he glanced up at the sun breaking through the rain clouds that had been threatening all day. "Promise," he added quietly, still staring up at the sky.

Funny how the lines radiating out from the corners of his eyes lent weight to that one quiet word. Like they took him from being an eager boy to . . . I don't know. Someone who was serious and absolutely meant what he said.

"I suppose you're hot and thirsty."

"Now that you mention it—" He met my gaze with a shy smile that brought the boy back to the surface. "The guy who answered the door when I first got here told me you'd be home in a few minutes—an hour ago."

"I helped teach an extra class today," I explained, gesturing to the bag and feeling mildly guilty. Sitting outside in midday May heat for over an hour? *Ugh.*

"Domenic didn't ask you inside?"

"He said he would, but he had to leave and no one else was home."

"Oh. Sorry."

He shrugged and reached down to pick up my dance bag. "Wasn't a big deal—I know I could've gone and come back, but I didn't want to risk missing you. Figured you'd get here eventually." We walked up the driveway to the side door. "Domenic? He's not your dad?"

I laughed at *that* thought. "Nope. He belongs to my grandmother. I don't have a dad." I unlocked the door into the kitchen, rolling my head around and feeling the blessed relief of the air conditioner wash over my skin as I crossed the threshold.

"You sprang fully formed like Athena?"

"How much of that mythology unit do you really think is going to be on the final?" I turned and took my bag from him, still feeling that mild sense of shock that I had to look up to meet his gaze. "I mean no parents in the traditional sense. Just me and my grandmother." And time to change the subject. "We've got Coke, iced tea . . . Water, of course."

"A Coke would be great, thanks."

"Okay, just give me a sec." I detoured into the laundry room, partly to dump out my dance bag, as usual, and if I was honest, to take an extra second to catch my breath, too. Couldn't remember the last time anyone had asked about my family situation or forced me to remember it wasn't standard-issue.

Honestly, needed more than one deep breath, because I kept picturing how he'd looked, staring up into the sun. And then after . . . The shy little-boy smile.

Bending forward until my forehead quietly thunked against the washer, I muttered, "Either you stay back here and hyperventilate, girl, or you show some spine and deal," the words vibrating against the cool metal. "He is *just* a guy."

"Did you say something?"

Pasting a smile on my face, I went back to the kitchen where I promptly stuck my head in the fridge, pulling out a soda, the pitcher of iced tea, and as an afterthought, the sweet ham and Swiss cheese.

"I was asking if you want a sandwich? Nothing fancy, just ham and cheese."

He took the soda I offered. "Sure—if it's not too much trouble."

"It's not." As I split lengths of soft Cuban bread, I asked, "Okay, so what do you want me to see, and do you like pickles, mayo, mustard?"

"We need a DVD player. And yeah—all of it."

I finished the sandwiches and handed him a plate. "DVD's this way."

Balancing a glass, the pitcher of tea, and my sandwich, I took off for Mamacita's room where I found a note from her, as expected, letting me know she'd gone shopping with Tía Gracy.

Great. The two of them could shop until the next Ice Age and here I was, alone with a tall, crazy-intense boy wearing a dark blue T-shirt that made his eyes take on shades of the same color and stand out even more against the golden tan that definitely didn't look like he got it in a booth at some strip mall spa. *Nothing* about him suggested polish—not the lines around his eyes, or the ratty clothes or longish light brown hair that kept sliding down into his eyes. Even his beard stubble looked like what he'd woken up with and hadn't felt like shaving rather than something cultivated to look fashionably scruffy.

He was so utterly the opposite of the dancer boys.

*Justifications R Us . . .*

*Hush, you.*

Even the inner voice's evil laughing couldn't stop me from watching some more as he walked over to the TV and slipped a disc into the DVD player. As he dropped to the floor beside me, I reached back to the end table, snagged the remote, and handed it over.

"Okay, have at it, but I warn you, if it's porn, it's not gonna tip the scales in your favor."

"Well, damn, there goes my plan."

I stopped, sandwich halfway to my mouth, and glanced over to find him watching me, his expression stone cold serious except for edges of his mouth, turning up just a little, which had me fighting back a smile of my own. Then, just like last night, we burst into laughter at the same time even as I did a mental head shake. Bad enough he was cute, he had to have a sense of humor, too?

"Okay, so if not porn, then what?"

Although I'd already guessed, even before he said, "Last year's show from Finals," and a green field with a group assembled in a formation popped up on the screen.

The music was jazz—something loud and driving and bringing to mind images of smoky nightclubs and zoot suits—reverberating all the way down to my bones. And the . . . what did Jonathan call them? The guard? They were un*real*. Like Jonathan said, they danced—*ay Dios mío,* did they dance. At the same time, they handled beautiful streaming flags and machine-gun-looking props and even at one point, wooden folding chairs, opening and closing and leaping over them. It had the discipline and finesse I associated with classical dance, but also a wildness and raw energy that seemed so . . . free. *Then,* the camera zoomed in on a featured horn soloist—Jonathan, bent back, horn pointed at the night sky as he let loose with a wailing solo that should've blistered the paint straight off the walls. And the expression on his face as he finished and pumped his fist, said he knew it, too.

Never taking my eyes off the screen, I refilled my glass with tea and downed half of it in one desperate swallow.

As the final chords played out, I was nothing but ripples of goose bumps, my legs twitching in response to every leap and turn. More goose bumps rose as I felt his shoulder brush against mine.

"Wow." I kept staring at the screen, even though it'd gone dark.

I swore I could feel his breath against my cheek as he sighed. "Yeah, I know."

"Oh, you really don't play fair." Out of the corner of my eye, I could see him looking away from the screen and back again.

"Not when it comes to something that's important to me."

In the dead silence that followed his quiet words, I could *swear* it felt like he was talking about me. Even let myself believe it for a split second. But that was stupid.

"Please come audition, Soledad."

See? It was his corps that was important. Right? That he needed me for. He needed me to be Carmen. I wouldn't let myself think of anything else.

"What time do you want to pick me up?"

# heatwave

Ten minutes before eight and I was still moving in slow-mo, which is why the two polite knocks didn't quite register and why Mamacita beat me to the front door. From the kitchen where I was nibbling on a *tostada* and sipping a *café con leche,* I heard, "Uh, hi . . . My name is Jonathan. I'm supposed to be picking up Soledad."

Setting my buttered Cuban bread and my coffee down on the counter, I hot-footed it into the living room, going for the intercept before Mamacita started making him shuffle cards or God knows what else. Luckily, though, she'd simply left him standing peacefully in front of the packed bookshelves, head tilted as he read the titles. I was so unbelievably relieved, I nearly tripped over Mamacita herself, clearly on her way to find me. Her hands caught my upper arms as she murmured, *"Ya, m'ija, despacio."*

"Sorry," I apologized, immediately feeling calmer at her gentle touch. "Sorry," I repeated to Jonathan, who had looked up at my less-than-graceful entrance.

"For what? I'm a little early."

"Not by much—I'm almost ready to go. Come on back." Because no way was I leaving him by himself to poke around some more. My middle school portraits were in here, for God's sake.

*"Soledad, demuestra educación, por favor."*

Damn. And here I'd been hoping she'd let us slide on out of here without benefit of formalities.

*Of course—like she'd pass up the chance to actually meet the nice, "chévere" boy?*

"Sorry." I tried to make the introductions as quick and painless as possible. "Mamacita, this is Jonathan Crandall. He and I go to school together. Jonathan, this is Paloma Reyes, my grandmother."

Okay, I *could* cop to the introduction being kind of fun, watching his eyes go wide since, let's face it, the woman so didn't look like a grandmother.

She took his outstretched hand in both of hers, inclining her head like some exotic queen as he said, "Nice to meet you," and was smart enough to leave off "ma'am."

*"Igualmente."*

"And now, we *really* need to get going." I gestured toward the kitchen. "Let me pour my coffee into a travel mug and grab my bag. I don't know when I'll be back," I added for Mamacita's benefit. "I'll call when I have some idea."

"Okay, *mi vida.*" Leaning in, she brushed a kiss against my cheek and whispered, *"Es muy lindo."*

My cheeks went up in flames as I whirled and stalked into the kitchen.

Ay Dios mío, por favor, *let him not have heard or if he did, let him not have understood.*

Not like she was wrong or anything. He *was* pretty.

At the same time, though, he really did seem totally unaware of it. Or he was aware and just didn't care. My money was on option number two, because honestly? Jonathan didn't strike me as particularly stupid or disingenuous. He was just as clearly about the music as I was about dance. Not much room left for anything else.

It wasn't just his intensity in talking me into this crazy plan, either, that had me thinking that—if anything, it was more how he *looked* when he performed, which I'd gotten to observe more than a few times last night, since he'd been generous enough to leave the DVD with me. *God,* but that fierce expression was hot.

I shivered again, recalling that image, nearly spilling hot coffee and milk on my hand.

"You okay?"

"Ow, shit." *Now* I spilled. *Dork.* "I'm all right," I said, wiping the outside of the cup and my hand with a dish towel. "Adrenaline overload, I guess—" Damned cheerful rooster on the towel looked like he was laughing at me. I threw it on the counter, making sure his smarmy little feathered ass landed facedown.

Jonathan grinned from where he was leaning against the back door. "It'll be good."

"I hope so."

"Seriously, Soledad, relax. You'll be great." Reaching down, he picked up my bag from the floor, slinging it over his shoulder as I met him at the door, keys and coffee in one hand, the remains of my *tostada* in the other. "So, your grandmother doesn't speak English?"

I rolled my eyes as I popped the last bite of bread in my mouth. After swallowing, I said, "She speaks perfect English when she wants to—which isn't often."

"Why not?"

"I like to think of it as a way of maintaining identity, *m'ijo.*"

Only my quick, last-second swerve kept our heads from colliding as we turned in tandem to discover Mamacita in the doorway to the kitchen—and how long had she been lurking there eavesdropping, anyway? The woman had no shame, I swear. And poor Jonathan, turning all sorts of red.

"I— I'm sorry, Mrs. Reyes—," he stammered, looking like he was searching for more words even as she waved him off.

"*Ay,* don't worry so much, *niño.* It was an honest question." She lifted a shoulder. "As much as I've always encouraged her to be her own person and travel her own path, I've also always wanted to make sure that Soledad had a good foundation for knowing what and who she comes from—a touchstone, if you will. Language is but one means to the end."

Sure, on the surface it sounded kind of woo-woo and New Age, but there was so much more there. Our gazes met and I felt all her love and devotion wrapping around me. She might embarrass the hell out of me sometimes, but never did I doubt how much she cared. A quick glance at Jonathan showed him with his head tilted, this expression on his face of, I don't know, confusion, I guess. Like he couldn't quite register what he was hearing. But a second later, a different word popped into my head: longing. *That* was it. Eyes wide, mouth slightly open, he reminded me exactly of a little boy with his face pressed up against the window of a toy store at Christmas.

A second later, the quiet moment was gone, shattered by the blare of . . . "Mr. Roboto"?

*Ohh*-kay, then. Just call me equal parts stunned and amused, because, really, bad eighties cheese as a ringtone? However, my almost unholy urge to giggle faded just as soon as Jonathan flipped open his cell. "I'm *not* going to be late."

Wow. Odd way to answer. I exchanged a quick glance with

Mamacita, seeing by the little line between her eyebrows that she was thinking the same thing.

"No, sir, I won't have to speed. I told you, she lives behind Miami Dade College—right by the Parkway. I'll come that way. Yes, sir, I know—good examples. Yes, sir, I know it's on me. Yeah, I said I *know*."

He flipped the phone closed without so much as a good-bye and gave it this look that should've shorted out all its little circuits. I wanted to ask . . . but you know, maybe not—

"Is everything all right, *m'ijo*?"

Mamacita clearly didn't have any such reservations.

He lifted his head and smiled, nodding once. "Everything's fine. Just my father. He's seriously hardcore."

"He's going to be there?"

"Yeah, didn't I tell you?" His smile brightened as his gaze shifted from Mamacita to me, but it still didn't quite wash—his eyes were dull, the different shades leeched out of them. "He's the horn instructor. You ready to roll? I'm almost embarrassed to admit I'm actually more hardass than Dad for being on time."

Who? What? Roll where? I blinked, trying to remember my own name and what was the *matter* with me?

"Where are we going, anyway?" I asked once we were in his truck and on Gratigny Parkway.

He glanced away from the road. "Out past Sawgrass."

"And you live—?"

"Aventura."

"Coming to get me was kind of out of your way, wasn't it?"

"No. Not really." The corner of his mouth eased up as he returned his attention to the road and the crazy drivers who were out, even this early, on a Sunday. "So, you ready for your live intro to corps?"

No. Not really.

What I wanted was to know was what that half-smile was about and *why* he wanted to be absolutely certain that I'd make it to this audition, because I'd eat my tights if that wasn't what was behind the offer of a ride, because yeah, it *was* out of the way, no matter what he said. I wanted to know what the deal was with his dad, because clearly something hinky there, and you know, I think what I most wanted was to bag this audition and keep driving and find somewhere quiet to just talk, because all of a sudden, more than anything else, I wanted to really, truly get to know Jonathan Crandall.

Of course, I didn't say any of that. I just nodded and said, "Yeah, I'm juiced."

"Me, too." Before I could register that too completely and start wondering what he meant, he was asking, "You want to listen to something?" At my nod, he pushed a button on the steering wheel. "I think you'll like this, but if you don't, we can pick something else."

As sweet, low-key jazz drifted from the speakers he glanced over again, a sheepish grin on his face. "Figured something mellow would be good for settling the pre-audition nerves."

I listened, the gentle flow of the piano and mellow throb of the bass feeling like they were seeping through my skin and straight to my nerve-tense muscles, like a musical massage. "Sounds familiar."

"Vince Guaraldi—you know, the guy who did the Charlie Brown music? This is a chart called "Cast Your Fate to the Wind." A lot of people don't realize he did a lot more than just the cartoon scores."

"Count me among the Philistines." I leaned my head back and closed my eyes, trying to feel the music even more. The melody brought to mind journeys and unknown destinations, allowing yourself to go wherever the wind blew. The title really was fitting.

"Can you burn me a copy?"

"I'd be happy to." The words were soft, flowing with the same gentle vibe as the piano and sinking into my pores. Turning my head and opening my eyes, I met his gaze.

"Jonathan, the road."

His voice went even softer. "There's no one on it."

"We're on it. I'd like us to *stay* on it."

"Right." I watched the muscles of his throat tighten and relax as he swallowed, then returned his attention to the highway. So it wasn't just me. And I did my damnedest to keep the long breath I released as unnoticeable as possible.

It was almost a relief to let the music take over for the rest of the ride, keeping each of us quiet and lost in thought until we pulled into a massive parking lot. Silently, I took in the collection of barrel-roofed warehouses arranged around a large grassy area marked like a football field.

"Welcome to the home of the Florida Raiders."

"It's . . . enormous."

"One of our original members was South Florida's Donald Trump before Donald even conceived of his first comb-over. Unlike the Donald, though, he didn't marry any supermodels or begat any heirs, so the Raiders are it." He pulled into a parking spot near one of the warehouses and killed the engine, the bright sound of a horn running through a warm-up exercise drifting through the windows, underscored by a rapid burst of percussion.

"You saying he left it *all* to the corps?"

"Yep. It's a seriously sweet financial setup, in the form of a foundation. It's also the reason we're still all-male when so many corps have gone coed. A stipulation that requires we remain all-male. The old man was big on tradition."

"Then how am I—"

"There's always a loophole." He broke in with a shrug. "And bingo pays for a lot."

"Bingo?"

He nodded. "Yeah. As a not-for-profit, the organization can run the games, and we use the proceeds to supplement what the foundation gives us annually. It's more than enough to pay for you without touching foundation money."

"Thank God, then, for *viejitas* with deep pockets," I muttered as I slid from the truck and reached behind the seat for my bag, my hand grazing Jonathan's as he reached for his gig bag. We both froze.

"Thank God for what with deep pockets?" he finally said, breaking the spell.

"Um, little old ladies who love bingo," I managed to croak out. Grabbing my water bottle from the outside pocket of my bag, I took a long drink, then held it against my cheek. You'd think I'd never brushed against a hot guy before. God, but I was pathetic.

We fell into step together heading toward one of the buildings. "So—they're expecting you here in the guard building. I'll take you in and introduce you, but then I have to get to horn warm-up."

I stopped in my tracks. "You're not staying?" Not that I couldn't handle an audition on my own—always had before. But man, on *such* foreign turf, it would've been nice to have a familiar face around.

"I can't." He looked genuinely sorry about it, too. "I'm the horn line captain this year. I really do need to be in there before anyone else, making sure everything's ready and just setting a good example overall, especially since we have a lot of rookies this year.

The vets have to set the tone or else everything has this tendency to fall to shit."

"Right—sorry. Being a total drama queen here." I laughed, but it came out sounding more like a wheeze.

He reached out and pushed the strap of my bag higher up on my shoulder. "No, you're not. This is new and you're nervous. It's natural."

*Not for me.* But I didn't say it out loud. Because I wasn't so sure how to explain that. Or why this time was different. Auditions were auditions, right?

Seeing him waiting with the door open, I tried to shake it off, but as I crossed the threshold, cue the stopping dead in my tracks again as something like thirty guys in various forms of workout gear turned to eye me down. And as I stood there, feeling more and more like a bug trapped under a microscope, I felt a hand take mine.

"Just an audition, Soledad," he said quietly, his fingers impossibly warm as they gently squeezed.

And just like at every other audition, I got all sorts of vibes, from simple curiosity to the more challenging "prove yourself, bitch" from the guys watching as Jonathan released my hand and we made our way to a small group of teacher/instructor types. Funny thing, though. The vibes—especially the more hostile ones—settled me down. Felt familiar except that for the first time in my life, the scales were tipped more to the testosterone-y side.

"So this has to be the Soledad Reyes I've heard so much about."
*Whoa.*

Staring *not* cool, but I couldn't help it. The voice by itself was striking enough—bass-drum deep and rumbling with a slow Southern drawl, but it was the rest of him—*Wow.* Only years of stage training prevented a completely tacky *omigawd* double take.

Seriously. From the bleached blond hair to the incredibly delicate, beautiful face to the killer body that was halfway between dancer and linebacker—long, lean, and with *enormous* shoulders made even bigger by the most violently hideous Hawaiian shirt I'd ever set eyes on. This guy was easily one of the most singular men I'd ever seen. From a dancer? That was saying something.

"Yeah, this is her," Jonathan replied with a grin that made me wonder *what*, exactly, he'd been saying about me. But couldn't ponder too much, since he was proceeding with the formalities. "Soledad, this is Gray Sheffield—he's the corps director as well as the guard caption head—instructor," he clarified in response to the look I sent him at the odd term. "Your chief commandant."

"If she makes it," replied a new voice.

Still in the process of shaking Gray's hand, I glanced over into a pair of cool blue-gray eyes that narrowed as they studied me, then Jonathan. That's when I realized that Jonathan's hand was resting on my back. And as the moment stretched into something incredibly uncomfortable, I felt it tremble then drop away, leaving me feeling a little . . . exposed. To the point where I shivered and found myself fighting a serious urge to take a step closer to Jonathan.

"Not like we have 'em knocking down the door to help us out, Marc," Gray responded mildly. "And Jonathan says she's a tremendous performer."

"Jonathan says a lot of things," replied his dad, because who else could it be? From the narrow stare to the stick-up-the-ass posture to the short, iron-gray haircut, the guy had *hardcore* written all over him.

With a pointed stare at his watch, he added "Like how he's sure to be on time for warm-up so he can set a good example."

Man, how Jonathan didn't rise to that sort of bait, I don't know.

I mean, I was all about the discipline and working hard, but for this kind of treatment I would've told the dude where he could stick his good example.

But Jonathan just calmly smiled and directed his own pointed glance down at his watch. "I'm early. And I'm on my way." But he didn't immediately ditch, instead putting his hand on my back again and turning me away from the crowd, creating the sense that it was just the two of us. "Remember—just an audition. You're too good to let this throw you."

"It won't." The nerves—the unfamiliar ones, at any rate—were gone and all that was left was the nervous anticipation. The good stuff. "You'd better go," I said, smiling to reassure him I really was okay. "You don't want to piss your dad off."

His eyes narrowed in an eerie replica of his dad's stare. "He'll be fine."

"So will I."

"I know." His face relaxed as he backed away with a small wave. "I'll see you later."

"Later." Turning toward the bleachers lining one wall, I went over and found a reasonably clear space to set my bag.

"Where can I warm up?" I asked Gray.

"We'll all warm up together," he responded. "I use a modified version of the New York City Ballet Workout for warm-up, so it should be right up your alley," he added, gesturing to the portable barres already lined up in the middle of the battered, but clearly cared for, wood floor. I lightly bounced on the balls of my feet, smiling as I felt the slight give of suspended flooring. *Nice.*

"I take it you approve?"

"Oh yeah . . ." I bounced some more because I just couldn't get over it. "No offense, but it's kind of surprising—finding it here."

Gray crossed massive forearms over his chest and smiled. "Well, when I'm not doing the corps thing, I'm a physical therapist. I've seen too many injuries that could've been prevented just with proper equipment. So I'm pretty insistent on having anything that can preserve the corps' health and safety. Personal quirk."

"Nice quirk."

Digging through my dance bag, I found my soft ballet slippers and pulled them on. Clothes-wise, I hadn't dressed to impress but rather for comfort and ease of movement: nylon dance pants rolled up to my calves and a formfitting half-camisole with a loose tank top over. Okay, so while the pants and cami were standard-issue black, in a small concession to vanity I had chosen my favorite deep purple tank. Mamacita said it made me look like an exotic hothouse flower. Thank God she hadn't popped out with *that* in front of Jonathan.

The ritual of warming up was predictably soothing and incredibly welcome. Watching Gray, since his pattern of exercises was unfamiliar, helped to sharpen my focus. Concentrating on my body—bending over, feeling my back elongate, every little vertebra popping and settling into place as I slowly straightened and bent back, making sure that every muscle was warm and stretched and supple—took the rest of my attention. So yeah, I was more than a little shocked when, after Gray turned the volume down on the music and said, "Okay, everyone, relax and take a breather," I turned to find, oh, I don't know, about a hundred pairs of eyes focused on *me*. The owners of all those eyes crowded the bleachers, reminding me of . . . . owls or something, their heads swiveling in tandem as I walked a few steps—and how in hell had so many people managed to sneak into the building?

*All dance, all the time. You think you'd be used to it.*

Jolted by a fresh shot of adrenaline, I searched for the one pair of eyes I was hoping was there and not off somewhere else being responsible or anything crazy like that. There—from the top row of the bleachers, where he had a clear view over everyone else, he met my gaze, offering calm reassurance.

Smiling, he nodded and mouthed, *"Own it."*

I nodded.

*Already mine.*

# el tango

"Not to freak you out or anything . . ."

I looked away from the crowd gathered on the bleachers to find Gray standing beside me. As I raised an eyebrow, he shrugged. "Everyone's curious."

"A little warning might've been nice, but otherwise, no big. Do you have something specific in mind for me?"

He leaned in, saying in a quiet rumble, "Look, darlin', I'm flying fairly blind, too, so let's both play it like we know what we're doing, okay?"

Oh, I *liked* him.

"Got it." I pulled off my slippers and padded barefoot to my bag, where I exchanged them for the jazz shoes. Reaching back into the bag, I fished out a CD that I handed to him. "Let's go with track twelve."

He glanced down at the disc, whistling softly. "Interesting choice."

"Thanks." I pulled on the shoes. "It's something I've been playing around with, and from what Jonathan's told me, corps is all about creative exploration and pushing the envelope. Seemed apropos."

"Indeed." He winked as he turned and went to the stereo while I reached back into my bag for the small canister of powdered rosin I always carried. After applying some directly to my shoes and wiping up the excess, I rose to a *relevé* and down, sliding my feet back and forth, making sure the powder was evenly distributed. Warm enough now, I lost the pants, revealing a pair of form-fitting dance shorts beneath.

As I walked the length of the bleachers and out onto the floor, eyeballing the dimensions and staking out a good starting spot, I heard, "What do you want to bet she'll be kiss-ass predictable and do something from *Carmen*?" said fairly quiet, but not *that* quiet. My gut clenched some, but otherwise? Bitch, *please*. I met the offender's gaze head-on and smiled that smile I'd learned from Mamacita—the serene, "come too close and I'll cut you" smile.

He flinched, then caught himself and straightened, looking like he'd bitten into a lemon. The guy sitting next to him rolled his eyes and elbowed Miss Thing before getting up.

"Don't sweat it, baby," he said as he approached and crouched down to pick something up off the floor. Straightening, he showed me the scrap of paper trapped between two fingers. "Caught on your shoe," he explained with a cheerful grin. "You know, for as many big girls as there are in the guard, you'd be amazed at how old boys' club they can be. Some of them are flipping their dainty shit at the idea of a female in the midst, but they'll deal."

"It's okay. I don't bite." I waited a beat and added, "Much. And only if you ask nice."

He laughed, the sound almost as bright as the tiny ruby stud piercing his nose. "I'm Nataraj—Raj for short."

I couldn't help but grin back. "Soledad."

Huge dark eyes creased at the corners, but before he could say anything more, Gray's voice broke in—

"All right, people—I know y'all are curious about this little experiment. This is Soledad Reyes, a dance student at Biscayne, and we're going to see if my idea of using a real Carmen translates from brilliant concept to brilliant reality. One way or the other I'm brilliant, right? Right."

A laugh rippled through the crowd. Okay, joking. There was a first for an audition. I liked it.

"Soledad, you ready?"

While Raj backed away with a whispered "Break a leg," I ventured farther out onto the floor and assumed my opening pose, breathing deep as I sank into my zone.

Okay, yeah, it had been tempting to choose something from *Carmen,* in a *duh* sort of way. Or, if I wanted to stay within the realm of classical ballet, *Firebird,* especially since it was polished to a diamond shine for the showcase.

But the last couple of days, weighing the pros and cons of everything I had in my repertoire, I'd kept coming back to this one piece—"El Tango de Roxanne" from *Moulin Rouge*—as being perfect. Dangerous, raw, sexy, angry, and above all, passionate. All of it building from a deceptively quiet and mysterious introduction. Only way to make it better would be chocolate.

While the piano and guitar traded delicate riffs, I prowled the expanse of the floor in a rough figure eight. At the strings' dramatic entrance, my footwork mimicked the sharp staccato precision, my upper body remaining taut as a wire. In contrast, my arms were fluid and sinuous, mirroring the vocals in telling the story of a professional seductress, paid for her favors, forced by circumstance to hold herself aloof until she meets the one man who's so different, who *really* wants her for who she is and who desperately tries to convince her she no longer has to sell herself. As the narrator's passion and fury grew, that fluidity traveled down my fingers, through my arms, into my body and legs, the precise, deliberate movements giving way to something more, something untamed and wild, as I veered between the security of a wealthy customer and the temptation of unconditional love.

During one quiet passage, I skirted the edges of the floor, meeting all those eyes, weighing . . . deciding . . . finally extending a hand and pulling a smiling Raj—my chosen customer—up. Taking the cue, he fell into step with me, the two of us swaying together, perfectly matched for a few brief moments until the music crescendoed once again and I pushed him away, bursting free, covering the floor in a huge sweeping series of turning leaps. Soaring, feeling the familiar, glorious stretch and burn of my legs in full extension, lost in the beauty of the music, in the story, building toward that one moment—where the strings, the brass, the vocals all joined together in a brilliant cacophony, prompting one last series of rapid-fire steps before I began spinning on one leg, turning in the classic *fouetté en tournant,* my free leg whipping around and around, faster and faster, never touching the ground until the last, final crashing note where I dropped to both knees, head thrown back, both arms thrust up and out, imploring my lover to return.

My eyes closed, the only thing I was aware of was the sound of my own harsh breathing, whistling through my throat and nose. After a few seconds I managed to get my breathing under control, and still . . . nothing. My arms falling to my sides, I blinked, the room fuzzy and gray around the edges. As it sharpened, the first thing I saw was the owl convention in the bleachers, every last one of them focused on a tight group that included Gray and

Jonathan's dad, all of them whispering like a bunch of *viejitas* at one of my family's holiday barbecues. And clearly, they were whispering about me, since, well, they kept looking *over* at me and gesturing *at* me and then looking some more, the bleacher creatures following their every move.

"Um, hello?"

*Did I suck?*

*Don't be a moron. You didn't suck.*

I rocked back onto my heels and stood, fisting my hands on my hips and trying for bravado as all eyes turned my way. And really wishing I'd driven myself, 'cause if I had sucked, I wanted to eighty-six this joint in a hurry and there's no way that could happen, not with Jonathan having to play at Responsible Guy. I looked up at him and found that he seemed to be stuck staring at the small group of instructors with that intense gaze of his I'd first seen back in the dressing room at school. Like he was trying to *will* them to make a decision. The right decision.

"Anyone?"

*Finally.* Gray broke away, leaving the others huddled together and whispering. Handing me a towel and a bottle of water, he said, "You can quit looking like that, darlin'. You did fine. Better than fine, actually. And I think you know that."

"Thank you," I replied, meaning the bottle as well as the compliment. I took a long drink of water and ran the cold bottle along my forehead. "And yeah, it *felt* great, actually, but what do I know from your standards for suckage? Could be that it wasn't at all what you had in mind."

"No, it wasn't," he admitted, which sent my heart doing a dive into my stomach. Good—but not good enough. Or too different. Or something.

A part that *should* be mine, slipping away.

Again

*Damn.*

"But you know what it was?"

I couldn't look at him. Instead, I stared down, carefully pointing and flexing one foot against the floor. "What's that?"

"The missing piece."

Slowly, I lifted my head. "What?"

"Yeah. You've just changed the direction of the whole show."

My grip tightened on the water bottle, plastic giving beneath my fingers with a loud crack. "Say *what*?"

"Using 'El Tango' is a perfect way in which to bring in a contemporary twist yet still keep within the show, stylistically speaking. It's exactly what we've been missing—keeping *Carmen* from being the same old, same old, and it's brilliant because, really, Roxanne, Carmen . . . both opportunistic characters . . . it creates a beautiful symmetry." And no matter how slow and easy that drawl of his was, each word still sounded sharp and measured—this wasn't any kind of a whim. He knew exactly what he was saying. In the four minutes and forty-four seconds it had taken me to perform, he'd completely reformulated the corps' show. Wicked impressive, even if it left me feeling just this side of queasy.

"We'll have to get started on new arrangements right away, and new drill, and we'll need to start brainstorming your exact routine—and I can already see your costume." I swear, even the palm trees on that butt-ugly shirt were perking up with every idea he kept throwing out. The other instructors who'd joined us looked as hyped as Gray—all except for one whose expression was going more granite and hardass with every word.

"Three weeks before tour?"

"Not like we haven't done it before, Marc," Gray replied mildly.

"And what else are the first few weeks of tour for, other than tweaking? Come on, name me one corps that's ever come out of the gate with the final product? What we need to do right *now* is get this girl set up—get the forms filled out, arrange for the stipend—"

"Hel-*lo*, 'this girl' is still here, and what is the matter with you people that none of you know how to actually *ask* any damned thing?" I glared up at Jonathan in the bleachers, looking like he was going to crack up—and felt the temper that Mamacita kept warning would one day be my downfall ratchet up another notch.

"I mean, I haven't exactly said I'd do this yet."

# give me a reason

"I haven't exactly said I'd do this yet."

Said into the quiet dark of the cab of Jonathan's truck as we sat in my driveway after nearly twelve hours of rehearsal—mostly observed on my part, and I was *still* tired. Seriously—these guys gave dancers a run for their money.

"Did you like what you saw today?"

I could tell by the sound of his voice he already knew what my answer would be, even if I wasn't prefacing it with the longest, girliest sigh ever.

"You know I did, *cabrón.*"

"What did you just call me?"

"You don't want to know." I sighed again. "Jonathan, I just don't know. It's so different—"

"And that's just what you love."

The hard challenge in his voice had the intensity of a physical slap, leaving me stunned *again* that he'd figured that out about me—so fast. "I *do* love how different it is," I admitted slowly, staring at him, the faint blue light from the dashboard almost creating an aura around him. "And I love that Gray thinks I'm so right for it." Because yeah, a little ego stroking absolutely didn't hurt. "But it's *so* different." The tremendous urgency and fire, the artistic freedom, the beauty of so many disciplines melding together . . . I shook my head, hoping all these crazy thoughts would just fall into place, because right now?

*You could jeopardize your chances for New York—*

*Or improve them—*

*But you've been waiting your whole life to go on your own, show who you are, make your mark—*

*Who's to say I still can't do that—*

*This isn't you—*

*But maybe it is—*

*I don't know . . .*

*I don't know . . .*

Not so much with the sense making.

"I'm sorry, I'm just going to have to think about it some more. But thank you." Impulsively, I leaned forward and kissed his cheek. "Thank you for showing me your amazing world," I whispered against his skin.

I pulled away, reaching for the door handle.

"Soledad—wait. Please."

Turning back, I found him staring down at the steering wheel, his hands clenched tight around it.

"What?"

His shoulders rose and fell with a deep breath, his fingers curling and uncurling around the wheel.

"Jonathan, what is it?"

Releasing the wheel, he turned and stared into my face for a long, long moment, his body swaying forward slightly, then back, mine doing the same, like it was trying to help his make the decision. Finally, he leaned all the way forward, closing the distance between us. And as his mouth brushed against my cheek, my stomach swooped like I was on a roller coaster.

"You're welcome," he said, his breath ruffling the loose hair around my ear. A second kiss to the opposite cheek prompted a reverse swoop, my hands twisting into the front of his T-shirt.

"And I'm glad you enjoyed it." The whispered words teased my skin as his hands skimmed along my arms, to my neck, and finally to frame my face.

His "Please?" was even softer than a whisper—more a breath, really, traveling from his body to mine as our mouths finally touched. And honestly, wasn't that what I'd been waiting for? To see if he *really* wanted me to be a part of this?

*Tell the truth now.*

Okay. To see if he really wanted *me*. Wanted to get to know me as much as I wanted to get to know him.

His mouth was firm, lips slightly chapped from so many hours of practice, with a faint, sharp flavor from the Carmex I'd watched him apply throughout the day. He moved slow and gentle, a little tentative, maybe even a little afraid—and oh . . . God, there it was, that tiny bit of vulnerable creeping through that sucked me right in and had me carefully trailing my hands across his chest to his arms, feeling the muscles trembling beneath skin that still held the warmth of all the sun it had absorbed today. *So* warm, and I just wanted to burrow closer, my arms up around his neck, one hand sliding up into his hair, my fingers curving against his skull. The closer I got, the more my head tilted back; the more my head tilted, the more my mouth started to open under his.

Changing the angle of my head so the kiss could get even deeper and more intense, I shifted my hands to his waist, reaching beneath the hem of his T-shirt to stroke the broad, solid body I already knew was beautiful, since like most everyone else, he'd stripped off his shirt during the hottest hours of the outdoor rehearsal. Don't ask me what anyone else looked like, though.

One touch of my tongue to his and it was like a dam blowing wide open—his hands reaching around to my back and pulling me impossibly close, like he couldn't get enough. And I never knew a first kiss—any kiss, actually—could be that sweet and gentle and hungry and hot all at the same time. His breath was mine, mine was his—the most amazingly complete feeling I'd ever experienced.

I should've been scared. Never had I fallen so fast for a guy.

I *wasn't* scared. I wanted more.

My hands curled into fists as I dropped my head to his shoulder, trying to get my breathing back to something steady before I passed out.

"God, Soledad," he groaned against my neck, where he was currently exploring, making me shiver and arch against him, wanting more. But his hands stayed on my back, stroking and bunching up the fabric of my tank, like he wanted to go farther, but again, I sort of sensed . . . fear.

"Please, Jonathan."

A long sigh against my neck, and next thing I knew, my tank was up and off, his hands wandering over my now mostly bare back, covered only by the thin straps of my cropped camisole, and around to my stomach, his thumbs brushing the undersides of my breasts.

"I can't believe this is finally happening."

I lifted my head, meeting his gaze.

"Four years, you know?" he said quietly.

"Four years what?"

"Four years I've wanted—"

I leaned back as far as I could in the tight confines of the truck. Those beautiful gray eyes were serious and intent, without a single ounce of bullshit in them.

"Wanted . . ." My voice trailed off with the growing realization.

"You." The single word hung between us, draped in equal parts sadness and hope.

"Then why did you wait so long?" Four *years*?

He shook his head and let loose with one of those soft laughs that made my insides turn to flan. "Because for three of those years, I was a short, socially backwards music wonk with no real excuse other than maybe asking about English homework to speak to a girl who made me crazy. And even as a not-so-short music wonk I still couldn't come up with a good excuse to really speak to a girl who *still* made me crazy." Shrugging, he looked down at his hands, resting on my waist. "I guess I needed a good excuse."

"How about just saying hi? That's a good excuse." I swear, I wanted to thump his clueless, very cute ass.

His hands trembled against my skin, just like at the audition this morning. But unlike the audition, they stayed put—even tightened a little. Keeping his gaze down, he said, "Soledad, I don't have a lot of . . . experience with girls."

I nudged his chin gently until he finally lifted his head and looked at me. "You're gay?"

He rolled his eyes and hit me with a look that had me giggling. "I don't have a lot of experience, period. Come on, I've spent most of the last four years in an all-male corps. You saw today what kind of commitment it demands. And that's on top of school and practicing my horn like a damned robot. . . ."

One hand moved to my neck, holding me steady—not tight,

but more like he didn't want to let go anytime soon. "Don't get me wrong, I love music, but living it the way I have hasn't left a lot of time for . . . a life, you know?"

It was like slogging through mud, my mind trying to catch up with his words. "So what changed? You seemed so confident when you came after me in the dressing room. And at Mack and Mabel's."

He laughed again. "That wasn't confidence, that was desperation. My last shot. I'd known for three weeks that Gray wanted a Carmen and I still hadn't had the balls—" Goose bumps rose along my spine as his fingers traced a slow, wondering line from my neck to my waist. "I knew if I didn't make some sort of move right then, I'd never—" He stopped and took a deep breath. "But now we've got the chance to spend the summer together. More than anything, I *want* to spend the summer with you. Please?" he said again as he kissed me. And I *knew.*

Maybe I was jumping in with both feet without thinking it through. Maybe I was a little—a *lot*—crazy for doing this on impulse after a lifetime of planning, but most of all, what I felt as I kissed Jonathan back was the most tremendous sense of tenderness for this sensitive, beautiful boy, and underneath that was, well . . . he wanted *me.*

He wanted me *so* much and I could give that to him.

Tell me, how was I supposed to resist?

# hide and seek

*May 21*

*I'm scared—I think. The way I'm feeling, really it's indescribable. I must be ten kinds of out of my mind. . . .*

   I stopped and chewed on the end of my favorite purple pen as I tried to make sense of what I wanted to write. Normally, writing in my journal came so easy, but not today. Today, everything felt completely different. I kept chewing on my pen, my gaze wandering around the seniors' courtyard where I was spending lunch period on a palm-shaded bench. Even though there were a few other people scattered around the courtyard, they were all into their own thing, giving the area a peaceful, solitary vibe. It was so quiet, I could hear the waves of the bay, just beyond the retaining wall surrounding this side of the school. A reassuring sound that tended to lull me into a similar sort of zone as when I danced.

Slowly, though, a new sensation began weighing down my shoulders, like something was drawing closer, approaching. . . . Glancing over my shoulder, I was startled to find Jonathan standing directly behind me, brows drawn together.

"Hey, what's up?" I stood to give him a kiss but held back at the last second, my hand falling to my side instead of reaching for his the way I wanted to. For all I knew, he didn't dig public affection. There was so much that was foreign turf about this. I mean, he'd been affectionate enough at the audition yesterday, but that had been different. Before everything changed.

"Nothing." He let his backpack slide from his shoulder to his feet, glancing at the journal I was still clutching before casting his gaze down like L.L.Bean canvas was the niftiest thing ever. "You're busy, I should go."

"Busy?" I ducked my head, trying to get him to look at me. "No . . . not really."

"Could've fooled me. I've been standing behind you for a while. Called your name a couple of times, but you were just totally off in your own world."

This was too weird—especially after last night. How he'd called after he got home and we'd talked on the phone for hours, his soft voice telling me he couldn't believe this was happening, how this was going to be the best summer ever, until I finally drifted off, the deep, steady sound of his breathing making it seem as if he was right beside me on my pillow.

But it also meant my phone was good and dead this morning and English, the only class we shared, wasn't until fifth period. With seniors sequestered in our discipline classes all morning, this was the first chance I'd had to hook up with him and he was pulling a complete Jekyll and Hyde. Not at all the same Jonathan I'd whispered to and shared dreams with last night.

"So? If I'm in a zone it just means you have to try a little harder. Like in the dressing room, right? You didn't let it stop you then." I was going for lighthearted, but annoyed and confused bled through, painting the last few words with a challenging tone.

Glancing at him from beneath my lashes, I could see his profile, set and stubborn as he stared at the oak tree that dominated the center of the courtyard. "That was different."

"Not really." I took a deep breath. "Look, are you having second thoughts?" With another deep breath, I barreled on. "I mean, I know the reality hardly ever lives up to the fantasy and all, so if you're changing your mind, that's cool—"

No, not cool. After all that persistence in chasing after me to do corps, telling me he'd wanted me for four years—*now* maybe he was changing his mind and I couldn't believe how much the thought of that hurt. After what? Twelve hours?

*Idiota.*

"What?" The flat grayness of his voice finally gave way to something with tone and color. "What do you mean? Soledad—*no.*"

Now it was me who wouldn't look at him, turning away to stare at the huge, twisting oak branches.

"Soledad." All of a sudden, my view of the tree was blocked as he circled the bench to stand in front of me, his hands warm as they covered mine. Still wouldn't look into his face, though, so I focused higher, on the curtains of lacy, silver-green Spanish moss waving gently from the branches.

Carefully, he pried the pen and journal from my hands. Setting them on the bench, he took my hands again, patiently uncurling them until we were palm to palm, our fingers laced together. "Please look at me."

"Why?"

"Just . . . please?" One hand released mine so he could reach out and trace a line from the corner of my eye, down along my jaw and to my chin. "I'm so sorry. I was just . . . I'm sorry."

The words were barely above a whisper, but maybe that's why they sounded all the more honest.

I finally released the deep breath I'd been holding for what felt like hours. "You know, this is as new for me as it is for you, Jonathan. And it's *hard*." I lifted my free hand and brushed his hair back. "My life has been dance the same way yours has been music. I've never had anything like this before. Or even thought I wanted it, really. Until . . . now."

"With me," he said slowly, almost like a question.

"Well . . . yeah."

*Even if it still scares you shitless.*

He sighed and drew us down to the bench, still holding my hand. "God, I am *such* an ass. Freaking out over nothing like some nervous old lady."

"Ease up." I nudged his shoulder with mine. "It's new for both of us, and even if we are going the traditional boyfriend/girlfriend route, we did sort of cliff dive into it without a whole lot of the traditional"—I searched for the right word—"stuff."

"I suppose you've got a point."

We were quiet together for a few minutes, just holding hands, and at last things between us felt right—enough for me to close the little bit of distance between us and rest my head on his shoulder. "So—if you hadn't been hit with a slight attack of the freak-outs, what would you have done when you saw me out here?"

"Well . . . ," he said slowly, his shoulder rising and falling beneath my cheek. "I would have really liked to, you know . . ." His voice trailed off as his shoulder rose again.

"This?" I lifted my head off his shoulder just far enough to brush a kiss against his cheek.

He smiled down at me, a faint red streaking across his cheek-bones, highlighting a few freckles I hadn't noticed until now. "Yeah."

We sat some more, my heart beating faster as he released my hand and carefully slid his arm around my shoulders.

"Anything else?" I whispered. A second later he shifted on the bench and brushed his mouth gently against mine, *just* as the bell rang, signaling the end of lunch. Probably a good thing, because even that one little innocent kiss? *Whoa, mama.*

As we headed for the doors, he asked, "So what are you doing after school?"

"I've got a Latin dance Master class." And *almost* added that I'd ditch because he looked so incredibly disappointed and I hated having put that look on his face. Although . . . would it be bad if I admitted to loving it, too?

*Bad girl.*

"You?" I asked in a hurry before I could say I was ditching. I'd *never* deliberately ditched a class before in my life. Wasn't sure I'd ever even considered it.

"Practice for my trumpet final, I guess." He sighed. "Again."

"What about after that?"

He held the door open for me to pass through into the hallway. "I don't know . . . probably study for regular finals."

"You mean like . . . for English class?" As he fell into step beside me, his arm across my shoulders, I looked up at him with my eyebrows raised, waiting for the light bulb to go off. And . . . there it went.

"What time do you want me to come by?"

Oh, he was a smart boy, this one.

"I'm done at five." I did some quick calculations in my head, to account for driving home, taking a shower, and making myself look presentable in a casually sexy way. "Come by after six?"

He was all lit up again, smiling in a way that had my stomach doing that swooping thing. "Will you hate me if I tempt you with ice cream?"

"Are you kidding? You'll totally be my hero."

"Hero?" His blush was ten kinds of sweet, and so adorable I almost couldn't stand it. "I think I could get used to that."

# wild hope

"Sweep the leg . . . More precise . . . Snap the head sharply. . . . *Así . . . así . . .*" Señor Márquez's voice rang out through the studio as he led me through the tango, his voice building in intensity along with the music, as dark and dramatic as the dance.

"Now . . . lunge—deeper, deeper. Extend the leg and point the toes *y . . . aguanta. Yes.* Hold it just like that—with the eyes as well as the body. . . . You adore and loathe this man you're dancing with, Soledad. You'd kill him just as soon as make love to him."

I felt one of his hands between my shoulder blades and the other along my jaw. "Hold that passion right *there, mi niña. Así . . . perfecto.*"

Out of the corner of my eye I saw Madame smiling and nodding. "Well done, *chérie,* well *done.*"

Dude, Madame's praise had me wanting to break into a gleeful Snoopy dance, but I wouldn't shame her like that, so I held both the pose and the severe expression until Señor Márquez released his hold—my signal to relax and catch my breath. No doubt, the man who'd just led me in the tango was a biggie in the Latin dance world, an absolute *master*. Rumor had it that he was an *old* friend of Madame's in the "wicked, carefree past we never spoke of" sort of way, and that's why he was in our little obscure neck of the woods. Worked for me. Even in his fifties he had it going on, in a smoldering Antonio Banderas sort of way. With Madame divorced ages ago, if the two of them had rekindled their *thing* and we got to reap the benefits, I was all for it.

"*Muchas gracias,* everyone, for such a successful class, and hopefully I shall see you all again tomorrow evening, provided I haven't frightened you off." After a burst of laughter and a round of applause, the class broke off, most of the students swarming around Señor, trying to glean more nuggets of wisdom. Normally, I'd be swarming with the best of them—that tango had been scorching—but I was yanking off my shoes and throwing stuff in my dance bag, because *mira,* I had places to be. In a *hurry,* since it was already past five and Jonathan would no doubt show up on my doorstep on the dot of six. And I could *not* wait.

"Soledad, a moment?"

I paused with my hand on the outside door. "Yes, Madame?"

"In my office, *s'il vous plaît?*"

"Uh, I'm kind of in a . . . *Oui,* Madame," I amended myself mid-sentence as I saw one jet-black eyebrow slowly go high-rise. Because one simply didn't say *non* to Madame. Entering her office I was surprised to find Señor Márquez already seated on the small love seat, having somehow slid loose from the sycophants. Impressive.

Madame came around to stand in front of me, her hands reaching for mine while a smile creased her huge dark eyes. "We have wonderful news for you, *chérie.*"

"Yes?" And *we?* As in Señor Márquez being part of the *we?* Seeing as he was nodding and smiling, guess so.

"I am afraid we played a bit of a rotten trick on you, *mi vida*," he said, not looking in the slightest bit apologetic. "I was auditioning you today."

"Ex*cuse* me?"

"You're familiar with my company, yes?"

"Um . . . yes." As in, *duh*. Anyone who followed Latin dance knew of his small but super accomplished Argentine-based company.

"One of our soloists is retiring in the spring. As is our custom, a corps member is moving up to take her place. The corps position is yours if you wish."

"Uh . . ." Village Idiot Alert, but seriously, my brain was too busy trying to process *"The corps position is yours if you wish."*

Señor Márquez opted to ignore my non-response. "Even though Imelda doesn't retire until spring, you can join us immediately. We have a bit of a financial cushion and I can afford to have you along for our fall tour. We spend August rehearsing in Buenos Aires before we leave for Europe."

"Now you don't have to worry about saving money for New York and concern yourself with auditions." Madame led me over to the pair of chairs in front of her desk. "To have career security so quickly and save yourself from that soul-sucking heartbreak—what a beautiful gift."

I stared down at her hands, small and almost birdlike in my larger ones, trying to make sense of what she was saying. "But . . . *why?* What about the ballet companies—the auditions we were going to prepare for? Don't you think I can do it anymore? Make it with one of them?"

"I know you have the ability, *chérie*. You are a beautiful dancer and your ballet is exquisite. But I fear for what that world will demand of you in exchange. And the truth is, you are equally gifted as a Latin dancer." Her grip tightened. "There are *thousands* of girls who aspire to ballet but comparatively few who are drawn to Latin. All things being equal, why not take advantage, *non*? Especially since it's as much your passion as ballet. I have wondered if it's not even more so."

The words of passion and love for Latin dance barely registered. The only thing I heard was the doubt. "Right." I jerked my hands free.

"Soledad," she snapped, rising to stand over me. "You're not stupid. You must realize how you have been protected, *bébé*. No matter how tough your teachers at school have been, no matter how hard you think I am, you have been protected. I know what it is like—" She put her hand under my chin and forced my head up. "I lived the life you so desire. I danced on stages across the world and starved myself nearly to death in the process. I became the physical ideal, was able to dance beautifully, until my body failed me."

I shook my head, trying to break free, but she held tighter, her gaze practically pinning me to the chair.

"I abused my body, Soledad. And as a consequence, had to retire early. Was never able to have children."

My mouth opened, but before I could get a word out, she broke in. "Of course it's different for you. You know of anorexia and bulimia and all the names for the things we did and had no idea we were doing. It doesn't mean it won't happen. And I will *not* allow it, *chérie*. Not to any student of mine, and especially not to you." Finally, she released me and leaned back against the desk. "Don't you understand? If you take Rafael's offer, your abilities and gifts will be celebrated. Not denigrated and beaten down in an attempt to force you into an unrealistic ideal."

"You don't think I can do it." This woman who'd been my hero my entire life—my biggest cheerleader, the one person who'd kept me going whenever I thought it was too much and there was no way I *could* do it. . . .

She didn't think I could do it.

"And you are not listening." She dropped back into the chair, her lips pursed as she shook her head.

"If you make your mark under Rafael's guidance, as I know you can, in time the entire world of dance—including ballet—will be yours for the taking. Companies all over the world will beg for you to guest." Leaning forward, she gripped my forearms. "You are unique, Soledad. Celebrate it. Turn it to your advantage."

In other words—she didn't think I could do it.

*What about all that talk of exploring all forms of the art? What about what you're considering with corps? How is it any different?*

*It's totally different. It's my choice. Not anyone else's. And not because I can't do anything else.*

"Well, speaking of unique . . ." I shook off her hands and stood, picking up my dance bag and slinging it over my shoulder—buying time so my voice wouldn't break. "I hadn't had the chance to tell you yet, Madame, but an opportunity—a paid opportunity—to perform has come my way for this summer."

That eyebrow went up again, the closest thing I'd get to surprise from her, I knew. "Yes?"

"It's a discipline known as drum and bugle corps. They're performing *Carmen* and they need me. To dance."

She shook her head, clearly as unfamiliar with the concept as I'd been a week ago. I turned to Señor Márquez. "Thank you for your generous offer, *señor*—"

*Are you crazy?*

"But the corps tours until mid-August, so I'm afraid I wouldn't be able to join you in time."

*You* are *crazy.*

Nodding, he said, "As I said, the position doesn't truly come open until spring. Having you with us during the fall would have been a benefit." His gaze calmly shifted from me to Madame and back. "Perhaps it's better this way—allow you time to . . . weigh all your options?" He smiled, but his eyes narrowed. "I will, however, need to know by October at the very latest. I cannot keep the position open indefinitely."

I forced a smile. "*Gracias, señor*—for the offer and your understanding." Not sure I would've kept the snarky edge from that last word even if I could.

"Soledad—"

My fingers clenched around the doorjamb, I looked back over my shoulder at Madame.

"I would like to know more about this . . . corps. What sort of dancing is it?"

"Unique, Madame."

Made for a hell of an exit line.

# harder to breathe

Up or down?

I pulled up the sides of my hair, *again,* fastened it in a barrette, *again,* then after staring at myself in the mirror, pulled the stupid thing out, *again.*

*"Mi vida, te vas a dejar calva."*

I stuck my tongue out at Mamacita's reflection. "Might make this easier." Picking up my brush, I pulled it through the thick mess. "Oh, *ow,* dammit." I fought to unsnarl the brush from a tangle that had appeared out of nowhere. I swear, at this rate, I really was going to wind up bald.

*"Cálmate."* She grabbed my wrist and pried the brush from my grip. Beginning with short strokes, she worked through the tangle until the brush went from crown to waist in one smooth motion.

"So . . . *el niño lindo* is coming over?"

"You know, you *could* just call him Jonathan."

"Am I wrong when I call him pretty?"

"No," I muttered, fighting a grin. Reaching under the vanity, I pulled out my small bag of everyday makeup, selecting eyeliner and lip stain. Dabbing on the stain, I mumbled, "We're going to study for our English final."

"Ah, *bueno*." She let my hair fall into its natural off-center part before pulling it back into a loose ponytail at the nape of my neck. Holding my hair with one hand, she reached past me and snagged a dark blue scarf from the basket resting on the vanity. "I'm curious, *m'ija*—why did you never mention him before Friday?"

I waited for her to tie the scarf before leaning forward and lining my eyes with the pencil, smudging the purple along my lashes with a fingertip and leaning back to check out the overall effect. Much better than plain old black, the way it brought out the different shades of blue and green in my eyes—made them pop against my dark brown hair and eyebrows.

"We never talked much before he came to me with this corps thing." Which I still totally wanted to smack him for. "Didn't seem to have anything in common."

Mamacita's reflection smiled. "And now?"

I ducked my head, putting the makeup away and generally straightening up, but there was no disguising the blush I had going. Even my ears felt hot.

"Okay, yeah, we're, um . . . going out," I stammered, "like, dating each other. Exclusively." Argh. Face, meet palm.

*"No me digas."*

My glaring at her only deepened the all-knowing serenity of her smile. You know, there were times the woman was just plain mean.

"You know, you *could* try to act at least a little surprised." I stomped out of the bathroom and toward the kitchen. "What'd you do," I grumbled as I did a quick reconnaissance, making sure I didn't need to make any last-minute snack runs to 7-Eleven.

"Celtic Cross? Tree of Life? The lesser known Nosy Grand-mother?"

"*Ay mi vida,* I didn't need the cards," she said in a gentle tone that nevertheless sounded like she was on the verge of losing it. "Although now that you mention it, maybe when he arrives . . ."

"Don't you dare—" I slammed the refrigerator door shut and whirled to face her. "You wouldn't, would you? You're just messing with me, right?"

She'd totally given up the ghost, dropping into a chair and laughing her head off.

"You're just messing with me." I pushed off from the fridge and flopped into another chair at the table. "You know, malicious is so not a good look for you, and don't you have a date with Dom or something?"

But after a few seconds of total outrage and simply wanting to . . . shake her, I realized just how ridiculous I'd been, crazed and buzzing around the house for the last hour in a way that would put a Cuban housewife to shame.

"So you knew?"

"*Ay mi vida,*" she repeated as she reached out and stroked my cheek. "I can honestly say I've never seen you quite like this. Since Friday and escalating every day." Rising, she crossed to the stove where she occupied herself with the kettle and mugs and tea bags. "And yes, I am going out with Domenic tonight. Dinner and a movie since he has the night off. Perhaps the bookstore afterwards and a *cafecito.*"

Damn, that was smooth, how she managed that. Sighing, I propped my elbow on the table and rested my head in my hand. "Honestly, Mamacita, how you can trust me so much, I have no idea." The sudden hot, prickling sensation behind my lids had me blinking hard and glad I hadn't bothered with mascara.

"Because I know you."

Just then, the kettle whistled almost like she willed the thing to go off—a second later I heard the sound of an engine shutting off, followed by the slam of a door, like she'd willed that, too. The near-crying sensation gave way to me practically scrambling out of my chair, grinning like a loon and not really caring if she teased me about it.

"*El niño lindo* has you just a little crazy and that's all right." Her hand, warm from holding her mug, rubbed between my shoulder blades, soothing the nerves that were doing a wild samba. "A little crazy is maybe not such a bad thing for you right now." I barely heard that last bit, my brain more fixated on how was I going to answer the door? Should I casually lean in the open doorway? Wait for him to knock? Or . . . or . . . should I let Mamacita answer while I hung back, all cool?

"I'll be in the back until Domenic arrives."

*That* got my attention. "You're not staying out here?"

She paused in the doorway. "Do you want me to?"

"Just for a minute." Suddenly, it seemed really important to introduce Jonathan to Mamacita again. Really introduce him now that . . . well, that she knew.

At the two knocks, I forgot about cool or studied poses and made a beeline for the door, just about yanking it off the hinges.

"Hi." And boy was I glad I'd stayed barefoot. I *really* liked looking up at him.

"Hey." Then he just stopped and stared, his eyes widening.

"What?" God, I hadn't accidentally smeared the lip stain or anything, had I? I resisted the urge to rub at the corners of my lips or under my eyes.

"You look amazing."

Again, I fought an urge, this time to just toss out some coy

"Oh, I just threw this on" commentary. For one thing, I sucked at coy. Instead, I did a quick little pirouette, making the lavender baby-doll dress swirl around my thighs. "You like?"

He grinned and nodded. "I like."

I did my own checking out, taking in the khaki shorts that showed off *really* nice tanned legs and the white polo that made his eyes take on a slate blue cast, kind of absurdly pleased I hadn't been the only one to go to obvious effort. "You look pretty great, too."

"Thanks." He ducked his head, looking like he was just this side of kicking his shoe at some nonexistent pebble, before holding up a white bag with a distinctive hot pink and aqua logo. "I bring gifts. I hope dark chocolate's okay—I remembered that was the shake you got the other night."

I rose on tiptoe so I could give him a quick kiss. "You got Mack and Mabel's homemade ice cream," I said against his mouth, then gave him another kiss. "And I *love* dark chocolate."

"I did good then?" Another kiss, him initiating it this time as his arm went around my waist, pulling me in closer.

"Yep." And much as I wouldn't mind staying in the doorway and necking, I did want him to say hi to Mamacita—not to mention, get the ice cream into the freezer. Mack and Mabel's ice cream was the good stuff, man. He really *did* like me. Taking the bag from him, I said, "Just drop your backpack anywhere—Mamacita's in the kitchen waiting to say 'hi' before she goes out, then we can grab snacks and we get down to it."

"You mean we're really gonna study?"

Just shy of the kitchen door, I stopped and stared at him, my jaw dropping. Then laughed as he raised his hands and said, "Kidding—," and then with the most wicked cute grin, added, "Sort of," which had me wondering, how much did we have to *really* study for this test? I'd been carrying A's and B's all semester after all. . . .

Grabbing his hand, I led him into the kitchen, where as promised, Mamacita waited, leaning against the counter and sipping her tea.

"*Hola,* Mrs. Reyes."

"Hello, Jonathan, how are you tonight?"

"Fine. A little nervous about finals."

I grinned into the freezer as I stashed the ice cream. *So* cute, the two of them meeting halfway with the greetings.

"I'm sure you'll both do fine. *Bueno, mi vida,* I'll be in the back."

"Okay." I switched from the freezer to the fridge. "Coke?" I asked Jonathan, pulling out a Fresca for myself.

"Sure." Next thing I knew, he was beside me, taking the sodas and putting them on the counter. "What else can I help with?" he asked, his fingers trailing damp, cool lines down my bare arm to my hand, where they teased the inside of my palm.

Hanging on to the refrigerator's handle, I said, "I, um . . . have some chips and salsa . . . if you want. And Jonathan?"

"Yeah?" He lifted my hand and watching me the entire time, obviously wanting to make sure it was okay, brought it to his mouth and, oh . . . *kissed* the palm. Oh . . . *mama.*

"We really need to study—at least, I do. . . ."

"I've got a chem final on Wednesday."

The rough/soft combination of his lips brushed against the sensitive skin of my palm, making me drop my forehead to the cool metal of the fridge. The thought occurred that maybe I should just open the freezer and stick my head in. "I doubt it's this kind of chemistry."

I straightened, the move making him do the same and thankfully, take a couple steps back, giving me some breathing room. "*You* are being bad." I shook a finger his direction as I opened the pantry cabinet and grabbed a bag of chips and the jar of salsa.

After dumping the salsa into a bowl, I grabbed it and the chips and led the way out of the kitchen.

"So being bad isn't good?"

I didn't say anything until we got to my room, where I plunked the chips and salsa on the low square table I used as a desk.

"That's not what I said."

"So what did you say, then?" He set the sodas on the table and stood there, arms crossed.

"Look, I just want to be able to know we can hang out together too, you know? That it's not just about wanting to jump each other's bones."

"*Do* you?"

"Do I *what?*"

"Want to—" He snapped his mouth shut and dropped his head, locking his hands behind his neck. "Shit," he muttered, the tendons in his forearms standing out as his muscles tensed even more. "I'm sorry, Soledad. I'm being a total dick."

"It's okay." Strangely, it was. He was just super emotional—I got that. Any artist, their emotions tended to have a thinner veneer over them. It's what we tapped into to be really great, but at the same time made real life a pain, sometimes. And how could I be ticked, considering I was the cause of the high emotion?

"And to answer your question, of *course* I want to. Eventually."

It was a monumentally risky thing to be saying, even with the "eventually." It was just—being with Jonathan was *so* intoxicating. A look or a kiss at a weak moment, and all my good intentions to take things slow were likely to disappear faster than that ice cream he'd brought. And let's face it, say something like that to most guys, and they'd be making a move, like, *now*. But not Jonathan. Nothing more from him other than a soft "*Damn*."

His hands fell to his sides, his fingers flexing. "It's not just about that, I swear."

"I know it's not, Jonathan. But this is all so new for me—I guess I really want take our time. Savor it some." Not that that had ever seemed a big priority before. Just some weird artificial construct designed to play with people's minds when all you wanted to do was play with their bodies. Man, had I been off the mark. Big time. The anticipation might kill me but for the first time, I really felt as if the payoff would be *so* worth it. Hence, good intentions. Not that that had ever seemed a big priority before. Just some weird artificial construct designed to play with people's minds when all you wanted to do was play with their bodies. Man, had I been off the mark. Big time. The anticipation might kill me, but for the first time, I really felt as if the payoff would be *so* worth it. Hence, the good intentions.

"I think maybe the four-year wait is kind of catching up to me. Forgive me?"

*God*. Had to try to remember that. If my couple of days had me twitchy and crazy and entertaining wicked ideas, what must his four years feel like? "Of course."

"Oh, and maybe this'll earn me more forgiveness points." He reached into his backpack, and what he pulled out and dropped on the table had my jaw dropping.

"Jesus Christ, where—"

"I picked it up off the bench at lunch. You must have forgotten it."

"But I never . . ." Never. Ever. I *always* knew where my journal was. But no . . . there it was, resting on the table, purple pen neatly tucked into its elastic band. Like a fast rewind, I scrolled back to lunchtime, the patio, writing in my journal, then that bizarre sort of argument with Jonathan and making up, all before fifth period. But no memory of returning the journal to my back-pack. And that I hadn't even noticed it missing at all the rest of the day?

"Um . . . thanks. Seriously."

"Means a lot, huh?"

*You have no idea.*

"Well yeah, I guess. Probably sounds stupid." Tried for a casual shrug, even though the muscles in my neck and shoulders felt like the Tin Man trying to move before the WD-40. I could almost hear the creaking, sounding like a haunting *nooooo.*

"It doesn't." Jonathan took a step closer, reaching out, a little hesitantly, more like the Jonathan from last night, as he took my hand. "I didn't look. I swear."

"I didn't think—"

His eyebrows rose. "Yeah, you did."

"Yeah, I did." A nervous laugh escaped, high and breathy and totally unlike me. "Sorry."

"It's okay." He drew us down to the big cushions surrounding the table. "We're still in getting to know each other mode. But I promise, much as I want to know everything about you, I want to hear it from *you.* Not from some book."

"Thanks." Another laugh, relief that evolved into a sigh as his arms went around me and he drew me close. We held each other, his hands stroking my back as I rubbed my cheek against his shoulder every now and again, just to feel the friction and the warmth of his skin radiating through his shirt.

"You know, Jonathan, you're a lot better at this boyfriend/girlfriend stuff than you think you are."

"Good." His chest rose and fell beneath my cheek. "Because I want to be the best boyfriend. Ever."

# june

# any other way

"Relax."

"I can't." Mamacita was going to kill me. I was down to one nail I hadn't chewed into oblivion. At least I'd made it through the showcase last night with my manicure intact, so it wasn't like I *had* to keep them nice anymore. "How'd your trumpet final go, by the way?"

"Fine. Just like I told you yesterday after I took it."

*Oh, crap.* I had asked yesterday. Twice, as a matter of fact, remembering that I'd also asked backstage at the showcase. I squeezed my eyes shut, then opened one just far enough to see Jonathan glancing over with a grin on his face. "Sorry." I gnawed on the last intact nail until my hand was snatched away from my mouth and held in a firm grip.

"Relax," he repeated. "It's going to be fine."

"Right." I tried not to squeeze his hand too tight, but *oye,* I was crazy nervous. My first weekend camp—two full days of rehearsals.

Seeing how the guys *really* felt about having a girl around. I had *no* idea what to expect, not really, and it was freaking me straight off the charts, no matter how many times Jonathan told me to relax and that it would be okay.

"Tell me, how can I relax? This is my first test—heavy-duty immersion and seeing if I've got the right stuff and all that."

"Listen, do you want to bag this?"

"What?"

"If it's freaking you this hard, we don't have to do it."

"But—it's a required rehearsal."

"I mean, the whole thing."

Stunned, I stared at him, willing him to look at me so I could see his whole face, the expression in his eyes, but for once he kept his gaze fixed on the road.

"What do you mean?" I finally asked.

"Look, we don't need it anymore. Asking you to audition was what I needed to get off my ass and finally talk to you, but once I did—once *we* happened—that was it for me. If you really don't want to do this, we can bail. Stay home. Maybe travel. Whatever you want."

"*What?*" My throat slammed shut, the word rising to a squeak. "Are you serious? Corps is practically your life."

He lifted my hand, kissing the back. "It *was*." His gaze flickered away from the road to me. "Now, not so much."

I was a worm. Seriously—a worm. No matter how much I wanted to be doing this, couldn't deny that in the back of my mind I'd been stressing over walking away from Señor Márquez's offer. Even Mamacita, darn her, hadn't been any help—when I told her about it, I would've imagined her first move would've been to reach straight for the tarot. But *nooooo*. Instead, she simply made me a cup of tea and said, "It's your future, *m'ija*. You're the one who must be content with your choice. Whatever form it takes."

And to make matters worse, there were Señor Márquez and Madame at the showcase last night, Madame kissing me, giving me a huge bouquet of roses, and lavishing praise on my performances. Talk about making me feel ungrateful and, well . . . if I was honest, guilty. After all, it *was* a professional company—one that had recruited me, no less. What were the chances of something like that ever happening again?

Yet here Jonathan was, willing to toss something he so completely loved, that was so integral to who he was, totally aside, without thinking twice. For me. You know, I think I was glad I hadn't said anything to him about the job offer.

"I want to do this," I said quietly, staring out the truck's window at the blur of strip malls and palm trees and subdivisions. "I really do."

Releasing my hand, he reached over to stroke my neck. "Then it's a moot point. You and me—we can have it *all* this summer." Then he laughed, massaging the tense muscles beneath my skin. "If you'll just *relax*."


"My darling Carmen . . . I must have you . . . our destiny is to be together *always*." Raj—or rather, the show's newly minted Don José, Carmen's devoted and ultimately doomed lover—slid an arm around my waist and mock-groped as we waited in the lunch line.

Swatting at his hands, I spluttered, "I swear, I'm going to stab you with a fork if you don't stop." Since Gray had declared him Don José at this morning's rehearsal, he'd been crooning in my ear like some demented Pepé Le Pew, every chance he got. Except when we were actually practicing. Then, he was as dead serious about the work as me. For the most part, I was thinking this was going to work really well. If I didn't stab him with a fork first.

"Soledad—"

Still smacking Raj, I glanced up into a pair of warm brown eyes. "Yes, ma'am?"

"Finally. I so wanted to meet you last night at the showcase, but it was simply too chaotic." As the sweet-looking woman spoke, her smile broadened into one that was a near twin of another that was already super familiar. "I'm Linda Crandall. Jonathan's mom."

*Augh.* Sweaty, gross from rehearsing, and acting like a total dork. *Not* the way I envisioned a first meeting with my boyfriend's mom.

*Everyone's sweaty and gross, m'ija. Pull it together.*

"Hi, Mrs. Crandall." I grasped the hand she extended across the stainless-steel serving counter in a brief clasp. "Pleasure to meet you."

"No, dear, the pleasure's definitely mine." She leaned forward and lowered her voice. "Jonathan's such a typical boy—doesn't tend to say much, but he's been lit up in a way I've never seen since you joined the corps. I'm genuinely looking forward to getting to know you."

As we walked away, Raj sing-songed, "Well, don't you look like the proverbial cat who ate the canary with a side of cream?"

"Shut up." But I could *not* get rid of the smile that kept tugging at the corners of my mouth.

"Will not. This is going to make for a completely delicious summer, all hello, young lovers, and Mumsy even approves."

Cheeks burning, I said, "Hey, look, Gray wants us to sit with him." Raj let loose with another gleeful cackle, the little shit, but like during rehearsal, he knew when to quit. So we were able to spend a fairly peaceful lunch listening to Gray outlining his plans. Part of it had me working in unison with the rest of the guard, but mostly I was going to be performing individual routines that we'd begin blocking out after lunch.

"What I'm envisioning is the rest of the guard as a whole portraying Escamillo, not just as a cocky bullfighter vying for Carmen's attention, but rather a representation of all the multifaceted temptations the world provides, wooing her away from Don José."

"Kind of abstract, isn't it, having one person for one character, but many people for another?" Raj asked in between bites of grilled chicken.

"Yeah, it is, but it's so beautiful, too—this idea that it's only the most powerful love that could keep us from all those temptations. While the love might've been that strong and all-encompassing for Don José, for Carmen . . . not so much." Gray's hands were a blur as he indicated moving from one end of the emotional spectrum to the other.

I ducked as a piece of romaine went flying past. "You know, Gray, I'm wondering if you're not part Cuban, as much as you talk with your hands."

"Sorry." He popped the salad left on the fork into his mouth and chewed, his eyes narrowing, no doubt cooking up more schemes.

"Hey, room enough for a lowly horn player?"

"Hey—" I leaned my head back, finding a nice spot against Jonathan's stomach. "Of course, provided you don't mind flying salad as Gray plots."

"So I heard." Tugging gently on my braid, he tilted my head back a little farther, leaned down, and kissed the tip of my nose. "And see," he added, picking a piece of lettuce off the chair beside mine and tossing it onto the table before sitting down. He glanced down at my near-empty plate. "You ate, right?"

"Hello, have you met me?" With a grin, I forked up the last bite of my grilled chicken salad. "Of course I ate." After I swallowed, I leaned over and kissed his cheek, warm and slightly salty from being outside and sweating.

"Sorry, don't mean to hover," he mumbled around a bite of sandwich. "Rehearsals are just so intense."

"No kidding," I agreed with a laugh. "This morning's seriously kicked my ass as hard as any dance practice." Across the table, Gray smirked and lifted his glass in toast. Keeping a casual arm propped on Jonathan's shoulder, I gently scratched the back of his neck. "But I'm a big girl." Reaching across him with my free hand, I snagged one of his chips.

"Yeah, she seems pretty vigilant about keeping herself properly fed and hydrated, if the size of that salad she just totaled is any indicator," Raj cheerfully supplied.

"Bite me, Raj."

"My pleasure, babycakes." He blew a kiss across the table, looking totally unrepentant. What a ham.

Jonathan leaned back into my caress, forcing my fingers up into his hair. "I know you're a big girl, but it's something to watch out for, especially outdoor rehears—"

"Jonathan!"

His head jerked away from my hand as he whipped it around, looking for the source of the summons.

"Shit," he muttered under his breath, then louder, "yeah, Dad?"

Turning in my chair, I saw Dr. Crandall sitting at a table on the opposite side of the dining hall with what looked like some of the other horn kids.

"We're going over some changes to the 'Toreador' sextet."

"I just sat down," he replied mildly, waving a hand at his full tray.

"We're merely going over the score—we'll rehearse as soon as everyone's done eating."

Right. Code for Over Here. Now. Not that Jonathan cared. Turning back to the table, he said, "I'll be over as soon as I'm done," in this eerie-cool and calm voice that had goose bumps rising on my skin like someone had just turned the air way down. Following Jonathan's lead, I turned back to the table, but not before I caught Dr. Crandall's gaze sliding over me and boy, did it *not* feel comfortable. Especially since the whole dining room seemed to be staring in my direction as well.

"Jonathan, don't you think—"

"No." He took another bite of his sandwich, his fingers digging into the hoagie roll.

Leaning in, I dropped my voice further, not wanting to spark any more gossip. "Look, it's okay. We were just finishing up and going back to work. And I'll see you at dinner, right?" I rubbed between his shoulders as I spoke, trying to get him to relax, but it was like rubbing a marble slab.

"I'm not his puppet."

"But you are the horn captain," I countered, not even wanting to *touch* the puppet commentary. "What was it you told me? 'The vets have to set the tone or everything falls to shit'?"

Amazingly, his muscles gradually relaxed and he leaned back against my hand again. "God, I really don't want to." He sighed and dropped his sandwich to the plate. After wiping his hands on a napkin, he brushed his fingers across my cheek. "Suppose I should, though. But dinner for sure."

"Pinky swear." I held my hand out, pinky extended, and waited for him to hook his around mine, using our linked fingers to pull him closer for a quick kiss. He picked up his tray and crossed over to where his father sat with a score, looking like he was absorbed in talking to the other kids. The minute Jonathan hit the table, though, he looked up with this won-the-battle smirk.

Sometimes, doing the right thing *sucked*.

As Raj, Gray, and I made our way back to the guard building, I asked, "Is it weird for the different sections to mix?" I'd noticed that for the most part, the drummers hung with the drummers, the guard with the guard, horns with horns. Not to mention, the looks that had zeroed in on our table—from all over the room— when Jonathan had joined us.

"I suppose sections tend to stick with their own," Gray replied. "It's maybe more fluid in a coed corps, but that's mostly due to the inevitable hookups."

"Come on, you can't tell me there aren't hookups in an all-male corps."

"Oh, there are." Raj elbowed me with a leer and a wink. "If you want, I'll tell you *all* about them."

I elbowed him back. "Perv."

"You say that as if it's a bad thing."

Gray held the door to the guard building open, shaking his head at us. "Yeah, of course they happen—it's a byproduct of being in such close proximity. Generally, we kind of turn a blind eye. Especially if you're of age."

"So why all the curious gazes back there, then?"

This time, it was Raj who answered. "Because it's Jonathan."

Suspicion confirmed. "And his dad." Like some high-drama *telenovela*, I swear.

Gray nodded, rubbing the back of his neck. "Marc isn't exactly subtle about how important Jonathan's music career is to him."

He paused, then took a deep breath and added, "He sure isn't going to go out of his way to make things easy for you two."

A slow burn started twisting its way down my spine. Seriously—Jonathan and I were both adults. What could the old man really do? "Things not being easy is practically a way of life for me, Gray. Don't worry, I've dealt with worse."

"I don't doubt you sincerely believe that, darlin', but honestly? I'd be shocked if you had."

# pocketful of sunshine

After a couple weeks of rehearsals, I was starting to get the hang of the corps world. As well as discovering just how genuinely nuts Gray Sheffield was.

"The front needs to be lower," he declared.

"Are you *high*?" I spluttered, fisting my hands on my hips and flinching as I got poked by yet another pin. "Dude, any lower, and I'm liable to get arrested for solicitation."

"That's sort of the idea, isn't it?" he replied with this truly evil smile, walking around me to check out the already obscenely low back of my costume, then back around the front. "I think the nude insert in front should be sprinkled with more of the rhinestones that are scattered over the body of the dress. Draw attention to Carmen's . . . *attractions*."

"I am *not* a midway ride."

Next to him, Mrs. Crandall was rapidly jotting notes on a pad.

"I think, too, a rhinestone beaded strap on the diagonal across the back. Practical, with the added benefit of visual interest."

"Sounds good," Gray agreed, taking another turn around the stool, the lime-green and yellow surfboards and turquoise waves on tonight's Hawaiian shirt leaving me vaguely seasick. "And let's make sure we have plenty of floating chiffon panels for the skirt. I want her to appear as ethereal as possible, as if she could disappear in an instant."

*Ethereal. Heh.*

"And what are you grinning at?" Gray asked.

My smile got bigger. "Still adjusting to this new mind-set of ethereal."

He snorted in response—we'd been down this road already. "I keep telling you, you are absolutely going to love the staging a football field provides." Coming to a stop in front of me, he took my hands in his and held my arms out to the sides. "Have you got good freedom of movement with your arms?"

In response, I pulled my hands free and did a full extension above my head, wincing again as a pin poked my armpit, then carefully lowered my arms. "I will, as soon as everything is stitched together. No offense," I added to Mrs. Crandall.

"None taken." It never ceased to amaze me how her eyes and smile were as warm as her husband's were cold. More proof that opposites really did attract. "Do you want me to add beaded nude inserts along the shoulders and sleeves as well?" she asked Gray.

"Oh, or how about this—we make the entire left arm nude except for a beaded rose winding its way down her arm?" Her pencil made quick scratching noises on her pad. "What do you think?" She held the paper up, a rough sketch showing what she had in mind, her voice sounding light and excited, which had me doing a mental double take. I mean, generally, the woman was *so* mellow and low-key as to practically blend into the woodwork.

"Oh, yeah, Linda, that's perfect." Gray was nodding with that crazed grin on his face again. "Okay, I think we're set here."

"I'll do up a simpler version of the dress, too, as a backup."

"Perfect, again. Soledad, hurry up and change. Everyone will be back in here in a few for final announcements."

"Got it." Jumping off the stool, I headed toward the bathroom, Mrs. Crandall beside me. I glanced over at the sketch in her hand. "That's amazing, Mrs. Crandall, how fast you came up with that."

She smiled, her dark eyes creasing even more at the corners. "Why thank you, sweetheart. While I love working on the flag silks and guard uniforms, I have to tell you it's a real treat to design something so feminine." With another critical glance at the sketch, she pulled the pencil from behind her ear and added a few quick lines. "Gave me a legitimate excuse to go poring through all my books on couture design. Got the idea for this from a vintage Halston."

I giggled as I pushed open the door to the bathroom. "And you have the luck to wind up with a boy who lives in ratty T-shirts."

A small pair of dimples flashed. "I consider it an okay tradeoff."

Well, *yeah,* couldn't blame her, given that the tradeoff was Jonathan. As she helped me ease out of the white Lycra and chiffon dress without impaling myself on the pins, I asked, "Have you ever done it—design—professionally?"

"No." She carefully slid one sleeve down my arm, then the other. "It's really not the sort of career that easily lends itself to family life."

"I guess not." But . . .

*Something's not jibing.*

I mean, it's not as if she was . . . young, exactly. In fact, if I had to guess, I'd say she probably wasn't that far in age from Mamacita, maybe somewhere in her late fifties. Just figured her for one of those women who'd done the career thing and waited to have a family.

But Jonathan was an only, like me. And eighteen, like me. But I'd been raised by my grandmother and he hadn't, so . . . so . . . *So* none of my business. Maybe something to ask Jonathan— someday, but not tonight.

Tonight was about rehearsals and dress fittings and morale-boosting speeches from our instructors telling us how *fabulous* we were, learning all the new music and drill and equipment and choreography. But even more important, it was also about spending more time with Jonathan, a well-earned post-rehearsal movie date at my house.

But only once we got *out* of here.

"Jonathan!"

I glanced over my shoulder, recognizing one of the horn rookies, a sweet kid who clearly had a case of hero worship for Jonathan, coming in for the intercept just as we were trying to make our escape.

"Damn," Jonathan muttered. "I'll just be a sec, okay?"

Nodding, I drifted away, scanning the sheets on the mounted cork-board we used for announcements. Copies of the lists of supplies we'd need for tour, copies of the tour stops and locations where we could pick up care packages mailed from home. *Tons* of fliers for year-end concerts at the different high schools and colleges all of us went to.

Jonathan appeared beside me. "Sorry about that."

"No problem. I needed an extra copy of this anyway." I held up the tour list. "For Mamacita."

"Cool—well, let's go, before Dave comes after me again." He grinned and rolled his eyes. "Rookies."

"Hey!" I jabbed an elbow into his ribs.

"Hey, yourself." He grabbed my arm before I could jab again and raised it high enough to tickle my side with his other hand. "Rookie."

"Ah, stop it!" I tried to get at his ribs, but he kept backing just out of reach, even as he kept a hold on me, managing to sneak in little tickling jabs. Damned long arms. "Jonathan, stop it! I'm going to get the hiccups, you jerk."

"Jonathan."

"Yeah, Mom?" *Por fin,* he quit tickling but still kept hold, sliding his hand up from my elbow to rest on the back of my neck.

"Are you coming straight home after you drop off Soledad?"

"No. Why?"

"Just needed to know if I should set the house alarm right away."

He shifted, his arm sliding all the way across my shoulders. "Go ahead and set it—I don't know when I'll be getting in."

"All right."

All right? *Oye,* if I said something like that to Mamacita, she'd at least expect to know what we were going to be doing and where we were going to be doing it. And make me swear in blood that my phone was turned on. And if I said it in *that* tone of voice, it would definitely be accompanied by a slap upside the head.

"We're watching movies at my house, Mrs. Crandall." With every word, Jonathan's arm got more and more tense across my shoulders, until it felt like dead weight. Honestly, he needed to chill. This was only holding us up a few extra seconds and it was his *mother,* for God's sake.

"Sounds like fun." She spared me a quick glance and a smile, then looked back at Jonathan again. "Do you need any money?"

"No."

What was *up* with him? She was only trying to be a mom. A *nice* mom. I jabbed an elbow into his ribs and gave him a version of Mamacita's Evil Eye. He stared at me, clearly confused, but as I turned up the volume on the look and shot a quick glance Mrs. Crandall's direction, his eyes widened.

"But thanks, Mom—I'm good." Leaning down, he brushed a quick kiss across her cheek before tugging me toward the door.

When I chanced a quick glance back over my shoulder, she was still standing in the same spot, hand to her cheek. There was no reason I should've felt like crying, right?

# world where you live

Finally, we were out the door and making a beeline for Jonathan's truck and freedom.

"Jonathan!"

He let loose with an explosive breath. "*God,* what now?" He turned to the rookie who'd blocked our initial escape. "What is it, Dave?"

"Yeah, um, your Dad just snagged the other guys from the sextet. Wants to run through it again." Little dude looked like an eager puppy, all bounce and enthusiasm.

"How nice for him."

Dave flinched and Jonathan sighed. "Look, dude, I've already practiced more than four hours today, on top of what we did tonight. My chops aren't exactly trashed, but I'm beat and I want to go."

Dave glanced over at me, then stared down at the parking lot. "Yeah, I get it. I'll tell your dad." And you could just tell by the tone of his voice that was the *last* thing he wanted to do. Poor little rookie.

But as he started trudging off, Jonathan slid an apologetic glance my way. "Yo, Dave, hold up." Slipping the truck keys in my hand, he promised, "Fifteen minutes."

I rubbed his shoulder, trying to settle the restless twitching. "Go. It's okay." Although call me paranoid and fit me for a tin foil hat, because I just couldn't help but smell conspiracy. Last thing I was going to do, though, was complain about an extra fifteen minutes. Which turned out to be closer to a half-hour, but again, not complaining—especially after I saw how flushed and giddy Jonathan came back afterwards. His dad might drive him bats, but the music, at least, always had a way of trumping the crazy. Thank God.

*Finally,* we made it to my house, settling in with sodas and popcorn in the back room.

"Okay, I've got *Holy Grail* and the last season of *The Sopranos,*" he said, holding up the cases.

I wrinkled my nose. "I always pass out halfway through *Holy Grail,* and watching blood and gore mafioso style? Right—because that makes for such a romantic night in with my boyfriend. How about *Notting Hill* or *Hairspray*?" Giggling madly, I fell back against the cushions of the sofa. "Oh man, your *face.* You're almost the color of the sofa."

"Nice. A girlfriend with a vicious streak," he complained to the ceiling. He rested his chin on my shoulder, his mouth brushing against my jaw as he suggested, "How about *Princess Bride*?"

The giggles died away. "You remembered?"

"Yeah, of course." He ran his fingers through my loose ponytail, tugging the elastic off. "Would I sound like a giant dweeb if I said I think of that night sort of like our first date?"

Wow. Just . . . wow.

"A boyfriend who's a total softie." Resting my palm against his cheek, I traced the curve of his lower lip with my thumb. "How about after Westley and Buttercup's happily-ever-after we watch one of the Bourne movies?"

He hit me with a hopeful stare. "Seriously?"

Laughing, I reached over the arm of the sofa for the cases. "Mamacita's got a thing for spy thriller movies and Matt Damon's butt."

"Jesus, Soledad, TMI."

I laughed harder. "I know, believe me, but she did get me hooked."

Those thick, straight brows drew together. "On Matt Damon's butt?"

"The *movies*."

His face relaxed. "I'd be pretty pathetic if I admitted to a sense of relief, right?"

"You're much hotter."

But I never got the chance to prove the many different ways his empirical hotness trumped Matt's because Jonathan never even made it past Westley and Inigo dueling swords and witty repartee, passing completely *out,* head in my lap. Carefully shifting so I could stretch out beside him, I stroked my fingers through his hair with wonderment. He was *here*. He trusted me enough to fall asleep in my arms, leaving himself completely open and vulnerable. Leaving me feeling like I was blasting off on the Mission: SPACE ride at Epcot, light-headed and with my stomach somewhere in the vicinity of my throat.

Slipping from the sofa, I went to get my journal, then settled myself at the opposite end of the couch from Jonathan. With a blanket over our legs, my feet gently rubbing against his, I lost myself in the familiar rhythms of writing, trying to capture all the sensations and emotions of these firsts before they were diluted by other experiences. Supplanted by other first moments.

"What time is it?"

I glanced up to find him propped on an elbow, rubbing his eyes and shoving his hair from his face. "Just after midnight."

"Wow, some date I turn out to be." He rolled onto his back and yawned.

"It's okay. Do you need to call or anything?"

He looked momentarily confused. "You mean, like home?"

"Yeah."

"Nah—Dad might be ticked that I'm out late, but since I told Mom, it's not like he can complain. Much." He laughed and I tried to, but a twinge of nervousness had me clutching my pen just a little tighter. However, I almost immediately forgot about it as he hit me with a sleepy half-smile. "I really am sorry I zonked. You must think I'm a complete loser."

"No." Looking down, I fiddled with my pen, doodling a design on a page of my journal. "Actually, I . . . I liked it—watching you sleep."

He slid across the sofa until he was right beside me, pulling me onto his lap. "God, Soledad, how do you *do* that? Make me feel so amazing," he whispered, pressing a soft kiss against my neck.

*Guh.* Yeah, totally mutual, especially with the way he kept caressing my neck, his late-night stubble leaving tingly little scratches in the wake of his kisses.

"Jonathan," I gasped, "you'd better stop."

Another kiss, this one on the crazy-sensitive spot behind my ear. "Why?"

"Because I'm not sure *I* can."

I could feel him smiling against my neck just before he lowered his head to the base of my throat and bit, just a tiny little nip, that he soothed with another kiss.

"*Jonathan.*"

"Sorry," he breathed against my neck, making me shiver.

"Are not." *Cabrón*. But as good as he felt, as good as he made *me* feel, it wasn't the right time. "Please, Jonathan. Don't hate me, but I just want everything to be, I don't know . . . perfect."

"Don't be crazy, I could never hate you." His thumb stroked the spot he'd just been kissing. Where my pulse was going insane. "But . . . can you at least help me out with understanding perfect? Are we talking, like, candlelight and flowers?"

"No. Not that kind of perfect. I mean, not that I'm objecting to candles and flowers, but that's not what it's about." I sighed. "It's hard to explain." Especially since I wasn't all that clear on it myself. "It's just . . . I just want—I want it to feel right."

"Okay." He nodded slowly. "Am I a total dog for wishing that feeling right was right now?"

Warmth hit me again, low and sweet. "No."

*And not the only one.*

"Good. Then don't worry. We'll figure it out." He shifted so he was cradling me in a way that was more comforting than anything else, then shifted again, one hand reaching behind his back. "This again? Do I have competition for your attention?"

I lifted my head to find him holding my journal. "You weren't available," I joked even as my fingers itched to snatch the book back. The memory of having left it sitting on that bench was still pretty fresh. "It's no big. Writing helps calm my mind. Kind of a Zen thing."

"Guess it works." His fingers traced the embossed design on the cover. "You seem pretty into it."

"You can blame Mamacita for that," I said with a smile as I recalled the memory. "As soon as I could write, she gave me my first Hello Kitty journal and told me to put all my most secret thoughts and wishes in it. That was pretty much it. Never could get me

110

interested in tarot, but writing? That sort of mystical connection I could totally buy."

"Mystical how?"

I fidgeted, trying to find a comfortable spot, feeling a little backed into a corner. *So* not accustomed to this sort of heart-to-heart—at least, not with a person. "It's like dance in that it allows me to release emotion . . . but in a different way." But unlike dance, it wasn't anything I felt comfortable sharing. With anyone. Not even Mamacita asked what I wrote.

"Well, maybe now you'll have other outlets for all those emotions." He dropped the journal to the floor, then wrapped his arms around me, one hand playing through my hair. "Be a lot more fun than writing."

"No doubt." Because the writing—it wasn't necessarily fun. Sometimes, sure, but it was a lot more than just . . . fun. Like dance. Like Jonathan, although of a *whole* different magnitude.

"Can I ask you something?"

I stretched and rearranged myself, pulling the blanket back over our legs. "Sure."

*As long as it's not about writing.*

*Chill. I think he got the message.*

*We'll see.*

"How did you wind up raised by your grandmother?"

*See? Much easier to answer.*

*Says you.*

"Um . . . well, short answer is, my mother dumped me at Mamacita's when I was two days old and I have no clue who my father is, except for he's who I must've gotten these from." I tapped my cheek beneath one of my eyes—the blue-green so different from everyone else in my immediate family.

"Whoa."

"Yeah." I sighed.

"Why do I get the feeling there's more to it than that?"

"Well . . . yeah. But you don't really want to hear about it, do you?"

"Why not?"

Why not? How about too many details and nuances and things that were probably boring if you just said them out loud. Not that I ever had. But there he was, watching me with that gaze that was open and curious and zeroed in on me with that same laser-beam intensity that had sucked me in that very first day.

"Um, well . . . my grandparents were your usual flavor of Cuban immigrants—came over with nothing, worked their asses off to make something, total American Dream. My mother was the youngest of three, the only girl *and* the only one born here. They were *so* proud of that—and because they were big on assimilation, they decided not to impose any of the typical Cuban parent restrictions. No speaking only Spanish at home, no chaperones, no asking too many questions when she stayed out late, because none of her American friends ever got grilled by their parents that way." My voice went up and down in the sing-song I imagined my bratty mother must have used.

Jonathan's eyes were wide. "So what happened?"

"Hell if I know for sure." My legs twitched beneath the blanket until one of Jonathan's came to rest over them, warm and secure. "All anyone really knows is when she was about fifteen, she started spending more and more time away from home. And who knows what she was doing and who she was doing it with." Now I let my voice take on the suspicious lilt my aunts used whenever my mom came up in conversation. "Until finally she didn't come home. And then she did."

"With you?" he guessed.

"Yeah." My fingers twisted the blanket, curling into the soft cotton weave—*Dios mío,* but I was freezing all of a sudden. "Sick as all get-out, looking like total shit, and to this day no one knows what she dropped or snorted or swallowed when she was pregnant with me, but I guarantee you, it wasn't prenatal vitamins. Or even Flintstones vitamins. A couple nights later, she bailed, never to be heard from again. To this day, we have no idea if she's dead or alive somewhere." I hoped she was dead, actually. Because if she was alive and had never once said anything? To *do* that to Mamcita? To do that to *me*? I'd probably kill her myself if she ever showed up.

"Anyhow, my *abuelo* wanted to give me up to Child Services, Mamacita refused—*he* bailed. Just couldn't take it. I mean, who knows what kind of devil spawned me, right? What might be *wrong* with me? And you know, after all his hard work, to have that kind of failure staring back at him every day? Cuban men kind of have issues with failure."

I tried not to sound bitter—much.

"Jesus, Soledad." He held me closer, one hand rhythmically stroking the length of my hair, the other low on my back, an anchor I let myself lean into.

"Hey, at least she didn't leave me in a Dumpster." I tried to go bright side, lighten the moment, but my voice was shaking. "And you know, Mamacita—she's been all the mother and father I could want. She's given me *everything.*"

"Everything?" His voice was soft as his gaze searched my face.

The moment hung between us as I studied his face in return. "Everything I've needed to this point," I said slowly, the intoxicating rush of falling into the unknown getting stronger with each word. "The future, though . . . I guess that's wide open."

# have you got it in you

"You can't do this, Jonathan."

"Really?"

"Do *not* take that tone with me."

"Back off, Dad. It's just the freakin' bus seating."

"And you're supposed to be on one of the horn buses."

"Unwritten code—*not* a rule."

"Except that you're the horn captain."

"Yeah, *and*? I'm their leader on the field, not their goddamned babysitter. What I want to do with my free time is my business."

"I can imagine what you want to do. You know, Brian never pulled crap like this."

"You mean he always toed the line and followed orders."

"He *listened* when offered sound advice."

"And here we go again. Jesus, you'd think you'd let the school thing go already. Indiana has one of the best music schools in the country."

"For a state university."

"So?"

"Considering you could have had Juilliard or Berklee?"

"*Your* choices. Like you chose Biscayne. For God's sake, I'm still going to do music, isn't that enough for you? I just want something closer to normal for once."

"You don't know what you want."

*Oh, God.* It was just shit luck I happened to be in a bathroom that shared a wall with the corps admin office and where, apparently, Jonathan and Dr. Crandall had gone to have their little throwdown. Over buses. And me. And Jonathan's school of choice. And Brian, whoever *he* was.

"Oh, yeah, I do know. I know exactly what I want. And that's what's bugging the shit out of you."

"That girl's got you acting like a stupid fool."

I cringed at the sheer venom in Dr. Crandall's voice.

"How? Because I want to *be* with her?"

"At the expense of your responsibilities. Tell me how that's not foolish."

"Hours of practice a day, enough to land a full-ride scholarship to Indiana, not to mention your exalted Juilliard and Berklee. Rehearsing by myself, with the corps, with the full horn line, with the sextet, when it's scheduled and even when it's not." Jonathan's voice took on the scary calm tone that only showed whenever he spoke with his dad. "I do everything that's asked of me and hell of a lot that's not. Tell *me,* Dad, how am I slacking?"

*Ay Dios mío,* I really needed to get out of here. My heart pounding from all the anger and emotion bleeding through the walls, I checked the hall outside the bathroom and took off at a fast, but hopefully casual, walk, making my way back to the guard building where I was meeting with Raj to continue coaching him on the finer points of the tango.

Because he wasn't a formally trained dancer, we had a lot of basics to cover, but he was as honest-to-God natural as anyone I'd ever worked with—not to mention funny and snarky and full of some of the sharpest observations ever. I'd be anticipating it if I wasn't so busy worrying about Jonathan and this weird, angry tension with his dad that I noticed more and more as the days went by.

"Hey, girl. Ready to get going?"

I extended one leg along the barre, sliding until the burn of the stretch sent welcome heat from hip to ankle. "You're late."

Raj got right up into my face, ducking so I'd be forced to look at him, and held up three fingers, wiggling them. "Just by this many minutes, baby."

"Sorry." I sighed, grabbing the towel I had hanging beside me and my water bottle from the floor. "I'm a little . . . tense."

"Would've thought Jonathan had taken care of that by now." He winked and made kissy faces while I tried to smile, but remembering what I'd overhead . . . my stomach clenched, hitting me with another wave of nausea. I took small sips of water, trying to will it away.

"Hey, hey . . . what's up? Tell Uncle Raj all about it." He dropped to the floor and patted the spot beside him, blinking in a way that I think he *thought* made him look wise and all-knowing.

"Uncle? You're barely a year older." Managing a smile that was thankfully sans Tilt-A-Whirl nausea, I sat beside him and smacked his shoulder. "And stop that—you're going to sprain your eyelash-batting muscles, and what a waste with me."

"I'm equal opportunity," he replied easily. "Okay, give me the gory details."

Fidgeting with the label on my water bottle until I pulled a corner free, I finally admitted, "I accidentally overheard Jonathan

116

and his dad arguing." I concentrated really hard on pulling a long unbroken strip off the label. "About me—and the buses."

Raj's eyebrows headed up. "Okay . . ."

I finally twisted the cap off and took a long drink. "Jonathan and I are planning on sitting together, and his dad's completely hacked."

"Well," he drawled, "considering this is Crandall, the Commandant, we're talking about—*and* considering that vets with Jonathan's time can usually cop a seat to themselves in which to concentrate on the show and nothing but, or at the very least don't have to be all cramped up and drooling on a seatmate, I get why the old man is hacked. Especially since the seatmate is you and the show's the last thing he's gonna be thinking about." After a dirty grin that had me slapping his shoulder again, he pursed his lips and tapped a finger against them, reminding me in a seriously eerie way of Mamacita. "However, I'm getting the distinct impression that's not all of it. What else did Herr Commandant bitch about?"

Chewing on a nail, I considered how much I could repeat without feeling like some old lady *chismosa*. "Well, this is really stupid, but it seemed like a big thing was about Jonathan riding the guard bus."

"Well, kiss my ass—Jonny's gonna actually *bail* on the horns to ride with the likes of us?" Raj looked beyond cheerful. "Well, hell—no wonder the old man's so cheesed."

"If it's such a big deal, couldn't I just ride the horn bus?"

He wrinkled his nose and pulled a face that had me choking on the sip of water I'd just taken. "Sure, if you'd actually want to put up with their collective tight-assed selves." He propped an arm on an upraised knee. "Eh, just kidding—sort of. They're okay, most of them. But Jonathan's not stupid, babycakes—he's aware that some of the guys in the corps haven't been nuts about your inclusion. And he's probably also aware that with respect to the guard, you're slowly but surely becoming a part of us. I'd bet my favorite Madonna CD he doesn't want anything to get in the way of that, ergo, you should be with us. But the boy's also going to make sure you're with *him*."

The evil little twerp laughed and leaned forward, putting his cool palms against my flaming cheeks. "Sweetie, the boy's been walking around with a metaphorical hard-on for the last three weeks. It's adorable."

Yeah, well . . . not just metaphorical. But that right moment—still eluding us. And had to admit, too, the anticipation was . . . nice. Frustrating, but in a good way.

And *definitely* not any of Raj's business, no matter how pathetic and pleading the puppy-dog eyes were.

"You're crazier than all my *tías* if you think I'm giving you any dirt." I stood and held my hand out, hauling him up.

"Can't blame a girl for trying. The boy is seriously hot." His shrug was as good-natured as his grin was cheesy. What a goof. Almost immediately, though, all that dropped away. "You know, just to give you the four-one-one—some of the truly uptight horns might be just a wee bit peeved that he's not with them. A lot of time gets spent on the buses—leads to a lot of that male bonding shit."

His entire demeanor was *so* subdued, I had no choice but to take what he was saying seriously. But still . . . it was a *bus*.

"Raj, I so don't get some of this stuff—these things that seem so important, but I don't know. . . . In the overall scheme of things, what do they ultimately have to do with the show?"

He moved to the barre and began stretching. "Dancers have a

lot of rituals and superstitions, right? Stuff that doesn't have a thing to do with actual dancing?"

Almost against my will, I touched the gold shooting-star pendant hanging around my neck, which I'd worn every day since Madame had given it to me for my tenth birthday. Thought about the fact that I always, *always* had to put on my dance shoes left foot first—don't ask me why. "Yeah, I guess," I admitted with a sheepish grin as I joined him at the barre.

"Same thing. When it's good, it gives us that extra added something that makes being a part of this so worth it. On the other hand, when it goes into overkill, it's enough to make even grown men act like jackasses." His theatrical eyeroll let me know exactly which grown man he meant. And while I laughed along with him, the Tilt-A-Whirl sensation was back—something Raj picked up on like he had radar.

"It'll be okay, Soledad. This thing we do—ultimately, it's supposed to be fun. Jonathan's not going to let anything get in the way of that any more than he's going to let anything get in the way of you two being together."

# somebody to love

*All of this has been . . . sweet and delicious and like nothing I've ever tasted before. It's amazing how I can get to him. A touch or even just a look is enough to get him to pause—and even if it's just for a split second, I know that I'm the absolute center of his universe.*

*He makes me feel fierce and yet so feminine at the same time. It's . . . dizzying. In such a good way.*

I closed the cover on the journal Mamacita had bought me for this new adventure, smoothing my hand over soft dove-gray leather. Subtle, she wasn't. Grinning, I capped my pen, slipped it into the loop on the cover's edge, and placed it in my backpack. For what seemed like the hundredth time tonight, I picked up the tour supply list and started checking things off. Halfway through counting my stack of camisoles and wondering if I shouldn't grab another two—or six—my phone started playing its new ring-tone—"Cast Your Fate to the Wind."

"Hey, gorgeous."

Nothing. Just the sound of a single harsh breath and some seri-ously tense vibes.

"Jonathan?"

Another breath, followed by a gravel-rough "Can I come over?"

"Yeah, sure. What's the ma—"

"I'll be there in twenty." Ending the call before I could finish ask-ing what in *hell* was going on. In just those few words sounding . . . *furious*.

Fifteen of the longest minutes of my life later—and I needed to remember to kill him for speeding that way—I heard first his stereo, loud, wailing Led Zeppelin, followed by sudden silence and the sharp slam of the truck's door. As soon as I'd heard the Zep I had made a beeline for the front door, waiting on the porch as he walked up the path, catching my breath at the sight. He *looked* calm and controlled, his face just set and still and so beau-tiful that even as I stressed over what had gone down, my insides were twisting themselves into knots that he was mine.

That steady, intense gaze never once looking away, he came right up to where I stood and before I could so much as get a squeak out, I found myself up against the wall, my brain short-circuiting from the intense lip-lock he was laying on me. His tongue stroked against mine, his body pressed hard against me, hands caressing from my thighs to my shoulders, sending short-circuit straight to full-body meltdown. And somewhere in all of that I managed to send up a split-second prayer that he did have me up so hard against the wall—otherwise, I would've dissolved into an ungraceful heap.

"Is your grandmother home?" he whispered when he finally

came up for air, nuzzling that incredibly sensitive spot right behind my ear.

"She's at . . ." I grabbed onto his biceps, my fingernails digging into his skin. "At Dom's bar. Probably . . . until . . . he's done."

"Good," he sighed. With that one word, the way he held me changed—instead of pushing me against the wall he shifted, pulling me close, resting his head on mine, and releasing another long breath, this one teasing the rim of my ear and making me burrow closer against him. "Can I . . ." His voice cracked and his breath hitched in his chest. "Let me stay?"

I wanted nothing more than to look at him, to see his face, but he was holding me so tight, like he was afraid to let go. Just in case the answer wasn't what he wanted. But I had to be sure of what he was asking.

"You mean—"

"Yeah." His voice was low and ragged. "Please, Soledad. I need you."

*I need you.*

*I need you.*

*I need you.*

It was like an echo that I never wanted to stop hearing.

*And you thought the fact he wanted you was the most amazing thing ever.*

I knew I should get to the bottom of what had him so upset. Knew I should figure out what brought him over here in the first place. But when I was finally able to pull back and search his face, I saw one thing. Whatever it was, right now, he needed something only *I* could give him. The rest—it could wait.

"Come on." Taking him by the hand, I led him into the house, locking the front door behind us. Funny, that click of the deadbolt— it sounded so final. He followed me into my room and waited while I turned on the bedside lamp and turned off the over-heads—

"It's probably not how you pictured perfect."

I turned from the stereo where I was putting on a CD. I mean, if we were going to do this, might as well set the stage at least a little. "It had nothing to do with how I pictured it, Jonathan. I told you that."

"I know." He shoved a hand through his hair. "It might've been easier if you'd wanted candlelight and flowers. I don't know what the hell I'm doing—"

"Do you feel like it's the right time?" I broke in.

A choked laugh escaped. "It's felt like the right time for weeks."

I smiled, but didn't let him off the hook. "Come on, Jonathan. You know what I mean—do you feel like it's *really* the right time?"

Our gazes met for what felt like a long, impossible moment, one where I desperately tried not to let on how I felt because I so wanted this to be about him. It needed to be. Finally, he nodded slowly. "Yes."

"So do I." I cleared stuff off the bed and sat. "That's what makes it perfect." He only took long enough to strip off his shirt before leaning over me, pushing me back into my pillows.

"Wait—" I pushed at his chest, then leaned over the edge of the mattress, stretching to reach my suitcase, sitting open on the floor. As I straightened and dropped the small box I'd unearthed on the night table, I felt a soft laugh rumbling through his body and into mine.

"What?"

"Great minds," he replied, reaching into his back pocket and pulling out his wallet, tossing it beside the box on the table. "I've been carrying some on me for at least the last week."

"God, but we are so completely out of control." I flopped back onto the pillows with a laugh.

"The way you make me feel?" Stroking my hair back from my face, he kissed me, light and gentle. "Definitely."

"Tour's not going to be easy, is it? Finding privacy—"

"We'll figure it out." He pushed up the loose hem of my shirt. "Later. But tonight—"

"Is ours." Gently, I scratched my nails down his back, rubbed my palms against his chest, loving how he felt.

"Soledad?"

"Hm?"

"It *really* doesn't bug you that I've never—" His gaze searched my face, one hand resting on my hip where his thumb traced a slow, crazy-making trail low on my stomach, but nothing more— almost like he wanted to give me an out.

*As if I could at this point.*

"No," I assured him, *again*. "It really doesn't bug you that I have?"

My heart stopped as his hand stopped moving completely and he looked away. Oh no . . . he'd *sworn*. And it's not like I could *do* anything about it—

"Jonathan?"

"It's good that one of us has experience." His voice was low as he kept his head turned away. Didn't matter. I didn't need to see his face to get the hurt. Not with the way it was coming off him in waves. "I guess I am a little jealous, though, that . . . *God,* this is probably stupid—" He stopped and then, in a voice that was so soft it nearly got lost in the background music I heard, "I wish I was your first, too."

My heart broke just a little at that. He wanted so *much* to feel like he came first for somebody. To matter more than anything.

"Jonathan . . . It's like I told you—when I got curious about sex, I tried it. It's not something I've done a lot, and when I have, it hasn't really been a whole lot more than a physical thing. Learning more about my body." *Ay,* how to say this and not sound totally cold? "My body . . . it's *my* instrument. Sex was another way to be in tune with it and understand everything about how it works. That's all it was about, really."

*Shit*—it did sound cold and kind of awful. But it had never seemed cold or awful before. It was practical and made sense for me and my world, and that's what was so different about all of this. *Nothing* about being with Jonathan made any sense. At all. But it was happening and I couldn't imagine it any other way. I lifted a hand to his face and turned it to mine. "You *are* my first in a really important way."

Shaking his head, he tried to turn away again, but I held tight, his rough stubble scratching my palm and sending tingles along my arm. *"Jonathan—"* Finally, he caved and relaxed, even though his eyes remained closed, forcing me to put everything I was feeling into words. "Until you, I've never been in love."

*Aymadredediosomigod.* I couldn't believe I'd said it. But what else could it be? This odd, terrifying feeling of falling down Alice's rabbit hole into this unknown world. That made me want to laugh and cry and want to throw up and wrap myself in everything Jonathan represented all at the same time.

I'd never felt it before.

I never wanted to stop feeling it.

It had to be love. Just couldn't be anything else, as hurting and intense and leave-me-prickly-and-oversensitive as it all was.

"You love me?" Everything about his face had relaxed, his mouth hanging open slightly, but his body was tenser than ever as he breathed, fast and shallow, leaving trails of goose bumps across my sweat-damp skin.

"No, doofus, the mailman." He jerked back slightly, shock turning to a laugh. A heartbeat later, I pulled his head down to mine and kissed him hard. "Yes, I love *you*, Jonathan," I whispered against his mouth.

Couldn't deny it got easier with each breath. That easier transformed into absolutely magical with his whispered, "I love you." Everything inside me relaxed, allowing me to sink into enjoying touch and taste, how our bodies seemed made for each other, because no matter what I did to him, he knew just what to do in return to make me *feel* that little bit more. Just before we crossed that final line, I used my last operating brain cell to ask, "You okay? You know . . . I mean, I can sort of take control, if you want."

Holding my hands, his body covering mine, he laughed—sort of nervous. Definitely excited. "Hey, I'm inexperienced, but I know where the parts go."

I laughed as well, enjoying the weight of him on me, how the vibrations from my laughing made him shiver, which made me shiver right back. "All right, then."

A few seconds later— "Soledad?"

"Yeah?"

"This is . . ."

I sighed and stretched and smiled. "Oh, *yeah*. It is."

"I'm thinking—" His voice was wound as tight and hard as his body. "Maybe you'd better take control."

"Nuh-uh. You're doing fine."

The soft light from the bedside lamp blended with his eyes, different shades of silver and blue, but it couldn't totally mask the happy gleam in them. Of course, the grin nearly splitting his face in half might've also been a clue. "Yeah?"

"Oh . . . *yeah*."

"What happened?"

I felt him smile against the back of my shoulder. "You've already forgotten?"

I changed the gentle stroking of his thigh to a pinch. "Jonathan—"

He sighed, his arms tightening around my waist. Sighed again, like he was trying to buy time.

"It's your dad, isn't it?" I turned and eased back on the pillows to where we could look at each other.

In the dim light, the whites of his eyes looked eerie and haunted. "Who else?" Misery cloaked those two words, making my fists clench into the sheets. I *hated* how the man made his son feel—and for what?

"Look, I want to ask you something, but first, there's something I think you should know." Even so, I hesitated.

*Trust him,* m'ija.

He lay back on the pillows, watching, his eyes narrow and wary, making my jaw clench. He *didn't* deserve this.

Putting my hand on his forearm and stroking gently, I confessed. "I was in the bathroom at the complex the other day and overheard you two arguing. Adding a quick, "by accident," because last thing he needed was to think I was hovering.

His arm jerked slightly beneath my hand. "Shit." He pushed himself up to a sitting position, pulling me along so I was cradled against him. "How much did you hear?"

"A lot," I admitted. "Enough to know that he's beyond steamed about your signing up for the guard bus." I ran my fingers through his hair, down his neck, across his shoulders, rubbing at all the tense knots. "I just don't want it to be a problem."

"Too late." Jonathan's voice was low and hard. "But it's his problem."

"Does it have anything to do with tonight?"

It did. It was all over his face, the way his mouth tightened, completely eradicating the full curve I loved to kiss.

"Funny that you overheard us. I overheard *him* tonight—on the phone—trying to talk Gray into requiring the sections to stay together on the buses."

"Is he high?" I mean, it wasn't like Jonathan was the only one cross-pollinating. There were friendships and hookups going on across sections with seating choices happening accordingly, so it wasn't quite as rigid and toe-the-line as I'd been afraid it would be.

"My God, Jonathan, if he talks Gray into doing that, I'll have to quit—everyone will hate my ass." Which was exactly what the old man was counting on.

Jonathan snorted. "Gray told him to get a grip."

My turn to snort. I could so hear Gray saying that and sounding polite as hell in the process. "And you know this, how?"

"I picked up one of the extensions once I figured out who Dad was talking to and about what." He sighed again, his chest rising and falling beneath the hand I had resting on it. "There's more."

Oh, joy.

"He was also trying to talk Gray into segregating you on the tour—making you bunk down with the moms as opposed to the rest of us."

"Oh, for God's *sake*—" I exploded, sitting straight up. "We've been *through* all of this."

The first week I'd been a member. All sides and options and opinions had been weighed and debated and finally, the board and instructors, who were all mostly veterans of coed corps, basically threw their hands up and said, "Who cares?" Legally, I was an adult, but more important, I was a member of the corps, period. Final verdict was no isolation, and as far as the practical stuff, all of the school gyms where we'd be staying on tour would have ladies' locker rooms. Besides, with my dancer's background, it wasn't like guys stripping or wandering around in their dainties would make me go all shaky and stupid.

Well, *most* guys wouldn't.

Jonathan cocked his head to the side. "What is it?"

I kept staring. "You are so gorgeous." I pulled the sheet down his body, watching his skin flush, stroking the long line of his leg. Resting my head on his stomach, I pressed light kisses against muscles that twitched in response.

"And very distracting." Fairly sure I'd had a train of thought going somewhere before I got utterly derailed.

"You don't say?" I glanced up in time to catch the slight grin that crossed that pretty face before it faded. "Look—please don't worry, Soledad. I eavesdropped long enough to know Gray's not caving. He made it clear the decisions are final and it's too late to go changing things now for no damned good reason other than Dad having a massive stick shoved up his ass."

Right. That's where my train of thought had been headed. "I hate that I'm the cause of all of this, though." And much as it pissed me off, nervous about being in any kind of proximity to Dr. Crandall.

"No." His fingers wrapped around my arms as he pulled me back up to the pillows. "Dad and I . . ." He released me and rolled to his back, pillowing his head on his arm. "If you overheard a lot of our argument, then you know there's more going on than just you, and it's been going on a long time."

"Okay, yes, I could tell there was a lot going on that didn't have anything to do with me. Stuff about college and you not wanting to go to Biscayne for high school." *God.* I would never have known him—at all. My heart beating faster, I pulled the sheet up over us. A cocoon, keeping us safe.

"It's not that I didn't want to go to Biscayne. I simply wasn't given a choice." He stared up at the ceiling fan. "But college is different. I can get the same quality music education at Indiana as at Berklee or Juilliard, and he damn well knows it. It's just not *his* choice."

He paused, a pensive look on his face. Waiting for me to ask about Brian. Who he was and what he had to do with any of this. If I didn't know anything else, I knew that. And he really, really didn't want to answer. That stubborn set of his jaw made that totally clear. And you know, realizing even *I* wasn't enough to make him want to share voluntarily—stupid as it was, it kind of hurt.

So yeah, I wanted to know. Couldn't deny that. But it couldn't be right now. He had to want to share.

"So you've got some way-back issues, but right now I'm the catalyst that's making everything worse." I glanced past his shoulder to my open suitcase and dance bag. Just beyond them, the rolled-up Aero mattress and my backpack with my new journal just visible in the open pocket. "Maybe I shouldn't—"

"Don't even think it." My hand was in his, his grip almost painful. "I am *not* his fucking puppet." He sounded even more rock solid about that than the first time I'd heard him say it. "And neither are you. The two of us together—we're strong, Soledad, and he knows that. That's what's got him so pissed off." He released my hand and put his arms around me, holding me close. His breath was warm against my ear as he whispered, "He knows we're together and that there's not a damned thing he can do about it."

# you give me something

"Oh, Mamacita . . . no . . . *no puedo.*"

"*Quieta, mi vida.*" One hand stroked the long braid I'd brushed my hair back into after the corps' farewell performance for family and friends, while the other folded my fingers over the envelope she'd just handed me. "You're not taking anything from me."

"But—"

"*Shhh, te lo juro,* it's fine. This isn't just from me—*es de la familia.*" She kept stroking and like always, her touch calmed me. "*Mira,* you wouldn't let us throw you a graduation party, but the family wanted to do *something.* Don't you understand, *m'ija,* how proud everyone is of you?"

I'd quit trying to shove the envelope back in her hands, knowing it was a lost cause. Staring down at the envelope as I turned it over in my hands, I decided to change the topic, instead. Because if I tried to talk about how much it meant that the family was willing to do this for me, I'd cry. "It was nice of you to bring Domenic today."

A surprise, since Mamacita had never been one to bring the boy-friends to family things. But he'd come to the senior showcase performance and now the corps farewell. Interesting.

"*Bueno,* now that you mention it." Holy cats, was she *blushing*? "He's going to be moving in—" My eyebrows shot up. "I was saying how I was going to be missing you, and one thing led to another, and well, he's just . . ." Look at that, she *was* blushing, a beautiful delicate pink, as she glanced over her shoulder to where Domenic was standing by the buses talking to Jonathan. "*Él es muy* . . . very . . . *¿tú sabes?*"

"Yes, he is *very,*" I said with a laugh as I hugged her tight. "I'm glad you won't be alone," I whispered. Not that she wasn't totally able to take care of herself, but I was glad she was letting someone else in. It'd been too long. "Hopefully it *won't* be temporary."

She drew back and lifted one shoulder, covered today in a white gauze blouse that should've looked completely inappropriate but somehow didn't. "We'll see." Then winked in a way that probably should have made me shudder, considering she *was* my grandmother and pushing sixty, but you know, sixty was the new forty, and besides it was pure Mamacita—and because it was, all I did was laugh. And shudder a little.

"I'm glad you, too, are no longer alone, *mi vida.*"

I stared at her. "I've never been alone." Independent, maybe, but never alone. How could I be, with Mamacita?

"Soledad . . . *mi querida.*" Her smile was all sorts of knowing. "*El niño lindo*—you love him very much. And he loves you."

Stared some more. Jonathan had been gone by the time she got home the other night, but the way she was glancing over at him, then back at me . . . there was no doubt she *knew.* Not that it was bad, that she knew, and I probably would've talked to her about it eventually, but— It was just so new and still so . . . I don't know, fragile, and I wanted to keep it close and protected. And again, she understood, because she didn't say anything more. Just gave me another hug and handed me a small package.

"Here. From Madame."

Throat tight, I lifted the lid of the narrow box, running a fingertip over the unmarred pink satin of the pointe shoes, ribbons wound neatly. Tucked inside one was a piece of paper. Drawing it out and unfolding it, I smiled, the words on the page as elegant and precise as if they themselves were dancing: *Don't forget to practice!*

"*Y una cosita más.*"

The tears that had been threatening were swallowed by helpless giggling as I looked inside the bag she shoved in my hand. "*Te quiero tanto.*"

"And I love you, *mi niñita bella.*" She took me in her arms again, all strength and love and devotion wrapped up in one small package.

*Mi niña,*

*As you embark on your adventure, I want you to remember to take the time to enjoy it and, above all, to savor and cherish everything about what led you to this place. The first time you fall in love—with anything or anyone—it's such a beautiful thing. Don't hold back. Experience all the joy—and the pain. In the end, it will matter more than you can begin to imagine.*

I read it all one more time, shaking my head at Mamacita's unabashed woo-wooisms. Raising the heavy sheet of stationery to my lips, I inhaled the cool citrus perfume that was so simply *her,* then pressed a kiss against the words before tucking it, along with the note from Madame, into my journal and slipping it into my backpack.

"What've you got there?"

I grinned down at Jonathan. "Twizzlers, " I replied, grabbing one of the jumbo bags from the overhead compartment. Since the candy was something I felt comfortable sharing. "Going-away present from Mamacita. Appeasing the wicked sweet tooth."

"Yeah, but chocolate's your poison." He grinned as he accepted the cherry licorice stick I held out.

"Yeah, it is, and if I ate as much of it as I wanted, I'd weigh four hundred pounds and so not a good look for Carmen and that just-this-side-of-legal costume Gray and your mom cooked up. These"—I held a stick up—"are full of sugary goodness, yet fat-free, therefore a compromise."

Grabbing a handful of candy, I shoved the bag back into the overhead compartment and settled down in the comfortable back-seat nest we'd made with pillows and blankets. The whole setup was a lot cozier than I might have imagined—engines rumbling behind us, my back against Jonathan's chest where I could feel his heartbeat, slow and steady, his arms holding me close. No doubt, I was a happy camper. So the view currently sucked—scrubby pine trees and *flat* for days, as we cruised up the Turnpike—but really, who needed a view?

"Anything else in the care package?"

"A copy of *Tarot for Dummies* and a deck of cards."

His laugh came out on an explosive puff of air, ruffling loose wisps of hair around my face. "I told you, you shouldn't have said anything about how long some of the bus rides were."

"I know, I know . . . she can't help herself."

"Guess she's hoping some of it eventually sticks."

"Guess so."

"So was that all?"

"No chocolate, so quit hinting." I tilted my head back against his shoulder, brushing a kiss against the underside of his jaw. "Just some stationery."

"Like for writing letters? Why? You can e-mail or call." He started rubbing my shoulders and neck, massaging out knots and kinks in a way that made me nearly forget my own name, let alone that he'd asked something.

"Mmm . . . because letter writing's a lost art. Ooh . . . right there." I moved his hand to a particularly tight spot. "It's a more considered practice. You have to slow down—gather your thoughts and take your time—when you write by hand." I bent forward, giving him access to my entire back, groaning as he walked his fingers down my spine. "And every month, as long as I can remember, she's written me a letter, telling me what I've done that she's proud of and, when she needs to, telling me stuff she feels I could do better."

And you know, seeing the words, written in her precise, old-fashioned script, made both criticism and praise resonate more. Those letters—they were so *real*. And I kept each and every one of them. Talismans.

"I'd write her a letter in return and that's how I got started on the habit. Probably why I like journaling so much. It's like writing letters to myself."

"Huh."

Could tell he didn't get it. It's okay. Not sure I always did, either. It was simply one of those things that *was*.

"You know . . . Seems as if you have someone right *there*— someone important—you shouldn't have to rely on something like letters or a journal." His tone was thoughtful, measured. Maybe he didn't get it, but he was obviously trying, and right then I fell in love just a little bit more.

"Yes . . . and no. Writing—and dance, too, when it comes down to it—provide a different kind of constant." I arched my back and pointed my toes, thinking of the new pointe shoes in their box, waiting to be broken in. "They're a part of who I am. Something *I* create, that . . ." I struggled for the words. "That I put *all* of myself into."

"Which makes it more personal. That you create it."

"Yeah." I stretched again before relaxing into a limp, boneless heap against Jonathan, taking his hands in mine. "Well, I guess more accurately, dance created me. I just follow its lead."

"Created you?"

"Yeah, I know," I said. "Sounds high drama—but it's the truth." Staring down at our hands, I smiled at the memory. "I was physically weak as a kid—my legs especially. Doctors suggested if I did something like exercise or dance, it might help."

And that was it.

Like it was yesterday, I could recall walking into Madame's studio, not quite five years old, and insanely shy and scared. And we'd walked in and the first thing I remembered noticing was the cool, damp, air-conditioned inside—totally different from the fry-an-egg-on-the-sidewalk-hot outside. Then the smells: powdery rosin and warm, stale sweat tickling the insides of my nose until I was rubbing at it with the hand that wasn't clutching Mamacita's. But the most vivid memory, the one I could *still* feel, was the floor—that beautiful, long expanse that had looked like it went on forever and that I'd just had to touch. It was a different kind of cool from the air, and felt smooth and rich beneath my palms, and so . . . *alive,* that I'd wanted to feel it all over me. I laid right down and pressed my cheek against the boards as if I expected them to tell me all their secrets—and in return, I'd tell them mine. And then Madame had knelt in front of me and very carefully helped me stand,

and with the gentlest touch outside of Mamacita's, had arranged my feet into first position, not all the way, but only just as far as I could turn out, smoothing her hands up and down my legs.

*Yes, that's it,* petit. *Feel your body. We'll teach it to listen to you, and you'll learn how to listen to it, and together you'll be beautiful.*

"You know how sometimes, you just know things? That first day, I knew I'd found my world. My place." Every time someone would say I had the wrong build or called me fat or said I didn't have what it took to make it, I'd remember that first day and how *right* I'd felt.

"The writing's something I keep for myself, but dance—it's personal *and* it gives me the world. Maybe it sounds cheesy, but . . . it represents freedom. And identity. It's who I am, you know?" Each word came out slow and soft as I admitted for the first time, out loud and to another human, what I'd always felt.

He didn't answer for the longest time, just stared out the window and gently stroked my arm as I leaned against his shoulder, drifting in and out, exhausted from our farewell performance, from the adrenaline of finally getting on the road, from letting him in that little bit more.

"I think . . . I always thought of music like you think of dance."

Awareness tingled along my skin as I studied the stark lines of his profile. "Has something changed?"

He kept staring out the window, like he was confessing to the blurred stand of trees lining the highway. "I think that music's becoming more like writing is for you and—"

"And?" I softly asked.

He turned away from the window and buried his face against my neck, his breath warm against my skin.

"You're my dance." Dropping small kisses along the side of my neck up to my ear, he whispered in a voice full of wonder, "You've given me a whole new world, Soledad."

# all we are

"Okay, people, first show is tomorrow night. I know this isn't how you want to represent."

Breathing hard, sweat leaving clammy trails between my shoulder blades and down my bare stomach, I fisted my hands on my hips, more so I didn't throw one at some innocent bystander.

"Relax, baby. He's just trying to psych the troops," Raj muttered, arm around my waist in the pose in which we'd been called to a halt. However, his grip felt more like he was trying to make sure I wouldn't go charging after Gray, who had clearly borrowed Dr. Crandall's favorite stick for today's rehearsal.

"I've never had a dress rehearsal that didn't suck big wind and the performances wound up fine. Phenomenal, even," I grumbled back. "Why doesn't he just let it go? We'll regroup."

"Because from now on, every rehearsal's a dress rehearsal. We can't afford to let them all suck, and we won't always have a chance to regroup."

"Another word from you two," Gray snapped, "and it's twenty for the whole corps."

My jaw clenched, a nerve pulsing from just beneath my ear all the way up to my eyes. Great—a monster headache on top of the three straight hours we'd already been going in sticky, ninety-five-degree weather.

"Let's split off and work music for an hour, then we'll do full run-throughs before dinner. Guard, grab equipment for the 'El Tango' transition."

Still breathing hard, I watched as Gray turned and obviously took a deep breath, his big shoulders rising and falling, then rolling beneath one of his predictably hideous Hawaiian shirts. Seriously, I wanted to stay pissed at him—fourteen hours on a bus into the middle of North Carolina with all of an hour to grab a quick lunch and unwind, how could he expect us to perform well? But then again, this was the normal routine for this gig. I was the one who needed to adjust.

Slowly, I approached, grabbing two bottles of water from the cooler the moms kept stocked for us. "Sorry." I held one out as he turned, surprised.

"Thanks." He took the water and drained it in one long swallow. "Don't sweat it. I just can't treat you any different, darlin'."

Sucking down half the water in the bottle in one gulp, I immediately felt better—and had better perspective. "I know. I'm just still learning the ropes."

"Not much more than a lot of ass-bustin' work."

"And push-ups," I added, lifting my bottle in toast.

Deep creases radiated from the corners of his eyes as he grinned and returned the salute.

"What the fuck—you think you're gonna pick it up through osmosis?"

Gray and I both turned, my jaw dropping as I saw Jonathan stalking back and forth in front of the sopranos. Looked like the horns had broken off into their individual instrument sections to rehearse and he was running the sopranos through their paces. Or just chewing them out, and how.

"No, let me guess—you're saving your best for the show. Got news for you—it doesn't work that way. You play full out, give it your best, every time, or you get the hell out—we don't have time for this."

"*Coño* . . . ," I breathed.

And he wasn't stopping, either, pausing in front of every one of the guys, bucking up in their faces. "Every. Single. Time. You snap your horn up, you're crisp, you don't slouch, you do every horn flash and movement, you play every damned note, you give it a hundred percent every single time like there's a judge in a green shirt breathing down your damned neck."

"Asshole."

I sucked in a breath at the soft insult coming from Aaron, a rookie like me, but who was what I'd heard Raj call a "rookie/age-out," meaning that at twenty-one, he only had one year of corps eligibility. It kind of put him in a weird place, a music major who was probably the big shit in his world, but in this one a rookie in a pretty rigid caste system. Who clearly hated having to answer to Jonathan.

"Give me twenty."

Aaron deliberately glanced over his shoulder, catching my eye before he turned back to Jonathan. "Your dick waving might impress your girlfriend but doesn't do it for me."

Jonathan took a step closer. "Fifty."

"Aren't you going to do anything?" I whispered to Gray.

He shook his head. "I've been expecting this to go down. Jonathan's got to resolve it himself."

"How?"

But Gray was walking away, and that's when I got it—Jonathan had to resolve it by any means necessary, and the less Gray knew about how, the better. *Madre santísima,* no one told me I'd be wading into *Conan the Barbarian* territory.

"Do 'em."

"No."

"Suit yourself." Jonathan casually walked away from Aaron, the rest of the sopranos silently following, leaving Aaron standing by himself. About fifty feet away, they reassembled into a shallow arc around Jonathan and raised their horns. His own horn raised and ready, Jonathan counted off, quiet and even, although the tendons in his neck were standing out, sweat pooling in the hollow at the base. As the bold intro to *Carmen* rang out, Aaron's expression shifted from confusion, to understanding, then . . . anger.

Walking over to the arc, he tried to shoulder his way into his regular spot, but no one would move—when he tried to fall in at the end of the arc, they shifted as one, their message clear. He looked around, but it was amazing how all the instructors seemed to have vanished.

"You arrogant little shit." He reached for Jonathan's arm, jerking him around.

Oh, *God,* Jonathan's mouth. I got light-headed as he pulled the horn away, just in time. A second later, he handed it off to one of the other players and faced off with Aaron.

He was so going to kick his ass.

*No.* He couldn't—he wasn't capable of it. However, right now, with sweat running down his bare torso, every muscle in his shoulders and arms bunched and tense and that light turning his eyes dark and fierce?

*Still think he can't do it?*

"Damn straight I'm arrogant. I've earned it. If I suck, I expect them to call me on it," he said, nodding at the other sopranos. "But that hasn't happened yet because I bust ass and don't allow it to happen. It's why I'm the horn captain." Clenching his fists, he took a step closer, totally eradicating Aaron's personal space. "And it's why you do it *my* way."

"Come on, baby—break time over."

I resisted as Raj tried to pull me away. "But—"

Grabbing my shoulders, he forced me around and started guiding me to an adjacent field. "Let it go—" He was grinning, his little ruby nose stud sparkling in the sun. "Let the boys be boys."

"Jesus, I thought *dancers* were drama queens."

A sharp crack sounded behind us but Raj kept propelling me along, one hand against my cheek, keeping me from glancing back.

"Girl, it's their drama—we have to rehearse."

*That* got me. Jonathan was a big boy, he could take care of himself. And Raj was right. *I* had to rehearse.

Didn't mean I didn't worry, though. Which pissed me off, because it sat there at the back of my mind, irritating, like an eyelash I couldn't quite get to.

By the time we got to dinner I was ready to slap Jonathan stupid, especially after I got a closer look. Sitting beside him, I bent over his hand and quietly said, "You had it won. You didn't need to hit him to prove your point."

"Actually, yeah, I did. Jackass couldn't leave well enough alone—had to try to get the last word in. About you."

"You hit him because of me? *Why?*"

"I won't let him talk about you."

"Jonathan, it'd be one thing if he said shit to my face—but honestly, what do I care what he says behind my back?"

His voice was low. "I care."

"God," I groaned. "You *don't* need to be making things more difficult for yourself. Or me."

"Soledad—"

I stood and shook my head, catching his expression out of the corner of my eye, a little hurt, a little angry, and a lot mystified as to why I wasn't thrilled he'd gone Conan on my behalf. Leaning down I whispered, "You know, maybe in some girly daydream, I might've thought I'd like the whole coming-to-my-defense shit, but—" Honestly, it just made me tense and crazy. "No matter what you think, this wasn't any kind of gallant move. You could've really gotten hurt and dammit, I *can* take care of myself."

Turning my back, I prayed he had the sense to not try to grab me or talk to me or *anything*. Because seriously, I couldn't deal with him right now.

# under a painted sky

*Mi querida Mamacita,*
*You know how you joke about how all the cousins suffer from*
*testosterone poisoning? Not just them. Tonight's the first contest*
*and everyone's nerves are on edge and we're all ready to kill each*
*other. But at the same time . . . during our last rehearsal, I could*
*feel it. The magic. Good thing, because I really needed something*
*to make this all worth it.*

A rose suddenly appeared across the page. A beautiful lavender
rose, rich and sweet with perfume. Smiling, I picked it up, held it
to my nose, and let the scent wrap around me like the cloak I'd be
wearing in just a little while.

"Where—"

"Ve haff our vays." Taking my stationery box and pen, Jonathan
carefully placed them in the overhead compartment above our
seat, then sat beside me. "You like it?"

"It's beautiful." I closed my eyes and stroked the velvet petals across my cheek, breathing deeply. "Seriously, how'd you swing this and why?"

Opening my eyes, I found him watching me, his chest rapidly rising and falling. His voice slightly hoarse, he said, "Mom helped, and because I'm sorry."

"You apologized last night. And this morning."

"But you were still mad."

I stared down at the flower, lightly scraping the pad of my thumb against an overlooked thorn. "I would've gotten over it."

"I hate having you upset with me, Soledad. Anyone else, I could care less, but it makes me crazy if I think you are."

"It's gonna happen. And you'll get mad at me."

"Impossible." His hands closed over my shoulders, warm and strong. Turning my head, I kissed the bruised knuckles on the one. Blockhead—but such an adorable, passionate blockhead.

"Close your eyes."

After a quick, curious glance, I did as he asked, feeling the absence of warmth as his hands moved from my shoulders, then shifted to my front, fumbling slightly as he stretched the neckline of my dress.

"Jonathan, be careful—your mother will have us both for breakfast if something happens to this dress."

"She'll be fine. Look." I opened my eyes and looked down, gasping.

"Oh . . ."

With a trembling finger, I touched the small silver pin he'd fastened right where the nude insert met the white fabric of my costume, close to my heart. From a distance, it would look like just another shiny ornament on the bodice, but up close it was the tiniest, most perfect rose.

"I want you to have a flower for every performance." His fingers brushed across mine and the rose at the same time, then skimmed down my side until his hand rested on my hip. "And this way, too, you always have a piece of me." Leaning in, he kissed me, then pulled back slightly, rubbing my shoulders again.

"Hey, relax. The show's going to be great. I can feel it."

"Yeah," I said, smiling, but really, couldn't relax. And it wasn't about the show, exactly. How could I say, without totally hurting his feelings, that I didn't need to *have* something in order for him to be a part of me? How could he not understand that he already was?

And frankly, it was annoying—having my mind crowded with worrying about his feelings when all I wanted to do was start thinking about the show. Get into the zone. And there was guilt, for being annoyed. And for feeling ungrateful.

*Shit.*

A pounding sounded along the side of the bus, Gray's voice yelling, "Come on, Raiders. Concert arc in front of the buses— five minutes!"

Pulling away from Jonathan, I wiped away the lipstick I'd left behind. Found a smile, because really, he was just expressing how he felt. "Showtime."

"This is where it gets good, you know—" He stood and zipped his uniform jacket closed. "You'll see, the minute we hit that field. It'll be like nothing else."

"So you've said. Again and again." I grabbed my black cloak. "I'm so ready to find out for myself."

The bus was all of a sudden alive—excitement becoming this palpable thing as we all gathered our stuff and emerged onto a parking lot thick with diesel fumes from dozens of buses and noisy with the sounds of horns and percussion warming up and the distinctive ripple of flag silks being tossed and rifles hitting gloved palms as voices counted off beats. A few hundred yards away was the stadium where we'd be performing, the lights barely visible against the early-evening dusk.

"What's that?" I asked Jonathan as I fastened my cloak and pulled my hood up so no one could see me. We were trying to keep my presence as much a surprise as possible for this first show, even from the other corps.

Buzzing through his mouthpiece to warm up his lips, he followed my stare to the group streaming past where we were gathering. "Dunno. Definitely not a corps."

Peering from under my hood, I took note of the short-sleeve jerseys with numbers on the back, paired with matching shorts. "Soccer players, maybe?"

"Well, we're at a county fair." He inclined his head toward the flashing lights of the midway on the opposite side of the huge parking lot. "Anything's possible—greased pigs, ferret races. Anything to entertain the crowds." Fitting his mouthpiece into his horn, he took my hand and led me toward where the concert arc was forming. Still curious, I glanced over my shoulder at the group weaving their way through the buses toward the stadium.

Yeah, they *were* soccer players, all loose and chattering and kicking black-and-white balls up in the air and back and forth. As I watched, one lean ponytailed guy fidgeted with the ball and kicked it up in the air, laughing as it bounced off a teammate's ass and back into his hands. *Boys.*

Turning away, I went to step into my place in the concert arc but felt a slight tug on the back of my cloak. *What the—?* A split second later, the tension disappeared, making me stumble slightly as I fought to regain my balance. Twisting around to look over my shoulder, I discovered a distinct, gray footprint, glaring against the otherwise pristine black fabric. Annoyed, I jerked my head up, hood falling back, and found ponytail boy a couple steps away. In what seemed like a single breath, he was down on one knee, brushing the dust away, leaving the fabric unmarred. Gracefully rising, he met my gaze and would you believe, *winked*?

A second later, he was gone.

"Performing their program, *Carmen, Revealed* . . . the Florida Raiders!"

Breathing from my core, trying to keep loose, I stood, dead center of the abstract star that was our opening formation, wrapped in my cloak, waiting for the drum major to count off. The first melodic chimes rang out, echoing through the hushed stadium waiting to see what we had in store for them. It was our signal to begin moving, a series of light, gliding steps, before the entire corps blew the lid off with the full, glorious introduction to *Carmen.*

The roaring of the crowd was already almost overwhelming—the music just slamming the listener straight in the gut—but beneath my cloak hood, I was smiling like mad. Little did *they* know. The guard ran to the front of the formation, turned our backs to the audience, extending our arms so our cloaks formed a solid wall, then, throwing off the cloaks, we turned to face the crowd. And the second my sparkling, formfitting dress was revealed, stark white against the black of the rest of the guard's uniforms combined with the fact that there was an actual *girl* filling it out?

I believe "apeshit" was the apropos word here.

Adrenaline surged, making me throw my head back with a new ferocity, adding power to my movements as I flirted with Raj, with the rest of the guard, with the audience. Leaping and turning across the enormous expanse of the field—it brought an enormous sense of exhilaration and freedom, my every performance dream come true.

As we progressed through the show, too, I could sense that as much as the reaction was about my part of the performance, it was also about the whole package. The movement, the music, all of us working together in perfect synchronicity—it was theater on *such* a grand scale.

My lungs burning from the last series of steps, I did a jazz run to the sidelines and waited, catching my breath and watching the beginning of the finale unfold, the guard spinning flat wood props that, one by one, they would lay down on the fifty-yard line, front and center, creating a dance floor where I'd perform my final tango with Don José.

Raj, his red military jacket hanging open over his black jumpsuit, hair falling over his forehead, extended a hand and I took it, following him to our impromptu floor, haughty, secure in the knowledge that I was granting him one final dance before sending him on his way, because really, what more did he have to offer?

We tangoed smoothly, our bodies close in this most intimate of dances, before I shoved him away, extending an arm, sweeping it in a large arc, showing him all the Escamillos twirling black capes like bullfighters, the linings all revealing a different, brilliant color—all the different possibilities the world had to offer beyond his love. As he watched, his features twisting in rage, I took center stage for myself, reaching out to grab everything the world was ready to give me. I turned and turned, spinning in the *fouetté en tournant*—the move that had led to Gray figuring out how to build this dance floor so I could best perform it because—

"Darlin', that move is what's gonna bring the damned house down, every single night."

Music and movement and the roar of the crowd swirled in breathtaking symmetry as Raj charged during that final turn, miming the fatal stab. Perfectly timed so as not to hurt either of us and concluding with my falling to my knees, then to my side, my head in Raj's lap as he gazed at the heavens, heartbroken. Then, in the midst of all the chaos, a special, private moment as Jonathan marched right past me in those last few measures, glancing down and winking—our secret signal—as "El Tango de Roxanne" ended and segued into the final chords from *Carmen,* the chimes ringing like mournful church bells.

The crowd noise abruptly hushed into a brief moment of stunned silence before erupting all over again, the wild cheering and whistles penetrating the veil of Carmen which I'd worn for the past ten minutes.

Oh, yeah—we *nailed* it.

Taking Raj's outstretched hand, I stood and took his arm, falling into formation with the rest of the corps as we prepared to march off the field, but it was Jonathan's gaze I found, him I shared the moment with as the crowd went insane around us, whistling and clapping, a raucous "Go, Carmen—you *rule!*" making the tiny hairs on the back of my neck rise.

As we made our way around the track and exited the stadium, we were met by the moms, handing out bottles of water as soon as we arranged ourselves in a concert arc beside the buses for the quickie post-show shakedown.

"For a first performance? Not bad."

Not bad? Not freakin' *bad*? I know I couldn't possibly have heard Gray right. Not that I was expecting gushing declarations of perfection, but come *on*—certainly we merited better than "not bad."

"Don't get sucked in by the crowd's reaction—it's great that you punched them in the gut emotionally, but it's the judges who give the scores. And for that, you need precise control combined with all that emotion. I don't care if it's a four-corps show in East Bum-fuck—or that it's the first night of tour. From now on, you need to treat every show like it's Finals night at Championships." He stalked from one end of the concert arc to the other, his ball cap turned backwards and tonight's hideous coral, black, and turquoise Hawai-ian shirt half unbuttoned, like always, though he might as well have been wearing Raj's Don José uniform for the attitude he projected.

"I know it's hot and it's muggy and you feel like wet washcloths, but it's not gonna get any better. Everyone else is marching under the same conditions, so *this* is when you have to start pushing your-self further and harder. There is no half-assed effort—not for the Raiders."

He stopped, dead center, eyes narrowed. "If this was easy, a lot more people would do it. *You* are the elite. Remember that."

A gift, really—managing to tell us how much better we could be while at the same time making us feel like we were the best, releasing us on an adrenaline high.

"Did you *see*?" Jonathan strode toward me, energy practically crackling off him. "How you drove them all crazy?"

I fell into his embrace, kissing him hard and twisting my fin-gers into the hair at the back of his neck. "It was soooo fun, Jona-than. Just completely indescribable."

"Told you." His face was flushed and sweaty, eyes sparkling with the same post-performance high I was coasting on. "Look, I have to powwow with the horns for a few. Meet you back here in about fifteen minutes, then we'll go watch the other shows?"

"Absolutely," I managed to gasp out before I found myself bent back by the sheer force of his kiss.

"You were so beautiful out there. I love you," he murmured in my ear.

As he released me, I slumped back against the side of the bus and watched him walk off, my fingers pressed against my mouth. Stayed propped against the bus, watching the people bustling back and forth, the buzz and hum of conversation sounding as if it were coming from behind a wall of water.

Given the hazy state of my brain, water actually sounded like a really good idea. Pushing off from the bus, I took a step, stumbling as my knee unexpectedly gave way.

"Your turn to fall at my feet?"

I found myself staring into a pair of dark eyes that immediately brought to mind laughter—and chocolate. "But I didn't fall."

"No, you didn't," he replied in a lightly accented voice. The pressure at my elbows increased as I was steered back against the bus. Retreating a few steps, my rescuer crossed his arms and grinned, and in that second I recognized him.

"Thank you for helping me." I grinned, because seriously, how I could I not, with the way he was checking me out, his eyebrows rising as his gaze followed the deep plunge of my neckline. "It makes up for your stepping on my cloak."

"An accident—" His smile grew wider. "But I am thinking a lucky one, no?"

"Depends on why you think it's lucky." Twisting my hair around my hand, I lifted the heavy mass of it off my neck, trying to cool off. Keeping it loose made for a great Carmen vibe, but an immensely hot one. Watching as Soccer Boy's eyes widened, I had to wonder if it wasn't hot in more ways than one. I filed the motion away for possible inclusion in the show's choreography.

I felt a cool touch on the back of my neck as Jonathan suddenly reappeared. "Hey."

"Hi, you done?" I smiled up at him but he wasn't looking at me.

"Yeah," he replied absentmindedly. Following his narrow-eyed stare, I saw he was eyeballing Soccer Boy, whose smile had faded only slightly as he stayed front and center, conveniently ignoring the "get the hell out" vibes Jonathan was giving off. Which . . . *really?* Overreact, much?

I shrugged, my gaze meeting my rescuer's in a silent apology that he responded to with a slight nod, the smile reaching his eyes again and making me relax muscles I hadn't even realized had gone tense. Unwinding my hair, I allowed it to fall over Jonathan's hand. "So you ready to go see the shows?"

Now, he looked down at me, his hand gently kneading the back of my neck. Another apology. "If you still want."

"Absolutely."

"You should be careful with your leg."

The gentle warning prompted me to meet that dark chocolate gaze once again. "I will."

With another nod and a quick glance at Jonathan— acknowledging his presence for the first time, I suddenly realized— he took off, disappearing between the buses.

"What's wrong with your leg?" Jonathan asked, the obvious concern in his voice forcing my attention back to him—and my knee.

"Nothing—" I straightened, gingerly putting weight on the leg. Darned humidity. I'd noticed my knee getting looser with all the outside practices. "I stumbled and nearly fell. He was nice enough to catch me before I totally faceplanted."

Immediately, Jonathan's hold changed, his hand moving from my neck to my elbow, gripping it tight. "Are you okay?"

"I'm *fine*," I insisted, my muscles twitching with the unexpected— and powerful—urge to shrug his hand off. "I think I just need more water."

"I'll get you some."

"We'll get some together," I insisted—gently, "I hoped. I bet you could use some, too." I lifted my hand to his cheek, which caused his to slip off my elbow. "You're really flushed, and while it makes you look incredibly sexy, I don't want you passing out from heat stroke."

His hand trapped mine against his cheek. "You look out for me." He gazed down at me, his eyes serious and intent.

"It's what people do when they love each other."

*Yeah, but do they smother?*

*He loves you. And what do you really know yet about being in love?*

# awake

We were in Tennessee—small town outside Nashville, I think.

*Think* being the operative word here.

It was official—two weeks into tour, there was one thing I *hated* about corps. This vile practice of driving half the night after a show and then spending what was left in the next gym du jour. I mean, it was just fundamentally wrong, especially if you were like me and hated interrupted sleep the way Dorothy hated the sight of flying monkeys.

What I wouldn't *give* for Mamacita's Cuban jet-fuel *café* right now. Preferably through an IV. At least we didn't have to jump right into rehearsal—not technically. We were having a rundown of last night's show in Natchez that had been recorded on a digital video cam. And lucky us—the instructors had hooked the cam to a big-ass monitor so our shredding could be done in high-def widescreen.

"You see what I mean about flat?"

This was our second time through—first had been an uninter-rupted watch and listen. Now, Gray and the other instructors were pausing—frequently—to point out music, drill, and visual issues. And pausing some more. And talking. . . .

"Soledad, pay attention here—"

Oh, man, *busted.* I blinked at Gray, who was waiting for me to wave or in some way indicate I had a pulse. Heat prickling along my shoulders, I shook my head, hard. "Yeah, sorry." I rubbed my eyes and shook my head again. "You were saying?"

"Nothing yet." Gray's wink said he understood the sleep-deprived fog. "I just want you to focus on this next section—your projection needs work."

Not completely following, I leaned forward and focused on the screen, watching myself, a shimmering white dot amid swirling color and movement.

"Right there." Gray pointed at the screen. "Watch, Soledad—it's a huge moment, you're realizing for the first time how Don José is limiting you, you're seeing the world beyond him." He paused the recording. "I'm not faulting your technique. You're playing fabulously in front of you and up to a certain degree, be-cause it's what you're accustomed to, but this isn't a theater, dar-lin'. It's a stadium with the seating going *way* up, instead of simply out. You need to make the press box your focal point at those mo-ments so all that gorgeous emotion pouring out of you can kick 'em where it counts."

As Gray rewound and started it again, I zeroed in, not on the technical aspects of the performance, but the emotional intangi-bles. The stuff that would take it from good to great. And saw that he was absolutely right. When Raj and I danced together, or during face-to-face interaction with the other guard members, I focused on them and it came off with an intimate vibe, which was good, but when I tried to play it grander, it didn't work. And thing is, it was *so* obvious. I swallowed hard against the lump in my throat. *Dios mío,* but I felt stupid. I dropped my elbows onto my raised knees and locked my fingers behind my neck, wishing that the floor would conveniently open up under me even as I forced myself to keep watching.

For the first time, I found myself longing for the familiar, intimate confines of a stage instead of that massive football field where I all of a sudden looked so damned naked. And small.

"Hey, ease up." Jonathan's breath was warm against my ear as he rubbed my back. "In the scheme of things, not that big. Playing to the press box is something that takes some getting used to. You'll get it."

"Jonathan."

We straightened in a hurry at the frosty tone.

"Gray, please back it up again—to the solo." The look Dr. Crandall zinged our way clearly adding, *Since you weren't paying a damn bit of attention because of* her.

"Your tone went a bit flat because your breath support isn't optimal. And consequently, your phrasing is suffering as well."

*The old man is high.*

Seriously—it sounded beautiful. Those long, elegant notes of the Second Intermezzo—the perfect accompaniment to Don José and Carmen's romantic interlude in their hideaway. Jonathan had this way of playing his soprano so that it didn't sound shrill and harsh but warm and sexy, and if you'd told me six weeks ago I'd be saying that about some oversized trumpet, not to mention the guy playing it—well, let's just say there would've been hysterical laughter. Possibly a question as to where you scored the funny mushrooms.

"Also here—" Having commandeered the remote from Gray,

Dr. Crandall raised the volume until it filled the entire gym. The aggressive "March of the Toreador" sextet segueing to "El Tango de Roxanne."

"Horns, are you hearing how it dragged and you momentarily lost sync with the percussion? It wasn't a huge issue last night, but it could easily become one—a larger stadium with more bounce-back, a louder crowd, and next thing you know, you're two, three beats off from each other and scrambling like hell to recover. That's something a young, inexperienced corps does—not a corps with our depth of experience and talent."

*Suuuure.*

On the surface, he was talking about the corps as a whole, but it was Jonathan he stared at longest and hardest as he made what was otherwise pretty mild commentary.

*So* obvious, at least to me—and judging by the expression on his face, to Jonathan as well—that Dr. Crandall was throwing down the gauntlet. Probably banking on Jonathan's overdeveloped sense of responsibility kicking in. And if anyone asked, he'd no doubt *swear* it was for the greater good of the corps. Not that *anyone* would dare question the Great and Terrible Crandall.

And once again, Jonathan's restraint in the face of his dad's less-than-subtle guilt campaign amazed me, until I realized it wasn't so much restraint as it was knowing what buttons to push. Like, when Dr. Crandall called a "voluntary" horn line practice session, even as the rest of the corps was being dismissed and given a few hours of downtime to catch back up on sleep or check out the nearby riverfront small-town charm. While most of the other horns, including a smarmy-faced Aaron, the asshole rookie/age-out, clustered around Dr. Crandall, Jonathan simply met his dad's gaze with a cool stare of his own, then shrugged and turned away, causing a dark, angry flush to overtake Dr. Crandall's face.

"I can practice later" was all he said.

Admittedly, the responsible part of me wanted to protest. I mean, that dedication to his art, his pursuit of perfection, was such a huge part of why I'd fallen for him in the first place. However, it had to compete with the part of me that got *such* a charge out of knowing I came first above all else with this beautiful boy.

Wasn't just about sex, either. Not that we weren't constantly looking for the time and privacy, but at this point being together for us was as much about solitude. Just having the freedom to say anything we wanted to each other without someone sitting in front of us or lying a few feet away. And even more, it was about being able to just sit and hold each other with nothing but peace around us.

With that kind of temptation, Responsible never stood a chance.

# give a little bit

"Let's do it, people!"

Damn straight. I was ready to hit practice with a vengeance—
ready to project out and up and any way necessary to own this
part. By the time we got to the full-corps run-throughs, I was totally juiced and into it—the *whole* corps was juiced. It was like
our little afternoon break had given us energy and perspective,
the hum of adrenaline running like a live wire between us and
stoking this ferocious passion that made the music that much
more rich, the percussion crisper, the guard's movements sharper
and ever more elegant, the whole of it adding an entirely new element into my performance. The instructors totally dug it, too, feeding off our energy and calling out encouragement and whooping
and whistling in a way they usually reserved for actual performances. And at one point, during Jonathan's solo, aching and
poignant, the notes floating on the warm afternoon air and sound-

ing like a lover's voice, I glanced up and saw Dr. Crandall standing off to one side, his eyes closed.

Abso-freakin'-lutely, it was worth closing your eyes for. I was glad that for once, Jonathan's dad was able to unclench enough to simply enjoy the pure beauty his son was capable of.

I noticed something else, too, as practice continued—little by little, an unfamiliar audience gathering along the sidelines, made up of people who definitely weren't of the music variety. Guys, most of them holding soccer balls and a few of them, more annoyingly, *messing* with the balls, bouncing them around.

I tried to ignore them, but damn, those black-and-white flashes I'd catch out of my peripheral vision were annoying as hell—like some demented soccer ADD.

*Especially* ADD-ish was the one who was currently parked on the sidelines right in front of me, bouncing the ball off his feet, then his knees, and even his head, for God's sake, like he meant to shoot it into the field, only snatching it back with his hands at the last possible second. And doing it all with this obnoxious grin on his face, like he knew I was keeping a wary eye on his ass. Then . . . he . . . he *winked*.

*Ohhh* . . . First show. North Carolina. Dusty cleat marks on my cloak. A brash, ponytailed soccer player who'd winked and dropped to a knee like a gallant knight. Who'd lent a helping hand and flirted with laughing, chocolate eyes.

However, any previous goodwill was totally out the window now.

*Come on, I dare you to come a little closer,* pendejo. *I'll show you some footwork and balls.*

"That's it, Soledad—now, up a little more, shoot all that attitude you've got up toward me, darlin'."

I swished imaginary skirts and lifted my chin up toward where Gray was situated at the top of the bleachers, flicking my wrist in a dismissive gesture aimed right at Soccer Boy at the same time I pushed Raj away and began my final solo.

After the last note faded away and the call came to relax, I rolled to my back with a groan and stretched. Sitting up, I brushed off the grass and dirt clinging to my skin. Dinner or a shower first? Tough choice, because my stomach was starting to rumble, but I felt gross.

"All right, people, concert arc."

We arranged ourselves, facing Gray in the center of the field, our backs to the bleachers.

"Okay, quick stretch." Cooling us down, mentally and physically, with a couple of minutes of deep, controlled breathing, then—

"All right now, tell me how much you guys love me," Gray said. He stood there in his blinding lemon-yellow and fuchsia Hawaiian shirt, arms out.

"We love you more than bunnies, Gray," we intoned. No one seemed to know when or how the comeback had become a tradition, it just was. Just like singing the last verse of "This Is the Moment" from *Jekyll & Hyde* as our final ritual before hitting the field. You know, I was finally getting the tradition thing—the feeling of camaraderie, even with the people you didn't get along with otherwise. Because on the field, we were all Raiders. We all had a common goal. This was all so cool and different from dance, where there was tradition and ritual up the butt, but the camaraderie? Not so much. Too much investment in personal gain and careers to allow for any meaningful bonds.

"Of *course* you love me more than bunnies," he responded with a cheesetastic grin. "Especially since you guys busted ass this af-

ternoon and we don't have a show tonight, I managed to convince
the rest of your slave-driving staff who wanted to be all Spanish
Inquisition and keep torturing you that you truly deserve the
night off."

As we whooped and hollered, he added, "Yes, yes, I know . . .
I'm fabulous. Now get out of here before they change my mind."

I wove through the chattering hordes, excitedly making plans,
trying to make my way to Jonathan. More time alone. How totally
bonus was this?

*"Mira que peligrosa. Quema desde aquí."*

My head whipped around looking for the source of the "dangerous hot stuff" commentary so rudely interrupting the quality
daydreams. I mean, I knew who all the Spanish-speakers were in
our corps, and that smart-ass remark had been delivered in a
voice I absolutely didn't recognize.

Well, well—look at that. Soccer Boy standing a few feet away
with his fellow jesters, all with stupid grins and expressions on
their faces I could only describe as . . . oh, *ugh*—ogling. Had he
ogled like that back in North Carolina? God, I had to have been
high on performance adrenaline to respond to *that*.

*"¿Perdóname?"* And it's not even like the scathing tone threw
them—just made them grin that much bigger, with Soccer Boy,
oh God, *posing,* foot propped on a soccer ball like some conquis-
tador. In shorts. These fools were acting like they hadn't seen
anything with dual X chromosomes in way too long. Kind of like
prisoners.

*"Parece que entiende,"* one of the lesser soccer boys said, elbow-
ing his cohorts.

Didn't seem to bother Soccer Boy in the slightest that I understood them, since all he did was cock his head—the move drawing attention to the shocking streak of silver cutting through his

dark hair. "Even better, then," he replied to his buddies, still in Spanish, although his stare remained locked on me. *"Porque yo quiero saber qué habré hecho para merecer tan preciosura."*

My jaw literally dropped. This chump had just referred to me as "precious." To other people. *And* wondered what he'd done to deserve me. And judging by the grin I'm sure he thought was charming, had absolutely *no* shame over it.

*Ay, bendito*—a Latin boy to the nth degree, this one. Actually put my cousins to shame with the macho swagger and "I'm too hot for color TV" 'tude, complete with cheesy pickup lines that no American boy in his right mind would ever try to use. And it was so utterly outrageous, I did the only thing I could do.

I laughed my ass off.

His smile got a little bigger. "You think I am funny?" he asked in the lilting English I remembered from our first encounter. Like *that* would work.

"Hilarious." Reaching the bleachers, I grabbed my towel along with a bottle of water from the nearby cooler. After a long drink I lifted the bottle higher and poured water over my head, sighing as the icy liquid penetrated my French braid to my scalp, rolling down my neck and shoulders. How the water didn't sizzle and evaporate right off my skin was a mystery.

"A total riot—especially with *that*," I snapped, nodding at the ball that even now he was fooling with, kicking it lightly from foot to foot.

In a neat trick, much as it pained me to admit it, he flicked the ball up, caught it, and handed it off to one of his buddies. It was all so smooth, he was standing in front of me before I'd even finished processing the sequence of actions.

"I am sorry. It's a . . . *manía nerviosa.*" Now he smiled, full out, showing off straight white teeth and making a tiny crescent of a dimple appear beside one corner of his mouth that I would *not* find charming. No way.

"Whatever." I lifted the shoulder I was currently toweling off. "It was kind of obnoxious."

Dark eyes narrowed as his smile faded. Guess he wasn't used to the charming smile plus dimple not working. *"Por favor, discúlpa—"* he said in a much softer voice that echoed the boy I'd met in North Carolina. "I *am* very sorry."

"Look, forget it." Working with distractions was part of the game, right? My gaze wandered, trying to find Jonathan, who I finally spotted, clustered with the rest of the sextet behind the bleachers. Looked like they wanted to do a little more rehearsing before breaking for the night. As the first notes of the "Toreador" rang out, I closed my eyes, automatically revisiting that section of the show and my choreography. A second later, I nearly jumped out of my skin at the brush of fingers against my arm.

*"¿A lo mejor podemos empezar otra vez?"*

I whirled to find Soccer Boy still standing there. "What?"

"Could we perhaps start again?" He held a hand out, the charming smile back on his face but toned down a notch to something approaching sincere. *"Me llamo Taz."*

*Is he serious? He can't be serious. Who has a name like Taz, anyway?*

*A guy who can pull off wearing some major diamond studs and flirt like whoa. Come on . . . He's kind of cute. And actually seems nice.*

"Soledad." I grasped his hand, then nearly fell over as he moved in and kissed one cheek, then the other, before stepping back and releasing my hand. Again, very smooth and so fast, my brain almost couldn't keep up. This guy was *good.*

"It is very nice to meet you, Soledad, and I am sorry I— I—" He stopped, his eyes narrowing again like he was searching for the right word.

"Distracted me?" Hey, at least I didn't say "acted like a jackass." Waving my hand, I let him off the hook. *"No te preocupes."* See? I could be gracious, too. Besides, had to confess I was finding him amusing in that dorky, endearing Latin boy sort of way.

His face cleared and he nodded. *"Gracias."*

Nodding in return, I started to turn away again, then stopped as I heard him say, "You are a very good *bailarina—muy apacionada."*

My eyes just about rolled out of my head, I swear. *Just* like my boy cousins in that didn't know how to quit when he was breaking even sort of way. I fought back a smile as I faced him again and replied, "Thank you."

"You know—" His voice was very soft. "To be Carmen so completely, it has to come from . . ." He tapped his chest. "Inside. *Tu alma."*

*"You* know *Carmen?"*

*"Sí,* I know *Carmen."* Nothing more than that—just a smile that seemed to add, "And what of it?"

Oh, *crap.* Snob alert. Seriously uncool culture snob alert. After all, what the hell did I know about soccer?

"Well . . ." I bent over to exchange my jazz shoes for a pair of flip-flops, trying to hide the blush I was pretty sure was competing with the heat flush from working out. Trying to come up with something to say that wasn't utterly lame or even more snotty. Straightening, I said, "Then you know what a great character she is."

Well, at least it wasn't snotty.

"It is *you."* The smile ratcheted back up, and damn, but it was charming. So much so, I couldn't help but grin back, shaking my head at the same time.

"Thank you. Again." I fiddled with the cap on my water bottle, twisting it off and on. "How do you—," I started, before catching myself at the last possible second. Because seriously, saying it *would* be snotty, no question.

Didn't seem to bother him, though. All he did was cock his head to the side as he reached back with his foot for the ball his teammates had left abandoned. Back and forth, he kicked it, establishing a mesmerizing rhythm. "My mother loves opera," he finally said, switching back to Spanish. "All of the arts, really. And she passed on that love to our whole family. Unfortunately, I have been less successful in my attempts to convince her of the artistic merits of *fútbol*." Another few lightning-quick flicks of his feet and then, like magic, the ball was in the air, suspended for a moment before he caught it with a flourish.

"I don't know why she wouldn't . . ." The rest faded as I caught Jonathan rounding the front of the bleachers out of the corner of my eye.

"Uh . . . it was nice meeting you, Taz."

*"Igualmente."*

I nodded and started to turn away, then stopped. "Thank you. Really," I said softly. "For what you said about my dancing."

A quiet *"Hasta la próxima vez, Soledad"* drifted toward me as I met Jonathan at the other end of the bleachers with a kiss.

"Who was that?" he asked, wiping a stray trickle of water from my neck.

"A soccer player—remember the guys from North Carolina?"

"Yeah. Is that the same one who was talking to you then?"

I put a finger to his chin and steered his head down so his gaze was directed at me rather than behind me. "Yes, actually."

"Why was he talking to you now?"

I wrapped my arms around his waist, resting my head against his shoulder because, suddenly, the last of the adrenaline rush from rehearsal was gone. *So* tired . . . and my knee had that wobbly Jell-O sensation that seemed to come more and more after the hard rehearsals. Closing my eyes, I leaned more completely against him, feeling like I could fall asleep right there.

"I don't know. Does it matter?"

"Thought you didn't like stalker behavior." I pushed myself to a more upright position to find Jonathan smiling. With his mouth, at least.

"Oh, please, two conversations that amount to maybe five minutes total hardly constitute stalker behavior."

Time to change the subject. "Think you can help steer me in the direction of a shower in the hopes it'll wake me up enough for us to go get some dinner, and maybe chocolate for dessert?"

No one could ever accuse the boy of being stupid, seeing how he winced. "Sorry—I'm being a jealous ass, aren't I?"

"It's not totally without its charms. So long as you don't make a habit of it." My shoulders rolled and relaxed beneath Jonathan's touch. "Seriously—all he was doing was complimenting me on my performance."

*To be Carmen so completely, it has to come from . . . inside.* Tu alma.

The soft words echoed in my mind, prompting an involuntary shiver.

Misinterpreting the shivering, Jonathan turned us toward the gym, saying, "Okay then, I can take a hint. You definitely need that shower before your muscles seize up and leave you sore and cranky and you blame me because I was being an ass." With a wicked smile, he leaned in close, his lips against my ear. "And don't I wish I could steer myself into the shower with you. To, you know, make up for being an ass."

*Okay,* then. I blinked at the wide, sweaty expanse of his chest as his words rattled around in my overtired brain and *yeah*, I had heard him right and . . . and . . . whoa, *mama*.

"You have got a *great* imagination."

"Does that have its charms, too?" he replied, draping an arm over my shoulders.

"Oh, yeah." I hugged him close, reaching up to kiss him again. "And it's definitely something you can make a habit of."

As we headed toward the gym, a blur of movement rushed past my peripheral vision. I glanced over my shoulder in time to see Taz's leg reach back and connect with the ball, sending it in a long, graceful arc that just whizzed past the goalie's outstretched hands and into the net. A split second before it landed, he pivoted, gaze meeting mine for a fleeting second before he smiled, bowed slightly, then turned to run down the field.

# you are

"So, who was that hunka hunka burnin' love yesterday?"

I stared at Raj as we warmed up on opposite sides of the barre. "The wha—?" Extending one leg high behind me, I bent forward until my forehead touched my opposite knee.

Almost as flexible as me, he bent over, copying the vertical extension. "The pretty boy after rehearsal."

"Oh, him." Immediately my mind conjured the sleek black ponytail and the cocky grin. And little dimple. "Some soccer player."

"All-star team from Spain. Twenty and unders. They're touring cross-country with American all-stars, playing exhibitions, in order to raise awareness of the sport for the heathen Yanks."

I straightened and turned to face the barre, bending forward until my back was perfectly parallel with the floor. "If you already know, why are you grilling me, and how'd you find all this out anyway?"

"Gray talked to their coaches. Doing some friendly new-neighbor chat across the fence."

"Neighbor what?" Stepping away from the barre, I carefully rose into a *relevé* and back down, then *chasséd* lightly, testing the surface of the unfamiliar floor.

"We're going to keep running into them." After hitting Play on the iPod hooked into portable speakers, he joined me on the floor, facing me as we listened to the show's intro. "In a massive stroke of luck and coinkydinks, they're doing the fair circuit. So when we have fair shows, they'll be there, playing with their balls."

I groaned as I continued to listen for our cue. "That's awful, Raj."

"Not from where I sit," he retorted with a cheerful leer. "Watching pretty Spanish boys play soccer beats the hell out of the bearded lady." An instant later he lifted his chin and wasn't Raj, my buddy, but Don José, straight-laced officer, strutting toward me, rifle in hand, spinning it in a way designed to both capture my attention and let me know he was all business. During the show, the rifle routine was done in unison with the rest of the guard, but we were rehearsing by ourselves because Gray wanted to add a new element to Don José and Carmen's first meeting. I was to toss a silk rose with a weight attached to it so it would sail gracefully across to Don José and he'd snatch it out of the air. *Very* dramatic, and a perfect punctuation to the conclusion of the "Habañera."

Of course, Gray being Gray, wanted Raj to be in the middle of some impossible rifle toss, turn, capture the rose with one hand, then the rifle with the other. My job would be to learn how to toss the rose so that it didn't take out an eye, or otherwise damage Raj. Oh—and not lose my balance because I'd be tossing it at the end of a dramatic leap.

This was gonna take some doing. And doing. And doing over, through the sweat and burn of tired muscles—business as usual.

"Come on, Raj, let's do it again."

"No."

I dropped my arms from my opening pose. "What? Why not?"

"Something's the matter, you're not moving right. The last couple run-throughs, you didn't seem as secure on some of the moves."

I took a deep breath, trying to ignore the sudden jump and skip in my heart rate. "Hey, that's normal for working through new choreography. I'm okay."

*Liar.*

"Liar."

What was he, reading my mind or something? Just what I needed—another Mamacita.

Heaving a sigh, I executed a pirouette and lunge, not wobbling as I landed only by sheer force of will and even managing a brilliant, blind-'em-from-the-stage smile. "See? I'm fine."

Spoken to thin air, since Raj was already at the other end of the huge double gym where Gray was rehearsing the rest of the guard, and deep in conversation. I shook my head and stomped over to grab my water bottle as the two of them swiveled their heads my direction, then started my way.

"I'm *fine.*"

"Not according to Raj."

My arms crossed over my chest, I let loose with another sigh. "Now he's a doctor?"

"I'm your partner," he shot back, his pose mirroring mine. "And who else is gonna keep an eye on you when you're so damned pigheaded? And *why* are you being so damned pigheaded? This is your livelihood, girl."

*Damn—*

My arms dropped to my sides, although I wasn't completely ready to give in. "Really, guys, I'm okay," I protested, even as Gray eased me onto the bleachers. Dropping to a knee in front of me, he extended my legs, looking from one knee to the other, corps director giving way to the physical therapist from his non-corps life.

"Does it hurt?"

"No," I sighed, finally resigned to admitting that it wasn't completely okay.

"The right's a little swollen, though." He pushed around the area, slow and careful, doing his PT thing. "How does it feel?"

"Kinda wobbly." I curled my hands around the edge of the bench, the cool metal ridges biting into my palms. "I honestly think it's just the humidity." I watched as he took my ankle in his hand and lifted my leg slightly, flexing, then straightening my knee, then flexing again, testing the range of motion. "Or maybe all the different surfaces?" The different gym floors, the parking lots we warmed up on, the different fields. Just not something my body was accustomed to.

"Yeah, that probably has more to do with it than the humidity. All those changes can be brutal on the joints even when you're used to it." He set my leg down and stood, his angel's face turning stern.

*Uh-oh.*

"I want you to wrap that knee and keep it elevated until we do final run-throughs this afternoon. I don't want to risk losing you for tonight's show."

"But what about the rose trick?"

"We weren't gonna add that for at least another week, so don't even go there, girl." Raj, doing his own version of stern and even managing to pull it off.

"Ditto on the not adding it and don't even go there." Gray shook his finger at me. "Wrap, cold pack for fifteen on, thirty off, and elevation. At lunch I'll hit a drugstore and see about getting you a brace to wear during rehearsals, and performances, if needed."

"But—"

"No," Gray and Raj both chorused and damn, but they were bossy. Still, couldn't deny that the idea of putting my leg up was sounding mighty tempting, although I'd walk on hot coals before admitting just *how* good it sounded. I hated feeling weak almost as much as I hated not nailing something. But also not about to jeopardize my career because of pride. Wasn't *that* stupid.

"Raj, stick with her."

"You don't trust me?"

"Honey, it's not that I don't trust you, it's that I *was* you." The severe expression softened—as did his voice. "In drive and attitude, if not in talent. So I wouldn't be surprised if the thought crossed your mind to sneak off and do just a little more practicing if you thought none of us were looking."

Our gazes met for a moment before I felt a smile coming on—barely. "Busted." Turning to Raj, who was looking disgustingly pleased with himself, I said, "Come on, let's go get a cold pack and Ace bandage from the moms. Then we're watching rehearsal." That pretty mouth opened, but before one word even escaped, I pointed out, "All Gray said was that I had to keep it elevated—not where. Right?"

Lips pressed tight and turning up ever so slightly at the corners, Gray nodded.

"Okay, then. I'm a part of the corps, I at least watch rehearsal. I don't want the guys thinking I'm slacking."

"You don't want *one* guy thinking you're slacking," Raj teased as we left the gym.

"No, it's all of them." No matter what the little smart-ass thought. "If anything, Jonathan knows better than anyone how I am. But the others . . ." Tugging at the hem of my tank, my gaze ranged over the field where everyone was gathering. My muscles twitched with the want. I was supposed to be out there. Even if it was for the best that I wasn't.

*Damn.*

"So far, I've busted ass as hard as anyone else, and they know it. I just don't want the guys to think that now that we've enjoyed some success, I'm going to be a total girl and wuss out or something—"

"Oh, baby." Surprisingly, Raj laughed and pulled my arm through his, tugging me close. "You so don't have to worry about that. I know some of the boys are assholes, but that's just a genetic defect. To the rest, you've more than proved how tough you are. You're one of us."

Funny how those four words made me feel almost as squooshy inside as a hug from Mamacita or a kiss from Jonathan.

After a pit stop at Mom Central, I carefully climbed up the bleachers, Raj behind me, clucking like a mother hen the whole way. Once he was satisfied I was comfortably situated, he settled in beside me, leaning back on his elbows.

"So."

I glanced over as I wrapped my knee in the stretchy bandage. "So?"

"Before we were so rudely interrupted, you were about to tell me about—" He tilted his head toward an adjoining field where a group of guys were lined up in a block, their backs to us, stretching. The soccer players, natch, as my gaze seemed to automatically land on one dark head with a ponytail.

"Was I now?"

Still staring over at the field with an avid expression, he replied, "Oh, you were."

"Good God, Raj, *really*."

"Good God, Soledad, were you not *looking* at him?"

"Okay, yeah," I admitted on a laugh, "I did notice he's built."

*And has a sweet smile.*

Raj's head swiveled back, his eyes so wide, a full ring of white was visible around the irises. "*Duh.*"

"Look, why didn't you just come over?"

"Please," he snorted. "He wouldn't have noticed, and if he had, would've been mightily annoyed."

"Come *on*. We're talking a Spanish guy here. Subspecies of *Latinus manus horninus*. The majority of 'em flirt with anything with boobs. I was convenient."

"That one was all about flirting with *you*, girl, and aren't you lucky?" Raj sighed. "He's seriously pretty."

I shrugged and stretched my leg along the bleacher. "Lot of pretty guys in the world, Raj."

"Yeah, but there's pretty and then there's *pretty*." Raj plopped the cold pack into my outstretched hand.

"He's okay." Arranging the pack over my knee, I looked back toward our field, catching Jonathan's concerned stare as he tried to listen to Gray at the same time. *"I'm all right,"* I mouthed. His expression didn't really relax, *pobrecito*, but there wasn't any other way for me to reassure him until a break was called.

"Well, color you all blasé," Raj muttered, punctuating the outrage with a sniff. "That boy is all kinds of hot." He sighed again.

My gaze wandered back over toward the other field and almost like he knew he was the subject of intense discussion, there he was, conveniently standing at the end of their bleachers closest to ours, drinking from a sports bottle. Reaching back over his head, he pulled off his T-shirt, showing off a nicely cut, lean torso with a tattoo inked on the back of one of his shoulders. And while part of me was thinking I should really be looking away now—

*Come on,* m'ija, *you're taken, not dead.*

From beneath my lashes, I took in the muscled legs and the deep tan with a small slice of pale skin showing where the waistband of his shorts had slipped, and the light sprinkling of hair across his chest and arrowing down the flat stomach. Noticed that among his teammates, he was one of the tallest, yet hadn't seemed all that much taller than me yesterday, and *how* was I remembering that?

Because pulling his shirt off had skewed his ponytail, he yanked the elastic off, pouring some water over his head and shaking it hard, water drops flying everywhere. I stifled a giggle at the image of a big, overgrown puppy that popped into my mind. And as he combed his fingers through what turned out to be shoulder-length hair and fastened just the top half of it in the elastic, I could clearly see the silver streak, shining in the sun.

"Thank you, God," Raj breathed out.

"His name is Taz, by the way." Figured I'd complete the image for his daydreams.

"Of course it is." And sounded like he was about two seconds away from sighing, "And he's so *dreamy.*"

"Raj!" Shading his eyes, Gray looked up into the bleachers. "Come down, please,—we have changes you need to be aware of. You"—he pointed at me with his free hand—"stay put."

Not like I could go anywhere—not with the way Raj's hand latched onto my shoulder "helping" to keep my ass planted firmly on the seat. "I wasn't going to—"

"Of course you weren't."

Lord, but it was tempting to "help" him off the bleachers. Instead, I sat on my hands and watched as he made his way down to the field and, after listening to Gray's instructions, blocked out the movements. From what I could tell, nothing major, so after watching for a few more minutes, I picked up my journal and pen.

*It's mind-boggling how I want every minute of every day with Jonathan to last a lifetime—even when he's acting like an idiot. That's part of the growing pains, though, right? You go through those rough patches and come out of it more devoted.*

*Or . . . hating each other?*

*Those soccer players*

"*Buenas, Soledad.*"

*Wha*—? My pen jerked, a purple line dribbling off the page, before it bounced off the bleachers with a sharp clang. Only reason my journal didn't follow was Taz's quick reflexes, catching the leather-bound book as it slid off my lap.

"Here—" He put the journal in my hands, asking "*¿Lo tienes?*" before ducking beneath the bleachers and reappearing a second later, pen in hand.

"Thank you." I accepted the pen and tucked it into the journal. Pushing myself up, I gradually put weight on the bad leg, testing its stability before carefully making my way down the bleachers.

Taz walked alongside as I descended, but didn't make a move to help or otherwise act as if I was helpless. Talk about refreshing, after the fragile damsel manner in which Raj and Gray had been treating me. Surprising, too—since, you know, Latin boys, at least the ones of my acquaintance, had this way of assuming *all* damsels were fragile.

Once on the ground, I turned to him. "Hi—again."

"*Hola*—again." He smiled and lifted his water. "We are going to start scrimmaging soon, but I saw you sitting with your leg up and wondered if you were all right." He shot a glance down at my wrapped knee, giving me a bird's-eye view of the silver streak. Not that I'd ever admit it to him, but Raj was right—way hot.

"¿La misma rodilla?"

"Uh—" I blinked. "Yeah, the same one," I finally managed. He remembered? From two weeks ago? Wow. My fingers brushed against the top of the bandage. "Just a precaution."

"Ah . . . chévere."

And like an eerie case of déjà vu, I felt a touch on the back of my neck as Jonathan appeared beside me.

"What happened?"

"Nothing. I'm okay."

But he wasn't buying the reassurances. Grasping my elbow, he tried to gently guide me back toward the bleachers. "Looks like you should be off it, though."

Every muscle tensed, my knee beginning to throb like it was trying to back him up. "I'm *fine*."

"What did your instructor advise?"

Both of us turned to Taz, whose presence I'd almost forgotten. But nope, there he was, standing patiently, like he had all the time in the world.

"Cold packs and elevation," I admitted, feeling a reluctant smile pulling at the corners of my mouth as one of his eyebrows rose. Subtle he wasn't, but then again, I got the impression it wasn't exactly the vibe he was going for.

"*Bueno,* I know it's not the most comfortable thing, especially when what you want most is to be out helping your team, but it's the best for the long term. I know from experience." While his words were as light as the smile accompanying them, his stare was intent. Not just looking at me, but rather into me. It should've felt weird and intrusive, but . . . no. It didn't.

"Speaking of helping your team, isn't that what you should be doing?" Jonathan's fingers convulsed slightly around my elbow as the pitch of his voice dropped with each word. I fought the temptation to pull free, not wanting to make a scene. Or embarrass him. He probably didn't even realize what he was doing.

Taz casually glanced over his shoulder to where his teammates milled around, drinking water and chatting as they remained on break.

"It would not appear as if they need me yet."

Why?

Why was he still standing here when he had to know that Jonathan wanted him gone, like, yesterday?

Oh. *Ohhh*.

I followed his stare to Jonathan's hand, still clutching my elbow. A hold I figured he wouldn't release until I let him help me down onto the bleachers. Easing down, I made a show of carefully swinging my leg up so it was elevated along the bench. His smile, as he sat beside me, was so gentle and caring, I couldn't help but feel like an overreacting bitch. He was just looking out for me. Taking his hand in mine, I turned to Taz, asking, "So, do you play tonight?" Trying, for God's sake, to shift attention away from me.

"This afternoon. It is why we have a light practice schedule this morning. We will scrimmage, then break for lunch at the stadium, made by the parents of the host athletic organization." He laughed. "The American parents are very nice, but the food they make is sometimes so heavy. And it is hard to play well if I eat the wrong things before a match." He held his hands up in a

"What can I do?" gesture. "They are only exhibition, but I . . . I feel—" Clearly struggling, he finished in a rush of Spanish. *"No me cae bien si no puedo dar esfuerzo máximo ¿tú sabes?"*

A slight twitch against my shoulder made me glance at Jonathan, his stare shifting between me and Taz, eyebrows drawn together. "It doesn't feel right if you don't go full out," I translated. "Just like us, right, Jonathan?" But it was Taz I smiled at, nodding in understanding, because boy did I *ever* get that. And I knew Jonathan did, too.

"Yeah, I guess." Pulling his hand free, he stood as Gray's piercing whistle echoed across the field, calling the troops back from break. "Except our performances count."

The words were casual. So casual, the "so bite me, loser" attitude came through loud and clear. And made me want to turn a hose on him. Talk about uncalled for.

"I never said ours did not."

Oh, *brother*. So Taz wasn't down with being insulted, and now he was making his point. Not that I could totally blame him. Judging by the narrowed eyes, Jonathan got it—*loud and clear*. While there might be some slight language comprehension barriers, it seemed guys had their own universal language that transcended the spoken word.

With a quiet *"Ciao,"* Taz touched his fingertips to his forehead in this salute move that was totally off the charts. But something about the expression in his eyes—the same one that brought to mind laughter—made me think he was completely aware just how cheesy the move was. And as he turned and jogged toward his field, I got my first clear look at the tat on his shoulder.

The Tasmanian Devil in a swirling tornado.

I laughed, loud enough that Taz turned, jogging backwards for a few steps with a goofy grin on his face, before turning forward again, giving me another look at that distinctive tattoo. Taz, indeed. *What* a dork. Charming, but definitely a dork.

The laughter died away as I turned to Jonathan and found him standing rigid, his gaze focused on Taz's retreating back before it shifted to me. And if the expression in Taz's eyes had made me think laughter, the expression in those gray eyes squeezed my heart, sharp and painful and all-encompassing.

I stood and touched his cheek. "I love you, you know."

He didn't say anything. Just let his eyes drift shut as his chest rose and fell, like it had just been set free.

july

# tears and rain

"He what?" I *know* I didn't just hear what I thought I heard. Staring up at Jonathan as he shoved stuff into the overhead compartment, I repeated, "He *what*?"

"Took me off the solo. 'Temporary, until you get your head screwed back on straight,' he said. And he gave it to freakin' Aaron. Jesus." He stripped off his uniform pants, balling them up and tossing them into the compartment. "Temporary . . . my . . . ass," he growled, shoving at the pants with every word. *"Dammit."*

"Jonathan, no!" Scrambling up onto my knees, I grabbed his arm just before his fist connected with the wall behind our seats. "Last thing you need is a broken hand."

"Like it matters."

"Matters to me." Brushing the backs of my fingers down his cheek, reaching up to kiss him, trying to ease that live-wire, angry hurt, at least enough so I could shove him down into the seat and keep him from hurting himself. Reaching into the overhead, I rummaged around in his duffel for a pair of sweats and a dry long-sleeve T-shirt, same as what I had on.

First, though, I handed him a towel, because it was seriously wet out there. A majorly chilly wet, with temps in the mid-fifties, since we were in Minnesota and *madre santísima*, what was *up* with that noise? It was July, for God's sake.

But while rain had fallen steadily the whole night, the much-feared lightning had stayed away, and since in corps, as in dance, the show *always* went on, we went out there and slogged on through. Gray did have us modify the dance floor routine down to the most basic tango moves and told me, "Under no circumstances are you to try anything you don't feel absolutely solid on, Soledad. Improvise, do whatever you need to do to stay safe."

Hey, you know—no arguments here. Performing on the slippery wood of the makeshift dance floor, or slick grass with wicked patches of mud lying in wait to trip my ass up, wasn't something I was hot to experience again anytime soon.

"I'll be right back," I said to Jonathan, who was sitting like a statue, totally ignoring the cold water dripping from his hair and into his eyes. Only his hands showed movement, slowly twisting the towel into a tight, vicious coil.

"Dry off, for God's sake, Jonathan. Or are you trying for pneumonia?"

"Wouldn't matter," he repeated, this time more in a dull monotone that had my throat closing.

I slid onto his lap and wrapped my arms around him, not caring that I was getting wet all over again. "Yes, it would," I said softly, my forehead pressed against his, running my fingers through his hair—*anything* to bring him back. Relaxing into him as I felt his chest rise and fall with a huge sigh, and his arms tighten around me.

"God, what would I do without you?" he whispered against my shoulder.

"Lucky for you, you won't have to find out." I took the towel and wiped the moisture from his forehead and neck, feeling fierce and protective as he rubbed his cheek against my shoulder, like a cat seeking comfort. "Now please, dry off and change. I'll be right back."

Grabbing his uniform and my costume, I shoved my feet into my sneakers and pulled on my hooded corps jacket. Luckily, our bus was parked closest to the food truck, so I only had to make a quick dash through the rain to where the moms were set up under the truck's extended awning, handing out paper cups of hot chocolate or tea, and collecting our uniforms for what was now a necessary A.M. laundry run.

"How is he?"

So she already knew. No big surprise, I guess. Corps bore a tremendous resemblance to a big, nosy Cuban family, and since she actually *was* family . . .

I turned to face Mrs. Crandall, who was standing a few feet behind me, holding two cups with a small paper plate balanced on top of one of them as corps members and staff and other parents streamed around and past us, cheerfully or not-so-cheerfully bitching about the cold and the rain and how muddy and terrible the field had been. And yet—as our gazes met—it felt like the two of us were alone in a bizarre sort of vacuum.

"He's pissed."

She sighed and closed her eyes, looking not sad or disappointed, like I might've expected, but . . . tired. Her lips moved, but I couldn't quite catch what she said—something like "It never ends."

*Huh?*

"Mrs. Crandall?"

Coming out of wherever she'd been in her head, she blinked and took another deep breath. "Make sure he dries off and puts on something warm and drinks this and— And . . . here, I'll trade you—" With some nice sleight-of-hand maneuvering, she managed to exchange the plate and cups for the mud-splattered clothes I held.

"Take care of him."

The cups were warm against my fingers, sweet-smelling steam curling into the damp air and bringing to mind comfort and blankets and how I felt cuddled against Jonathan, talking in whispers while the bus rumbled deep into the night on dark, endless highways.

I *really* wanted to get back.

"Yes, ma'am, I'll try."

"He'll listen to you—he wants to please you more than anyone." She seemed *real* interested in shaking out the clothes, draping them over her arm just so. "Get on back to the bus before the cocoa gets cold."

But back in the bus, any thought of finding out what had gone down was replaced with figuring out where Jonathan had disappeared to, although . . . come on, didn't take a rocket scientist.

*"Damn."* I shoved the cups and plate into a surprised Raj's hands as I did a 180 and started shoving past people to get back to the front of the bus.

"What is it?"

"I've got to find Jonathan and keep him from doing something monumentally stupid."

"What? Why?"

"His dad took the solo and gave it to Aaron."

"Oh, *damn*—wait up."

Finally off the bus, we ran through rain that was falling harder and getting colder. If the fates were trying to hit me over the head with symbolism, I had news for them—didn't need it. Already knew this was bad.

"This is complete bullshit, Dad, and you know it. When the hell are you going to get it—the head games that worked on Brian *don't* work on me."

The shifting beams of headlights as buses and trucks from other corps started pulling from the parking lot played over them as they faced off behind the equipment trailer, highlighting the sheets of falling rain. Silver curtains drawn around the ongoing drama between these two.

"I never played head games with Brian. Didn't have to." Dr. Crandall's voice was as cold as Jonathan's was heated. "He worked on his gift. And you, with even more natural ability, more drive—or so I thought—just pissing it away because you're more interested in fucking that girl than in developing your talent."

Blue eyes glared past Jonathan and bored right into me. "And in the end, she's going to break your heart, and then where will you be?"

"Jonathan—" I warned, reaching for his arm, surprised to find it relaxed. Downright shocked to see him smiling, although it wasn't a smile that necessarily inspired warm or happy sensations.

"You are so wrong. With all your crap. About her. About me. About every damned thing you *think* you know." Taking my hand, he led us away, calling back over his shoulder, "And since when do you give a shit about my heart?"

As we trudged back to the buses, I exchanged "What the hell just happened here?" glances with Raj, because seriously, tonight was just a big ball of surreal named Crandall.

# believe

Back at the bus we changed clothes again and drank the now-cold cocoa and watched the lights of the stadium grow smaller and more distant until they were swallowed by nighttime—all without saying a word. And knowing he still needed time, I waited, the two of us stretched out across our seats, my back to his chest, listening to the usual noises of the bus settling down for the night, the hum and buzz of multiple conversations dwindling down to silence, helped along by the soft jazz streaming from the bus's speakers and the steady drumming of rain against the windows.

It was only then, when we were as completely alone as we could get on a bus full of people, that I ventured to say anything.

"Jonathan?"

Silence. But he wasn't asleep. If the ragged, uneven breathing hadn't been a dead giveaway, the rapid tattoo of his heartbeat against my back would've done it. Like a time bomb, on the edge of blowing. "Jonathan, please, if you talk about it, you'll feel better."

"No." He huffed out an explosive breath, his chin scrubbing against the top of my head as he shook his. "Just . . . leave it alone, okay?"

"I can't." Sitting up, I unwound my hair from its braid, just to give myself something to do with my hands. "Look, I don't know all of what's gone down between you and your dad to make your relationship so bent, but you have to know I'm willing to listen. To anything." Combing my fingers through the damp length of it, I pulled it forward over one shoulder, staring down at the row of nightlights running along either side of the aisle. Looking like two tiny rows of spotlights. "You know . . . you expect me to tell you everything about myself, but you can't do the same for me. I know it's selfish, but . . . it hurts."

He reached for me, pulling me down until my head found its spot on his shoulder. "I've just never had anyone I could talk to about stuff like this, before."

I slid my hand just beneath the hem of his shirt, resting it against the warm skin of his stomach. "You do now. If you want."

All he did was stroke my hair, letting me know with his touch just how sorry he was. Soothing the hurt. And in his touch, I could feel he was as open and receptive as he was likely to get.

"So . . . it's not the solo, is it?"

"Nope." His chest rose and fell beneath my cheek with his deep sigh. "I mean, he's using the excuse that he thinks I'm not practicing enough as justification, but it's bullshit, and we both know it."

"Taking you off the solo and giving it to a guy you can't stand and who'll probably be an ass about it is his way of forcing you into practicing more?"

"Not really." He shoved a hand through his hair, then pillowed his head on his arm. "More like trying to guilt-trip me into spending less time with you. Best part is, he thinks I'm too stupid to get that that's what he's really after."

I let that sink in for a bit. Finally, I propped myself up on an elbow, studying his face. His eyes were closed, but he hadn't drifted off—his mouth was tense and straight, the curve I was used to looking at, to kissing, nowhere in sight.

"Why's he so hard on you?" Jonathan worked so hard and was so talented—and except for a few random, fleeting moments, Dr. Crandall didn't seem to appreciate that, at all. At least, not that I'd seen. It was so unfair. And I knew it wasn't just because of me, although my being part of Jonathan's life definitely seemed to be making things worse.

"Soledad—" He was staring at me with a pleading sort of expression—the words practically suspended in the air between us. *Don't want to talk.* I needed to get that through my thick skull and give him his space. Which . . . fine. But no law said I had to like it.

Heaving a deep sigh, I reached up into the overhead compartment, grabbing my journal and the booklight I used for writing at night. As I settled myself at the opposite end of the seat, I made sure the blanket was draped over both our legs so I could keep touching him. So he would know I was here, when he was ready. If ever.

*Maybe it's massively unrealistic, but I want him to share everything with me. I want him to trust me the way I trust him, and I just don't know how to make that happen. Sometimes I wish this was all simpler. More . . . normal—*

"Would you put that away?"

I glanced up, saw him glaring at the book in my lap. "Jonathan, I know you don't want to talk right now." I stopped short of saying it was okay, because you know, right now, it wasn't. In the tiny part of my brain that was still rational, I knew that wasn't fair, but rational didn't have shit to do with the heart. Maybe I didn't know much, but I knew that.

"I can't just hold it all in the way you do. I need *some* way to vent. And dancing's not exactly an option at the moment."

"Look, it's just that it's such a twisted situation—it's . . . hard."

"You think I don't get that?" Snapping the book shut, I turned off the light, and put both in his outstretched hand, watching as he reached up to stow them in my bag. "God, Jonathan, do you really think I don't understand how hard it is to open up and share stuff with someone you care about? Who might think differently about you, once they find out everything you've spent your whole life trying to forget? Letting someone else see how screwed up and scared you are? How utterly fucked your life or your family is?"

"Jesus, you know I'd never—"

"But you're assuming I would."

Everything went extremely still and quiet then. So much so, that I leaned my head against the back of the seat, my lids growing heavier, and I knew it was because I either had to fall asleep or burst into tears, and I was damned if I'd cry.

"It's because I'm not my brother."

His voice was soft and bitter.

"Brian." Clear as a bell, I could Dr. Crandall's voice again, invoking the name Brian the same way some of my *tías* invoked saints.

"Yeah."

"Where—?" Although . . . I had a feeling I knew.

"Dead."

I sat straight up, my heart taking a nosedive.

"Look, don't—I never knew him, any more than you knew your mom."

I stared at his face, at the heartbreaking expression etching it with a new beauty, and felt my heart doing that nosedive thing again.

Sitting up, he took my hand in one of his, the other tracing light patterns across the back of it. "I wasn't wanted, either. Not for myself. I'm Brian's replacement. Pretty lame one, I guess, if you ask my dad."

Didn't say a word, because seriously, what could I say?

"Hit-and-run in an intersection in Boston where he was going to Berklee. He was nineteen. I was born almost a year to the day after his funeral. My horn—it was his. My place as a leader in the corps. Pretty much everything musical. It's my legacy."

"Oh, God, Jonathan—"

He held up his free hand and I piped down because he was finally on a roll and needed to let it out, and I *knew* I was the first he'd ever told all of this to. "Dad and Mom got married really young and she got pregnant almost right away. Actually, I kind of suspect it was knocked up, then marriage, not that anyone's ever said out loud."

He stopped and took a deep breath. "The gypsy life of a professional musician doesn't really work so great when you've got a wife and kid to support, so Dad changed his major from performance to education. But luck was definitely on Dad's side when Brian was born with all the same musical gifts plus the drive and passion. Given that kind of second chance, Dad was going to make damned sure Brian had all the opportunities and didn't have to settle for being just a lowly college professor. He was going to be *more*—bigger than Wynton Marsalis and Maynard Ferguson put together. And big brother didn't disappoint. At least, not until the day he didn't check both ways before stepping into that intersection.

"Dad tinkered with the master plan after that. Figured that maybe he'd given Brian too much—made it too easy for him. That it made him careless. So, I was going to have to work a little harder." As our gazes met, a snippet of something teased the edges of my memory . . . from that first night. Our first argument. A heartbreaking smile crossed his face, making me hold tight to his hands.

"It's why you're on the corps scholarship, too—and why you busted ass to get the full ride to Indiana."

"Bingo." He turned his head to stare out the window. "In the world according to Marc Crandall, the busting ass will not only make me a better player, it'll make me look better with the side benefit of making me appreciate what I've got that much more. That I'll be more careful and presumably not go stepping off curbs with abandon. But all this time, and he still hasn't figured it out."

"What?"

He snorted. "That the more I rely on myself, the less I have to answer to *him*."

Again, I had to stop for a second—fight past the acid in Jonathan's voice and allow the words themselves to sink in. "Okay, so your dad's got some seriously freaky control issues, but at least your mom—"

"My mother feels guilty for being the reason my father gave up *his* dreams, so she's spent her entire life making it up to him by doing anything he wants, damn anyone else. She's a goddamned doormat."

I wouldn't have thought it was possible for his voice to go any colder.

"Jonathan, when you love someone, you do stuff—"

"You don't roll over and *die*, Soledad."

"She—," I started to argue, then stopped, because, *madre santísima*, the *look* on his face. I'd pushed enough tonight. And honestly, what did I *really* know about Linda Crandall?

"She loves you," I insisted. "If there's anything I can recognize, it's love for you."

In a soft, pained voice he said, "As much as she can love a do-over, I guess."

Unfortunately, I didn't have the words to argue with that. Not yet.

He stretched out across the seats again, cradling me close. "You're the first person who's ever wanted me just for who I am. No agendas. No bullshit." Closing his eyes, he said on a quiet sigh, "Just . . . me."

I traced my fingertip along the damp curve of his lashes. "Just for you."

"I love you so much, Soledad. More than music, more than *anything*."

His voice was soft but oh-so-intense, and the sheer thrill of the words themselves shivered through me. Inside and out, in a way that had him pulling me even closer, his body anxious and clearly wanting so much.

In that moment, I didn't care where we were.

# between the lines

*It's scary. Being in the center of that much love. So scary—and thrilling and . . . potent. And I know it goes both ways. My hold on him is as strong as his is on me. He'll never leave.*

"You're not going to say a thing, are you?"

I snapped my head back and forth. "You know I can't." Executed a sharp turn, a snap of the head, then lunged in Raj's arms as we practiced a new move for the tango.

"Figured as much."

And jeez, *what* a dramatic sigh as his hands caressed my body and slid under my arms, his elbows bending sharply beneath my shoulders, hands tangling in my hair. Slowly withdrawing, he released me so I could slide down the length of his body until I wound up in a full forward split, my hands grasping one of his thighs as he tossed his sabre and caught it just behind my neck. "But damn, that was some severe weirdness last night."

"Suffice it to say, you don't know the half of it."

As he stepped away, I swung my legs together and stood. "Want to practice the rose trick?" We were *so* close. Unfortunately, so close wasn't good enough when you were talking flying roses with weights attached and spinning rifles and blind turns. Second nature was what we needed because even one millisecond off and it could—no, *would*—be disastrous. But the idea of flirting with that kind of danger was what had me absolutely itching to add it. I mean, come *on*—it was totally the kind of move that would make the judges—not to mention, the crowds—lose their ever-lovin' minds.

Raj shook his head. "Can't. Gray's working equipment—adding more elements, the creative bastard. He told me to come find them as soon as we were done. Also wanted me to make sure you weren't hurting after last night's frolic through the rain. You aren't, are you?"

I wanted to say something snarky about Gray's old lady tendencies and Raj being his not-so-secret watchdog, but my throat was closed tight. It'd been such a limited thing, my entire life—people who protected me. Now, it was like my cup runneth over.

I swallowed hard. "I'm good, I promise."

"Okay." Raj gathered up his sabre and rifle while I rolled the legs of my nylon pants down to my ankles and grabbed one of my cardigans. According to the itinerary I had stashed inside my journal, today's locale was Golden, Colorado, where we'd pulled into our host school this morning after the all-night drive and a quickie breakfast at a Mickey D's somewhere in . . . well, *some*where where Mickey D's was the only option at seven A.M.

*Bleah.*

I'd stuck to yogurt and juice, which, once upon a time, might've been enough, but all of this fresh air and intense working out often left me with a wicked appetite. On the upside, though, it was also keeping my weight and fitness the best they'd ever been, so I could afford to eat more. Even chocolate.

Going back to normal dance routines was going to be a royal bitch.

But—

*Admit it. . . .*

I missed them, too. A lot. There'd been a letter from Madame at our last mail stop, a short note—she was hoping I was doing well and admonishing me again to "practice!"—tucked inside a manila envelope filled with pictures she'd taken at the senior showcase. The ones of me as Firebird were mind-boggling, more because the first word that had popped into my head when I saw them was *ethereal.* Captured in the glossy shots wearing my fiery costume, legs fully extended in a soaring *grand jeté* and looking downright other-worldly.

But it was the photographs of the flamenco number that had me kind of gaping in shock. I looked *so* fierce and passionate. Like a painting come to life, Raj said when I showed him the pictures. And ever since, I'd found myself wondering *what now.* More and more I'd wondered if I wasn't a complete idiot for walking away from a sure thing—brought home all the harder with the ragingly obvious evidence in those photographs. Madame—she'd been right. Performing ballet I looked intent and serious and completely committed to getting it right. But the flamenco number had clearly had a fluidity and grace and ease that transcended technique. I'd performed from the heart and didn't even realize it.

But at the beginning of the summer, October had seemed so far off. And Jonathan so new, and I hadn't wanted to lose what he was offering, either. Now, though . . . I *had* to seriously start thinking about giving Señor Márquez an answer.

Stepping outside, I took a deep breath, trying to clear my head—and get used to the new surroundings. While it wasn't cold, the mountain air had an unfamiliar feel. Thin and sharp, like it could cut right through me.

"By the way, I already knew I didn't know the half of it."

I stared at Raj, feeling very Twilight Zone.

"About Jonny," he clarified. "He's always had that still waters run deep vibe about him."

"You could say that." I looked up into the bluest sky I'd ever seen. "You like him, though, right, Raj?"

Maybe a weird, out-of-nowhere question, but oddly enough, Raj didn't seem thrown. "I didn't used to," he answered, each word coming out measured. "Didn't think he was a guy I could ever relate to on any level. But now that I've actually had a chance to get to know him this year, yeah, I like him."

I fought back the automatic defense. Raj was entitled, after all, and he *had* said he liked him. Now. "What's so different about this year?"

Raj leaned up against the outside wall of the gym, staring out at the jagged mountain peaks that seemed distant but like they were closing in at the same time. Kind of awe-inspiring, if a little on the claustrophobic side. It slammed into me, in a sudden rush, just how much I was missing the wide sweeping beaches and endless expanse of my Atlantic.

"Look, this is my third year in, right? And for the first time, he's . . . well, the only way to say it is, human." He shot me a sidelong glance. "Pinocchio's finally a Real Boy, and it's all about you."

"Get out." I shoved at him even as I grinned.

"Get out, yourself, girl." Raj shoved back with a shoulder. "The boy's crazy about you. And with you he's a different person." He stretched his arms over his head, then bent over at the waist. "So what are you going to do with yourself while the rest of us work equipment?" he asked, as he straightened.

Madame's *practice!* flashed in my mind. "I was thinking I might go back inside and practice. My ballet technique is probably going all to hell."

"Please—you haven't exactly been slacking," he scoffed. "Those slippers that started out so shiny and new are looking like they've been thrown under a train—twice."

Okay, yeah. But as pretty as new pointe shoes were, they didn't look right to me until they had some wear.

"I don't know that you have enough time to do much before run-throughs, babycakes," Raj mused, looking down at his watch. "You're probably just better off going over to the stadium and walking laps outside. This altitude's a bitch—you should probably get used to it."

Not a bad idea. Especially since just rehearsing inside had left me a little light-headed. When I hit the stadium, though, surprise— already occupied. Surprise again—when I realized who was doing the occupying. And yeah, it *was* them, as my gaze immediately picked out a sleek, dark ponytail weaving and bobbing among the other bodies.

I figured we'd run into them—this show was at a fair. But I'd thought maybe it'd be at the fairgrounds. Like the first time. I'd even convinced myself we might not even see them at all—a lot of these fairs were ten days or more. . . . What were the odds, right? So I'd even processed through the disappointment.

I whirled, turning my back to the field and dropped to a knee. Tied and retied my laces, willing my hands not to shake, blaming the fact that they still did on the cool breeze.

God. I'd been *hoping* to run into them. See . . . him.

But I would *not* sit here and gawk like some ditz, waiting to be noticed. I had a job to do—a performance to prep for. Standing up and absolutely *not* looking toward the field, I took off at a measured walk, making three laps at a pretty decent clip, although . . . whoa, the air. This dry stuff had a way of feeling invigorating at the same time it was sucking the energy straight out. What I wouldn't *give* for sticky and humid right now. Seriously. At least it didn't fool you into thinking it was energizing.

*"Buenas, Soledad."*

I glanced to my left, dredging up a smile as Taz fell into step beside me. "Hi."

"It's nice to see you again."

"Uh-huh." Why did he look so bright-eyed and full of energy? He was soaked, his shirt sticking to his chest and sweat running down his face, but didn't even seem winded. So not fair. I picked up the pace, but he just adjusted his stride, no problem.

"Very nice."

"Uh-huh."

And if he didn't shut up and quit looking like some damned perky Energizer Bunny with earrings, he was going to get a not-so-nice surprise. As soon as I could freakin' *breathe* again.

"Are you all right?"

"Uh-huh." I was. Mostly. So what if my heart was thudding against my rib cage, little sparkly lights bobbing and weaving in front of my eyes—and *why* did it feel like my brain was suspended above my head? And spinning?

*"Oye, aguanta, chica—"* Funny, now I felt like I was swimming—my arms feeling like they were fighting against one of those nasty Atlantic currents. *"¡Tráiganme agua!* Now!"

Taz's voice sounded like it was coming through a wall of water. Lovely cool water. . . .

"*Siéntate, Soledad.*" I stared at Taz, who had a wobbly, fuzzy-around-the-edges appearance. Nifty. "Sit down before you fall."

"I don't fall."

His teeth were really white. "Uh-huh."

Now, why was he mocking me? Raj was all wrong. Taz wasn't pretty. His brows were really too heavy and his nose was big. . . . No, wait—not big. Broad, like his cheekbones. And his shoulders. But he was a weenie. With a dimple.

"Okay . . . *despacio.*"

A second later, I felt a rubbery, rough surface beneath my butt and hands as a bottle appeared at my lips.

Almost couldn't swallow, my mouth was just that dry. Only instinct forced the muscles into working as the cool water hit the back of my throat, coughing and spluttering when more than I could handle filled my mouth. "*Un buchito a la vez* . . . Drink slow . . . Just a little . . ." The low, soothing croon rose up and down, in sync with the rubbing on my back in a way that had me closing my eyes just so I could relax into it more.

The next sip I held in my mouth, trying to wipe out that stuffed-with-cotton-balls feel that was making it so hard to swallow. Another couple of sips and I slowly started coming back to reality and my surroundings. The track surface, rough and bumpy beneath my legs. That blue, blue sky above. What looked like a forest of hairy man-legs in knee socks and cleats surrounding me and directly behind, something firm and warm, but not heat-of-the-sun warm, more—

"Are you better now?"

I tilted my head back, at least as far as the shoulder behind me would allow, and looked into a pair of concerned dark eyes.

I scrambled to my feet, the forest of man-legs scattering. "Uh . . . yeah."

Uh . . . *no.*

The minute I hit my feet, I was swaying and feeling the freaky spinning sensation, and man, this was seriously starting to piss me off—

Hands gripped my waist from behind and steadied me before I became one with the track again. *"Qué cabezona."* Still keeping one hand on my waist, Taz circled around in front of me, shaking his head. *"Poquito más,"* he ordered, holding the water bottle up to my dry lips.

Closing my eyes, as much to stop the spinning as to keep from seeing the glaring "I told you so" across his face, I drank. Standing there, letting the water work its way through my system, I felt my equilibrium finally making a return appearance—at least enough so I could open my eyes and not feel like the world was hurtling sideways.

At this point, I should've said thank-you, right? Been gracious and mature, since he'd been so kind. Instead, I snapped, "Why aren't you dizzy and out of breath?"

*Nice,* m'ija.

"Sorry."

Didn't seem to bother him, though— he just tilted his head from side to side as if both my grumpy commentary and apology were pretty much equal. "We have been in Mexico for the last several days. I have had time to get used to it." He pulled the long sleeves of his T-shirt down to his wrists since the breeze was picking up, a little stronger than before, carrying with it a sharper edge. Shivering, I tucked my elbows in close to my sides.

*"Ven aquí."* One hand went under my elbow, the other around my waist, like he couldn't quite trust me to walk on my own, which I could—seriously, I *was* better, but he was Spanish, so why waste

valuable breath arguing? And wasn't I just thinking how nice it was to have people looking out for me?

He led me to a bench, gesturing that I should sit—but rather than urge me onto the seat as I might've expected from his bossy ass, he released me and let me make my own decision about it while he bent to rummage through a nearby duffel. As I eased down, I felt his hands on my shoulders, draping a jacket over them.

"So you do not catch . . ."

"A chill?" I filled in at his pause as I shoved my arms through the sleeves.

Straddling the bench, he sat, facing me. "*Mm . . . sí. Gracias.* I could not think of the right word in English."

"You could've just said it in Spanish."

"I could have, yes, but I have been making an effort to practice my English whenever possible on the tour." He smiled that wide, brilliant white smile, looking like a delighted little boy. "So again—thank you."

"No problem. And really, I'm the one who should be thanking you." I ducked my head on the premise of zipping the jacket up and pulling my braid free of the collar, but really, taking another quick whiff and hiding a smile. Yep, really there. Beneath the familiar smells of detergent and sweat, the nylon collar brushing my cheek definitely had an undertone of something spicy-sweet.

Honestly, only a Latin guy would wear cologne to work out.

"So . . . Mexico?"

He looked up from where he was bent over, rummaging in the bag again, and nodded. "Ciudad de Mexico. It is very high, like this, but the air *¡ay!*" He flicked one hand in a dramatic gesture. "It is so bad, so dirty, but it was tremendous to play somewhere they truly appreciate *fútbol*." He straightened and taking my hand, put a small, gold-foil-wrapped disk in the palm.

"*Valor*. My favorites. The sugar will help." He grinned and popped a piece of dark candy into his mouth. "You like chocolate, yes?"

Oh, if he only knew. I unwrapped the foil and bit into it like a woman too long deprived, closing my eyes so I could better savor the rich, bittersweet taste. At his laugh, my eyes flew open. He reached into his bag for another couple of pieces, handing one to me.

"*Los americanos* we play with," he said, picking up the conversation, "they rarely experience how crazy the fans are for *fútbol* in real life."

"Yeah, it's not so popular here." I didn't think, but what did I know from soccer—excuse me, *fútbol*?

But he was nodding in agreement. "*Y qué pena*—it is a beautiful sport, but here . . ." He made this disgusted noise deep in his throat and shook his head, the motion causing a long silver-black lock of hair to fall into his face.

"*Bueno*—" He yanked the elastic free and ran his fingers through his hair, pulling it back with jerky motions and fastening it again. "I should not be so critical. Everywhere we have been, people have been very nice. *Y los niños, qué lindos son*—they still want to learn because no one has told them yet it is a waste of time. What about you?"

His sudden shift from commentary to question had me blinking, and while I was feeling a lot better, it still took my altitude-addled brain a second to catch up. "What about me? I don't know a thing about soccer, but it looks interesting."

"It *is* interesting, but no—" He shook his head. "I mean, tell me about yourself. Where are you from? You're obviously Latina and an amazing dancer, and why are you the only woman with all those boys?" Somewhere between "Latina" and "dancer" he switched completely to Spanish, the questions coming out in a rapid-fire burst, that last one delivered with a nice dose of disapproval along with a narrowing of those dark eyes, like he was mentally revisiting the number of guys to my one female body.

Automatically replying in Spanish, I said, "From Miami, most of my family is Cuban—thank you again for the compliment, by the way—because they needed a female dancer to portray Carmen, and please don't worry about my delicate sensibilities, I can take care of myself. Anything else?"

A laugh exploded out of him, his head going back, the sun catching the streak of silver in his hair. I found I couldn't take my eyes off it. Couldn't take my eyes off *him*, period. He was just so . . . free. Laughing myself, I felt a giddy rush that I wished I could blame on the thin air.

"You are a perfect Carmen—*eres una fiera*. So independent. It is beautiful." Raising a foot to the bench, he propped his arm across his knee and hit me with a dark, steady gaze, like he was settling in, trying to figure me out.

*Goes both ways,* m'ija.

Yeah. It did. What a surprise. Who *was* this boy?

"My turn. What about you?"

"What about me? I am, as the Americans like to say, an open book."

"Where are you from, then? Aside from Spain," I added, fending off the potential smart-assery.

No smart-ass, though, just a wistful "Málaga," matching the faraway expression on his face. "It is in Andalucía, right on the Mediterranean. Very different from here." He glanced up at the mountains, his fingers toying with a silver medallion at his neck, sliding it back and forth on its chain. "*Estas montañas*—they are very beautiful and wild like the Pirineos—but I like the sea better. It is also wild, but more open—allows for more . . . dreams."

Okay, this? Wasn't some kind of cheesy line. Not unless he was just some kind of seriously good actor. His words sounded too raw . . . too honest.

And struck a responsive chord. Bringing on that surprisingly strong pang of homesickness all over again as I envisioned how the Atlantic looked right before a storm, the turbulent gray-green reaching out to meet the dark line of the horizon and capped with a deceptively innocent white as the waves broke fast and hard against the sand. "I miss walking on the beach," I confessed, propping my hands on the bench as I tilted my head back and stared up at the mountains bearing down on us, experiencing that slight claustrophobia again.

"Me, too." The distinctive metallic rasping of the medallion sliding along the chain made me glance over. His nearly perpetual smile had faded as his gaze darted around, to the mountains and the sky and the empty stadium before coming back to rest on me. "The traveling—it has been . . . *maravilloso*, but—"

"But?" I prompted.

"I'm tired." The medallion dropped to his chest. "I want to be in one place again," he admitted quietly, like he meant to share it with only me and the mountains. "I love traveling, but it's different when you *have* to do it."

Felt as if we had a whole conversation in the glance we exchanged in the silence following his words. But it was a teasing sort of exchange, the words in a language I wasn't quite comprehending. That I didn't really *want* to understand yet. But in a way, I did. At least, I wanted to try.

"Can I ask you something?"

"*Seguro.*"

"When we first met, why were you so . . ." *Obnoxious* was the word that came to mind, but that wasn't quite right. I finally settled on, "Outrageous?"

He shrugged and looked away. "When I'm nervous, I talk too much. Say stupid things."

*Please.* The boy probably hadn't had a nervous moment since the crib. Yet . . . in my mind's eye, I could clearly see him fidgeting with the soccer ball as he apologized for the yes, stupid, "precious" comment. And ever since that moment he'd been different.

"Also—" His voice was very soft as he leaned in close. "I knew if I made a show, it would be clear to my teammates that I—"

"What?"

He drew back, again, saying everything he wanted me to know with what he didn't say.

"Oh." And felt a warm glow begin, down low in the pit of my stomach. "Oh."

I dropped my gaze to his carved medallion, the silver mellow against the dark green of his T-shirt. Tentatively, I reached out and touched it, still warm from his hand. "This is pretty."

He glanced down, his chin grazing my fingers, his skin even warmer than the medallion. "It's San Rafael—my patron saint." His gaze rose, the laughter back in his eyes. "My *mamá* gave it to me for protection—he's one of the patron saints of travelers."

"*Baltazar ¡entra!*" Taz jerked his head toward the field. Man, I'd almost forgotten that the soccer players were still practicing, and here was Taz, babysitting me and talking to me and . . . and—My hands dropped to my lap like they were on fire.

"Aren't you supposed to be out there?"

"Substitute was in." He stood, shoving his sleeves back to his elbows and tucking the medallion inside his shirt as another *"Balt-azar ¡arranca, m'ijo!"* rang out.

"But now, I have to get back. Drink your water." He leaned down and quickly kissed both of my cheeks.

"Bye," I called as I watched him jog toward the field. *Duh.* Taz. Bal*t*azar. Wonder why he went by Taz? Because seriously, Balta-zar had to be one of the coolest, most exotic names I'd ever heard and totally fitting for a soccer player who walked along Mediter-ranean beaches and knew *Carmen* and could wax poetic. Then, as I watched him charge into the game, almost immediately going into hyperdrive, calling out orders and taking command of the ball when it finally reached him, the tat on his shoulder flashed in my mind.

Yeah, Taz worked, too.

I watched for a bit, fascinated by the chaos of bodies running and yelling, legs and heads reaching for the ball at the same time, the ball going from person to person in its own dance—sometimes short little steps, sometimes big, sweeping flights through the air and always, it seemed like someone was right there, waiting to direct it to do their bidding.

*So much like a dance. A crazy, undisciplined dance.*

*No . . . not so much undisciplined. It has its own rules. Its own beauty.*

I stayed on the bench a few minutes longer, my gaze somehow always managing to find that one dark head. It wasn't until he made this impossible kick, sending the ball into the goal, then glanced over and grinned like he expected to find me sitting there and star-ing like a goon—and why *was* I still sitting here staring like a goon?—that I stood from the bench and resumed walking. Breath-ing slow and deep, I went into a Zen sort of place until the sharp crack of a drumstick hitting a snare snapped me back to reality

Shocked, I realized that the field was empty, the soccer players having bailed without my ever having noticed, the corps now marching into the stadium. I ran to fall into my usual spot, all thoughts of soccer and high altitudes and Tasmanian Devils disappearing.

After we finished, we assembled in a concert arc and listened to Gray give his usual rundown before he excused us for show prep.

"What's with the jacket?"

"The what?" I glanced up at Jonathan as we walked side by side back to the gym, then down at my chest. God, I'd totally forgotten I had it on, and he hadn't bothered to ask for it back before he left. I ran my fingertips across ESPAÑA embroidered in script on the upper left chest, above a patch, before moving to the other side, tracing the embroidered BALTAZAR. Unzipping the jacket a bit more, I casually folded down the collar, mostly obscuring his name.

"That Spanish soccer team we've run into before loaned me one of their jackets when I got chilled and light-headed while I was working out earlier. They must've forgotten to get it back."

"Huh."

Heat started prickling along my neck, just below my hairline. "What?"

He didn't answer—not right away—instead occupying himself with blowing through his mouthpiece, emptying his spit valve, shaking his horn to make sure it was clean. "Nothing," he finally said. "Just didn't know they were around."

"Neither did I, until I got to the stadium and they were here practicing." I shoved my hands into the jacket's pockets. "I overdid it a little, warming up. They were nice enough to help out."

"Well, that's cool."

Right.

"Jonathan, they were just helping. This altitude kicked my ass and I felt sick and no one else was around." For him, I could admit to weakness. If it would wipe that look off his face.

"I'm sorry I wasn't." He pulled me close, his arm tight around my waist. The kiss he brushed against the top of my head was so gentle, so . . . *God.* I rubbed my cheek against his shoulder, which made him hold me tighter.

*He just wants to take care of you.*

*Wants to make sure you know it, too.*

I took a step away, but made sure to keep our hands linked, swinging them between us in a playful manner that had him smiling, relaxing his face into something boyish and carefree.

Later, in the privacy of the girls' locker room, I grabbed my journal and pulled out the itinerary. Four days. In four days, we'd be in Missouri and according to the schedule, that show was affiliated with a fair. It was possible we'd see them tonight, but if not—

*I'll make sure to return the jacket by Missouri. Such a sweet gesture.*

Carefully, I folded the jacket, ESPAÑA facing up, and slipped it, along with my journal, into my backpack. And as I finished applying my makeup, I could *swear* I caught the faintest hint of a spicy-sweet cologne.

# gravity

*Querida Mamacita—*

*We're in Wetten Landing, Missouri, today and Dios mío is this town tiny! There's only one enormous regional middle/high school—and let me tell you, it's one where they take their sports really seriously. Six athletic fields and four oversized gyms, can you imagine? So all five corps competing are being housed here, plus the soccer teams are practicing here, too. Really, who needs a carnival? All the musicians, the local band kids, curious people from the town, all crowded into the bleachers and along the sidelines, watching the soccer players scrimmage.*

*Ay, have I told you about the soccer players yet? We've run into them a few times as they tour around the country—two teams, one American, one Spanish. How funny is that? The Spanish guys crack me up, the way they make the cousins look like total amateurs in the machismo and 'tude department, but you know, at the same time, they're pretty sweet. For the most part, they have*

*beautiful manners and a sort of . . . I don't know, a sense of chiv-*
*alry that seems like it's not from this time.*

*By the way—how's Dom?*

What he was doing was impossible.

Seriously. Look . . . just *look* at how Taz was going, oh my *God*, airborne, his leg whipping around and actually connecting with that ball. I propped my chin in my hand and leaned forward, trying to figure out what was going on.

"Do you have any idea what's going on?" I muttered to Raj around bites of Twizzler.

"Not a clue," he replied, holding a hand out for a piece of candy, his eyes glued to the field. "And seriously, I don't care," he breathed out.

Slapping a piece of licorice into his open palm, I laughed. "You are so unbelievably shallow, I swear."

"Nope. Just appreciative of some fine, *fine* works of art."

He wasn't completely wrong—it was extremely artistic, if not in the way *he* was thinking. It wasn't the first time that watching them reminded me of a dance—everyone with a choreographed role—but every once in a while one of them could take off on an improvisational tear that was crazy and intense and made things happen, and even though it was just a practice, as the ball went flying straight into the goal we all stood up and cheered and whistled and stomped like it actually meant something. Looking at the way they high-fived and slapped each other's asses, I kind of got the feeling it really did matter in the same way a great run-through mattered to us.

After a few more minutes, a whistle blew and the teams separated to huddle with their coaches, things looking like they were winding down. As Raj and I made our way down the bleachers and to the field, he nodded to what I was holding and said, "So you gonna return the letterman's jacket?"

Since I still had it because I hadn't seen him in Colorado, the teams having played their exhibition and taken off for parts unknown before we even hit the fairgrounds. And because he was observant and nosy and because for some bizarre, inexplicable reason, I'd had to tell *someone,* Raj knew who, exactly, it belonged to.

"Stop it." Really, I shouldn't think about pushing him off the bleachers for being an ass. *I* was the one with the big mouth.

"I honestly don't think he wants it back."

"He probably just forgot it. Or was being a good, noble Spanish boy and not wanting to leave me freezing my ass off or something."

"Or he wants you to have something of his."

Down on the field I turned to face Raj. "Why?"

And all he did was roll his eyes, the shit. You know, it's not that I was being dense, but come on, I didn't even know this guy. Not really.

*Yeah, you do—and you want to know more.*

"Babycakes, that boy's been interested since day one. At the very least, it's an excuse to keep talking to you. Not that he really needs one."

I stared at Raj, mildly freaked because what he was saying about Taz echoed what that damned inside voice had just been saying about me. And he was standing there, grinning in a way that made me feel like he had some sort of window into my brain and *knew* it. Making some noise I didn't even know I was capable of, I stomped off, leaving his smirking ass behind.

Weaving my way through the crowd, I couldn't find Taz—not right away. Not such a surprise, really, considering how the girlies were descending on the soccer players like ants on a picnic lunch. He was probably three deep in adoring fangirls and loving every damned minute of it, flashing that dimple and cocking his head so the sun would catch the silver streak and diamond studs equally.

At least with Jonathan off practicing with the rest of the sopranos, I had enough time to wade through the estrogen and Aqua Net.

*Temper, temper . . .*

"No, no . . . *cariñita*—if you put your feet like this, it is easier to control the ball."

"But it feels funny, and besides, it goes farther if I kick it with the front."

"Ah, that's what you think. *Mira*—"

I watched as Taz lined up a soccer ball and kicked it with his foot pointing forward. It went pretty far. A second later though, the next ball, kicked with the inside of his foot, went twice as far.

Even from several yards away, I could see the little girl's blue eyes go absolutely huge. "Wow . . ." Then her head dropped. "But you're a boy. I could never do that."

"*Pfft.* Of course you can. *Vamos.*"

He set up another ball and showed her what part of her foot she should try to hit the ball with. After a couple of kicks that dribbled away from her, he made another adjustment, showed her how to approach the ball, and finally—on her fourth try, she sent the ball flying in a way that had her yelling "Yes!" and high-fiving Taz.

"I did it!"

"Of course you did."

"Ha—and my brothers said girls can't play."

Again he let loose with a disgusted "*Pfft*" as he dropped to a knee. "Do you know that your women's national team is one of the best in the world? They can beat a lot of men's teams. And you can tell your brothers I said so."

Those big blue eyes went even bigger. "Seriously?"

He nodded, the corners of his mouth twitching. "Seriously." Reaching out, he gently tugged a blonde braid, then stood and snagged one of the nearby soccer balls, casually handing it to her. "If you practice a lot . . . who knows? Maybe one day I will be watching *you* play."

She stared down at the ball, then back up at him, her eyes so unbelievably wide they looked like they were going to take over her face. "Oh, *cool*! Thank you!" She ran up to her parents, hanging on to that ball as if he'd given her the keys to the kingdom. Who knows—maybe he had. He'd at least planted the seed.

"That was really nice of you."

His head snapped around and he smiled—that full-out smile with the white teeth and the little dimple. "I always wanted *hermanitas*. Instead, I have older sisters who thought it was fun to dress me up like a doll. And my *mamá* wonders why I spent all my time playing *fútbol*." And yeah, sure, he rolled his eyes and looked every bit as exasperated as a little brother should, but still . . . the affection was obvious. And familiar.

*God*, but I missed Mamacita and Tía Gracy and Madame and my sorry cousins and just . . . everything. This time, Taz's kisses to my cheeks weren't just expected, they were welcome. A hint of the things I was so used to, the warmth of his hand on my arm reminding me of walks on the beach. Over his shoulder, I caught Raj staring as if he had that window into my head again. And smirking.

Oh, he was seriously working my last nerve. He'd be lucky if I didn't brain him on purpose with the rose tonight.

I took what I hoped was a graceful step back, swallowing hard as Taz's hand slowly slid down my arm before falling away. "So *¿cómo estás?*"

"Very tired." He laughed, but there were some pretty obvious dark shadows under his eyes. I could relate. More and more I was starting to feel like I was sporting carry-on luggage under my eyes. "And very hungry."

"Well, that should be easy to take care of," I replied, waving at the townspeople setting up a completely impromptu potluck lunch.

"*Bueno, sí, pero*—" Leaning in, he lowered his voice. "Perhaps you will laugh at me, but what I really want is my *mamá's* paella." He sighed. "Málaga has the *best* seafood."

"Oh, definitely not gonna laugh. Miami has great seafood, too. And what I wouldn't do for some grilled shrimp with *mojo*." Again, I felt that sharp, bittersweet pang of longing for home and Mamacita and everything familiar. The longer we were away, the more I missed it all. Absence really did make the heart grow fonder. Who knew?

"Miami will be our last stop before returning to Spain. I am very much looking forward to it."

"When's that?"

"About three weeks."

"Cool."

In about three weeks we'd be in Indianapolis, for Finals Week. For just a second, I felt . . . disappointment, I guess. There and gone, with relief unmistakably chasing hot on its heels. *Damn.* On both counts.

"*Perdóname*, but do you mind—"

I blinked away the momentary fog to see him gesturing at his shirt, pulling the hem out like he was trying to get air in under it.

"Oh, yeah, sure—" I waved that he should go ahead and tried not to stare.

Tried.

Honestly, I still wasn't convinced over the empirical prettiness of his facial features, but I'd never denied that the boy was built. Especially standing not two feet away, sans shirt, in all his buffed glory.

"Is something funny?"

"What?"

"You are smiling."

*I are— am . . . ?*

"Uh . . ." I scrambled for something . . . *anything.* "It's just— you weren't exactly shy before about being in front of me without a shirt." Truth, dammit.

"When—?" A little line appeared between his eyebrows, then disappeared just as quick. "Ah . . . the day your knee was bothering you. That was before I knew you." He nodded like that explained it all as he wiped his shirt over what seemed like an unending expanse of tanned skin and flexing muscles.

My eyebrows shot up even as my gaze followed the path of the shirt across his torso and up his neck where his medallion hung, silver against bronze, and I think I was seriously starting to lose my mind. "A bottle of water and some conversation doesn't mean you know me."

Another shrug as he slung the shirt over one shoulder. "We know each other better than before, no?"

"I—" Really? Okay, he was a soccer player from Spain and he missed his *mamá's* paella and wore a medallion she'd given him as protection. His real name was Baltazar and he was a pretty nice guy who maybe had some old-fashioned notions behind the brash soccer-boy façade. He liked the ocean. He was tired of traveling. He missed home. He was nice to little girls who maybe needed a shot of "You *can* do it."

As all this stuff crowded my mind, one right after another, I realized they were awfully close to the surface. Maybe more than they should've been. *Definitely* more than they should have been.

But still—they were *just* little things.

"I will make sure to come say hello tonight."

Thrown by the sudden shift in conversation, all I said was, "Tonight?"

"Our match isn't until tomorrow, so we are going to the fair tonight. *Jugar un poco.*"

"And you're coming to our show?" When he could be wandering the midway with his teammates, showing off by playing stupid fair games and charming small-town Midwestern girls? They'd probably fling panties with phone numbers scrawled on them in Revlon's finest if he so much as breathed near them.

He smiled, just a small, gentle curve of his mouth. So purely sweet, I felt myself stop breathing for a second. "I would like to see you perform. For real."

His words were still echoing in my head when Raj's voice intruded with "Well . . . that went well."

"What?"

He patted the jacket I still clutched in my hands. "Oh, *shit*," I groaned.

"Honey, I *told* you—he wants you to keep it."

"Give it a rest, Raj, wouldja?"

"When he wasn't looking at you like he was trying to memorize every tiny detail, he was looking down at it. He knew you had it, Soledad. He knew you meant to give it back. He had every chance to give you an in to say something and he didn't, did he?"

Not one word. And something about that shook something deep inside me. He really liked me. Maybe because I was a little taste of familiar in a world of unfamiliar for him, but he liked me. And I couldn't deny I liked *knowing* that he liked me.

Couldn't deny that I liked him, too. Goofy, sweet Latin boy.

"I'm not trying to be stupid, Raj—I've just—" I fought for the words. "Look, you know being with Jonathan has been a new thing for me—and complicated enough. Having another guy . . . well, I've never experienced anything quite like this—"

Raj waved his hand. "Oh, honey, relax—no one's saying you have to take the guy out behind the bleachers and give him a hummer. It's just a little harmless flirting."

I laughed at Raj's bluntness. God love him for being so honest. "True." I looked down at the jacket, the embroidered BALTAZAR facing up, not entirely sure it was completely harmless, but come on. Jonathan knew I'd never do anything on purpose that could hurt him. He *had* to know that.

"Okay, then." Raj slung an arm across my shoulders, his free hand reaching down to take the jacket from me. "So enjoy it for what it is. We'll probably see them a couple more times, then he'll go back to Spain, probably to one of those pro contracts I've been overhearing are coming his way, and you'll both have a nice memory of a summer flirtation. A what-might-have-been. Everyone needs at least one of those."

Pro contract. Not a surprise, really—all of the soccer players seemed good, but Taz had something . . . I don't know, special about him.

Like Jonathan—except . . . Oh, forget it. I really needed to stop thinking about Taz. Like Raj had said, he was going to be gone soon. Whereas Jonathan was right here. With me. I grinned as I spied him headed our way, looking relaxed and happy. Glancing down at the jacket Raj held, I asked, "Could you put that with my stuff, please?"

Harmless flirting was one thing, but I wasn't stupid enough to go inviting trouble.

"Yeah, of course." Raj's raised eyebrows communicated that he got where I was coming from. "You know—," he started, then stopped, staring at the jacket.

"What?"

His gaze, as he slowly lifted his head and met mine was dark and frankly, a little nerve-rattling. "I'm going to sound a lot more like your grandmother than you probably want, but you know, you never know exactly what's supposed to be. Keep your mind open, babycakes." With that, he peeled off before Jonathan got too close.

Trying to shake off the queasies, I ran at Jonathan. "Hey you—" I flung myself at him, wrapping my legs around his waist as he hoisted me up.

"Hey." His lips touched mine, gentle . . . then not so much. "Man, now I'm really sorry I called that practice."

"Mmm . . . I know what you mean." I burrowed my head against his neck as he gently set me back on my feet. "But then again, we *are* stuck in a school with three other corps. Not like there's a lot of opportunity for privacy."

"True. And we're traveling after the show." He looked disappointed, but resigned.

Right there with him. We'd had a lot of bus travel lately—not too many private moments we could catch that *weren't* on a bus.

"Well," I said slowly, "I'm sure we can figure something—"

"No, Soledad." Shaking his head he repeated more firmly, "No. What we've got—it deserves a hell of a lot better than dark corners or the back of a bus. You deserve more." His smile evolved from so tender that I felt like crying, to a wicked grin, complete with a naughty gleam in his eyes. "But what can I say? I can't get enough of you. Kind of makes me stupid."

"No. . . ." I reached up and kissed him. "Kind of makes you wonderful."

# front row

Mi querida niña,

I hope this finds you well. And that hopefully you have not killed Raj yet. You know as much as I love you, I cannot condone such violence, and besides, I'm not sure I have enough saved to bail you out. I know *how anxious you are to add the rose trick, and from everything you've described, it sounds as if it will be an amazing moment in the show. Pero acuérdate—paciencia, m'ija. And it will be fine.*

I drew a spread for you: Ace of Swords, Two of Coins, and Magician. If you've opened your tarot book at all during the trip, you'd know these are cards that have to do with clarity and creativity and—believe it or not—juggling. In other words, trust Raj.

And stop rolling your eyes.

Tell el niño lindo I said hello and to take very good care of you.

———

The roar was almost deafening.

And that was just as I produced the rose and the crowd realized what I was about to do. Carefully, I watched, narrow-eyed, calculating. With a flourish, I raised the flower high above my head, lowered it, pressed a kiss to the silk petals, and then as I whirled—

Deafening roar erupted into a massive yell as the flower arced through the air toward Don José. Growing louder and more frenzied as his rifle went airborne and he lunged, one hand snatching the rose out of midair and with the other, neatly catching the rifle behind his back. In one smooth motion, he rose to his full height, lifted the rose, and kissed the petals, just as I had, while I smiled and sashayed away, certain in the knowledge that I'd captured the young soldier's heart.

On the sidelines, waiting for my next cue, I breathed deep and snuck a peek into the stands, trying to catch sight of Gray. I *knew* the trick had gone off well, especially judging by the crowd's reaction, but I wanted *his* reaction. Ah, there was tonight's orange and purple Hawaiian shirt—halfway up the stands. Catching my eye, he flashed a quick grin and a thumbs-up.

As I started to return my attention to the field, another figure caught my eye. Much lower down in the stands—in fact, front row, just across the track from where I stood—Taz. As promised, here at the show, but he wasn't watching me. Not obviously, at any rate. Instead, he appeared to be leaning on the railing with what looked like a large pad propped in front of him. I glanced over to the field, then quickly—just for a second—let my gaze find him again. I couldn't watch—not now, not with my next cue coming up in just a few measures, but *what* was he doing?

A split second later, the percussion riff that signaled my next entrance sounded and Taz disappeared from my mind as I focused on my continued seduction of Don José and the eventual, ulti-mate tragic end to our story.

It'd been a good night. Regardless of what the scores would say—*this* was the kind of performance we grooved on, as a group and as individuals. We were starting to feel it more often, were able to call up that indefinable energy almost at will. It seemed no matter how tired we were, once the lights were on *us*, the judges' pens ready to write, we were able to turn it up that extra notch.

After breaking from our post-show concert arc, Jonathan met me halfway. "I need to shake down with the horns—just for a few minutes. Meet you by the souvenir booth?"

I tossed my empty water bottle into a nearby recycling bin. "Sure. I heard the new T-shirts your mom designed came in. I want to get one."

"Already taken care of." He smiled, then bit his lip in a shy ges-ture I hadn't seen from him in ages. "I got it as an extra-large so you can wear it as a sleep shirt. Mom's holding it at the booth for you."

Big things, little things—he was just *so* eager to make me happy.

His fingers trailed along my cheek. "That look on your face—I always want to be the one to put it there." With a quick kiss, he took off while I headed for our on-tour moneymaker, the booth where we sold T-shirts, patches, CDs, all sorts of souvenir-y stuff. All the corps had their own booths set up beneath the bleachers but I was loyal—only Raiders stuff for me.

As I approached the booth, I noticed a now-familiar figure, hair pulled back in its usual ponytail, but instead of being in athletic shorts and cleats, he was wearing jean shorts, a black T-shirt, and flip-flops as he stood by the tables studying the different items on display.

"Hi, Taz."

He glanced up, smiling, like he expected nothing less than to find me beside him. *"Hola, Soledad."* He started to lean in, but stopped short—his gaze following mine to Mrs. Crandall who, like the other moms in the booth, was busy helping customers, but who was also . . . well, right there. And not everyone *got* some Latin customs.

Good for Taz, noticing how I froze up, because he immediately eased back, smooth and subtle. "Hi, Mrs. Crandall," I called out, just so that she knew I was there. So that she knew *I* knew she was there.

"Hello, sweetheart," she said glancing up from making change with a smile. "I've got something for you."

"Yes, ma'am, I know. Jonathan told me."

She rummaged in the boxes set toward the back of booth, calling over her shoulder, "Do you want it as a sleep shirt or for regular wear?"

"Jonathan said he ordered it big."

She paused and looked more fully over her shoulder. "Yes, I know. But which do *you* want?"

I blinked, thrown for just a second. "Uh . . . sleep shirt, please." I took the shirt from her, shaking the black cotton out so I could see the full design: a rose at the apex of a pair of crossed sabres, CARMEN, REVEALED emblazoned in a silver foil script above the FLORIDA RAIDERS embroidered in a gorgeous, striking turquoise. I'd lay money we'd be seeing hordes of people with this shirt by the time Finals rolled around. This had iconic written all over it.

"Oh, Mrs. Crandall, you did a fantastic job. This is *so* beautiful."

As she smiled and ducked her head, Taz said, "It is beautiful—and appropriate, considering what I saw tonight. *Tu grupo es increíble.*"

226

I felt that fierce pride take over. Still amazed me how the corps as a whole getting compliments felt every bit as good as the individual props. *"Gracias."* Realizing Mrs. Crandall was still standing there and not wanting to be a complete rube, I turned to her. "Mrs. Crandall, this is Baltazar." Using his formal name and enjoying the lilt and roll of the syllables along my tongue. "He's one of the soccer players from the teams we've seen a couple of times?" As she smiled and nodded in recognition, I turned to Taz and said, "Taz, this is Mrs. Crandall, one of the corps moms."

He nodded, offered his hand, saying, "It is my pleasure, *señora.* You are the mother of one of the boys?"

Her smile deepened into that achingly sweet expression that came along with any mention of Jonathan. "Yes, my son is in the horn line."

"Ah, of course." His narrow, dark stare slid my way for a brief second.

"So I understand you boys are from Spain?"

While Taz gave his nice, polite Latin-boy answers, I cruised the perimeter of our booth, chatting with the other moms—and checking Taz out. Taking stock of him in a different environment. He spoke easily with Mrs. Crandall—his stance casual, but with a vibrating tension and energy that drew as many "check *him* out" looks from the giggling girls passing by as when he was on the field in full soccer player mode. Enough that it made me want to smack them—I mean, could they be any more obvious?

Somehow, though he remained totally apart from it, oblivious to the looks and whispers because he was so completely focused on his conversation. At least, completely focused except for that one glance my way that had me looking down at the stack of shirts in front of me as if cotton baby-doll tees were the most fascinating thing ever. But still—couldn't help another look, this time noticing him holding the large pad I'd seen him with from the field. A pad with a hand grasping a pencil on the cover.

He turned away from the table, his mom-grilling from Mrs. Crandall apparently complete.

"You were drawing. During the show."

He glanced down, then up, looking like a trapped rabbit. "*Sí*— but it is nothing . . . *una bobería.*"

"That's supposed to make me feel better?"

Which had his mouth opening and closing as he flushed a deep red and left me feeling about two inches tall.

"Hey—" I reached out and touched his arm. "I'm sorry, I was just teasing. *Fastidiando,*" I added, since he was shaking his head, looking absolutely pained. *"Estoy celosa."*

"Jealous?" He stopped, mid-shake, and cocked his head to the side. *"¿Pero por qué?"*

"Because I can't draw to save my life. I've always envied anyone who can capture life on paper. It's an amazing gift."

At that, he stood up straighter, and something about how he did it made me think peacock. Honestly, had to fight to keep from rolling my eyes. Okay, so I lost the battle, but I managed to keep it subtle. And it was in a good-natured sort of way, since I couldn't help but admit he was cute while unconsciously preening.

"I told you how my mother loves the arts. And drawing is easy for me. Something to do with my hands. Like you with your book. I thought maybe you drew, too." He raised one eyebrow, waiting.

*If he draws, stands to reason he'd be super observant.*

*There's the part where he's interested, too.*

"Um . . . no. Just write. *Boberías,*" I joked, drawing that smile from him. "Will you show me?" And proceeded to nearly swallow my tongue.

Idiota—*what if it's like your journal?*

But no . . . His grin broadening, he turned the cover back on the pad, eagerly flipping through the pages.

"This is one of my favorites."

"Taz!" I smiled down at the same exact image that was inked on his shoulder. "You drew Taz?"

He nodded. "I started learning how to draw and speak English from watching American cartoons. Which also made my mother crazy. All those visits to the Picasso Museum, and what inspired me was—" He rapidly flipped through the pages until he came to Bugs, standing in a classic pose, holding his carrot. "'Ehhh, what's up, Doc?'" he drawled in a high-pitched nasally voice that was so different from his low, even baritone that I doubled over laughing.

"Oh, God, that's perfect."

"Yeah, it's not bad."

I straightened up in a hurry. "Hi. Didn't see you."

"You were distracted." Jonathan's arm came around my shoulders and I leaned into him. Tightened my arm around his waist as his free hand touched the shirt I held. "I see you got your shirt."

"I did." I reached up and kissed his cheek. "Thank you—it's beautiful."

"I'm sure it'll look better on you." I breathed easier as the tension eased beneath my arm, that vulnerable note that never failed to break my heart creeping in beneath the casual tone of his voice. But *Dios mío*, I wished I didn't always have to . . . to . . .

Shit.

He knew I was his. He *knew* it.

"Guys, I know you haven't formally met. Taz, this is Jonathan Crandall, my boyfriend." As the final two words emerged, even more of the tension ebbed away, leaving him relaxed and confident, his fingers playing through my loose hair. "Jonathan, this is Taz."

Nothing really, from either of them beyond a mutual "Hey," and a pair of wary nods as they stared each other down. If a few minutes ago my animal metaphors had me thinking peacock, now I was thinking more . . . tomcats in a dark alley.

*Oye,* and here I'd thought I'd hit maximum testosterone overload, traveling with an all-male corps for the past month—forget it. Totally paled compared to what was flowing between these two. I held my breath, praying that Jonathan didn't go all irrational caveman like he had with Aaron. Not that he had a damned reason to, but who knew what went on in his mind sometimes. And if he did do something boneheaded, I had the distinct impression that if pushed, Taz wouldn't hesitate to push back—hard.

"*Bueno*—" Taz glanced down at his watch, a slim, elegant leather-and-gold thing—and again, my soccer jock surprised me, since I might've pegged him for big and gaudy—then smiled and met my gaze directly. "I need to meet up with some of my teammates."

I relaxed, gradually releasing that tense breath. "Where do you guys go next?"

"Boston, then Toronto."

"Cool."

Because we wouldn't be anywhere near. Nope, we'd be meandering through the Midwest, gradually making our way toward Indianapolis for the Finals. Maybe it was better this way—Taz just sort of disappearing and with any luck, keeping his distance if he did reappear.

*Luck? For who?*

*Mira,* so the flirting was a nice rush and I would've liked to enjoy it for a little longer. He was a *nice* guy. One I might've enjoyed getting to know better.

But was it really worth this kind of stress? Especially since he was going back to Spain anyway.

*But you could go to Europe, too. Couldn't you?*

All of a sudden feeling like I had in the thin, Colorado air, I mustered a faint *"Adiós"* as I watched Taz disappear into the flow of the people streaming in and out of the stadium.

"Thanks for saving the shirt, Mom."

"No worries, son." But it was me Mrs. Crandall smiled at from behind the table, her gaze meeting mine in a way that had me catching my breath.

Ay Dios mío, *she knows.*

*Knows what? That you and Taz flirt? Listen to what she's saying. No worries. She knows where your heart is.*

*God, I wish he did.*

His hand closing around my wrist, Jonathan led me away, his steps growing faster as he wove through the crowds, opposite from the direction Taz had taken, I noticed as we rushed past booths and milling groups of people with their soft pretzels and cotton candy and slushies and carefree, laughing voices.

"Jonathan?"

His grip tightened painfully as he kept pulling me until we were around the far side of the stadium and in an area that was dark and quiet, protected from the road by enormous trees. Pushing me up against one, he kissed me hard, his teeth digging into my lips.

"You love me, right?" His breath was hot against my ear as his hands burrowed into my hair, getting caught in the waves and pulling slightly as he held my head steady.

"You know I do."

"I'm sorry, I'm sorry—" He was saying it over and over, kissing my hair, my cheeks, my eyelids, my mouth again, the force of all that passion pushing me into the tree, the rough bark digging into the bare skin of my back. "I know I shouldn't even have to ask, but—God, Soledad, you're everything. *Everything.*"

Reversing our positions, he sank down, pulling me onto his lap so my costume didn't get dirty. As I dropped my head to his shoulder, his voice floated over me in a harsh, ragged whisper. "What the hell are we going to do?"

And there it was: the Big Question. With only three weeks left of tour, September loomed closer and after it, October. He had school and I had . . .

"You want to stay together?" My voice was thin, the words these light, fragile things dissipating into the hot, still summer air.

"God, yes!" Gently, he lifted my head so he could look into my eyes. "How could you even ask that?"

"Because you're going to Indiana and I'm—"

*Not.*

Oh, God. No matter what I chose, I hadn't *ever* considered following him as an option. Not once.

"I'm not going to go." The words rang out glaring and stark against the velvet dark of the night surrounding us. "I'm going to be a performer, not a teacher. Why do I even need school? I can bag it, move to New York with you—look for gigs while you audition. I won't have any trouble finding them. We can move in together—be together—wherever your career takes you, I can go, too."

I put my hand flat on his chest, trying to stop the flood of words, trying to throw something up against the fear. "Oh, God, Jonathan, *no*—you can't give up everything you've worked for."

"Oh hell yeah, I can." In the little bits of light coming off the occasional passing headlights, his eyes glowed a deep, intense gray. "Why should I waste time with school when I can get paid for what

I already know I'm good at? Right? You remember? You said that, and you were right." His fingers dug into my shoulders as he stared down into my face. "Seriously, who gives a shit about school in the real world? With what we do, life informs the art. And my life doesn't mean anything if we can't be together."

My head spun with what he was suggesting—all the scenarios and ramifications—complete with the echo of my own words coming back to haunt me. But it was different for him.

And so unbelievably overwhelming for me. Too much, too much . . .

"Jonathan, we're only eighteen—"

His shoulders twitched beneath his uniform jacket. "My parents got married when Mom was eighteen and Dad was twenty."

*And he's using them as an example? And* married?

His grip loosened, became a caress along my shoulders. "All I want is for us to be together."

Breathing a little easier—not much, given all the emotion churning between us, but a little—I stroked his hair, ran my fingertips across his face. "We don't have to decide right now." Shivered as he caught my hand and kissed the palm. "We've got time to figure it out, I promise." And hoped like hell I wasn't making an impossible promise.

"Okay." His sigh was deep and long and all kinds of relieved as he slumped against the tree, eyes closed. "Okay."

# august

# slow dancing
# in a burning room

*We're in a hold pattern. I love him more than I ever thought I could love another person. He loves me. But there's just so much going through my head, so many things to mull over and consider. So much I haven't had the courage to tell him. I know I want everything he offers, everything he represents.*

*But I can't deny I also want—*

*Want what? I'm not completely sure, but it feels as if there's something else. Or that maybe . . . there should be something else. But what? Or is it . . . who?*

*No. NO. How can I even be thinking that? What's the matter with me?*

"Get *out*," Raj breathed, turning in a slow circle beside me, his mouth hanging open.

"What?"

"This is so freaking *Back to the Future*, I'm *dying*." He turned in another circle, staring up at the dark, heavy wood beams crossing the ceiling.

"You looking for something?"

"The 'Enchantment Under the Sea' banner for the big dance, natch."

"Stop it."

He reared back and glared down his nose. "I will not. We are in small town, total Norman Rockwell Americana, Wisconsin, for God's sake. In a barn of a VFW hall, for the big celebration barbecue and *dance* to kick off the county fair. You gonna sit there and tell me you'd be surprised if Marty McFly and his DeLorean showed?"

Jonathan's gaze shifted from me to Raj and back to me. "Is he serious?"

My eyes tearing up, I nodded. "'Fraid so—the boy loves him some classic eighties flicks. Don't even get me started how many rehearsals I've had to listen to him dither about the collected works of John Hughes." One of the perils of having a film-major dance partner.

"Hey—*Pretty in Pink* with a young and bee-yoo-ti-ful James Spader and Andrew McCarthy? Don't get much better, children."

"He's not really serious."

"Trust me—you don't want to go there," I warned. "You'll get the unabridged version of his 'Evolution of Teen Cinema: From Gidget to Juno' term paper from last semester." I looked around at the plaques and banners and old military uniforms interspersed with festive balloons and twisted paper streamers. Honestly, Raj really wasn't so far off. There was a definite step-through-the-portal-and-into-another-time sense about the place.

"Hey, guys, come look—"

Raj and I made a beeline to where Jonathan stood at one of the lobby walls studying a classic black-and-white photograph—one of dozens—showing a group of young men marching in parade formation carrying old-fashioned side-slung drums behind a banner reading VFW POST # 629. The crowds on the street were waving little flags, the men all sporting hats—spiffy fedoras that were in odd contrast with the plain overalls some of them wore—while the women wore big-skirted dresses and oversized sunglasses, their short fluffy hairstyles held back with scarves. Above their heads, a banner strung between two fancy scrolled iron light poles proclaimed, HAPPY 4TH 1951! The whole thing looked straight out of one of my history textbooks.

"Check this out—" Jonathan pointed at the rows behind the drummers. "Look at the bugles."

Leaning in so he could take a closer look, Raj said, "No valves? That is seriously old-school."

"So that's an old corps?"

"Yeah." Next to me, Jonathan nodded. "You know, it was the VFW who sponsored some of the earliest versions of corps. The roots of the activity are all in places like this or in churches or—" He stopped and shoved his hands into the pockets of his khakis. "Hell."

"What?"

"Geek alert."

"Not hardly." I shook my head, moving along the wall to look at another picture, at the faces that looked as young as ours, but older at the same time. Reminiscent of the few black-and-white pictures Mamacita had carefully saved in an album at home. Pictures from when she was a young woman in Cuba. "I think it's cool."

"Really?" Jonathan's voice was soft as he leaned in close, like he was studying the picture as well, but sneaking a glance beneath my lashes showed his gaze was focused on me.

"Sure," I reassured him, reaching up to brush my fingertips across the slight blush on his cheekbones, tracing the scattering of freckles that had deepened over the summer. "It's part of you."

As his lips touched mine, an exasperated "All right, all right, you two break it up or find a room" came from behind me. As *if.* I let my kiss linger a little more before facing Raj and pulling off as innocent a smile as I could muster. Probably not very, but still, I tried.

"You were saying?"

"That I'm jealous I haven't found anyone to swap spit with this tour." He mock-pouted, then grinned as he started shooing us toward the doors. "Plus, in there, there's barbecue and hopefully some decent tune spinning with a DJ imported from the wilds of Milwaukee, which brings me to, I'd *love* to dance with you to something that's not a tango for a change." He batted his eyelashes with a sickening smile.

Just when I wanted to strangle him, he'd up and say something disturbingly sweet, the jerk. "I'd think you'd be sick of dancing with me." I shoved my shoulder into his as the three of us walked into the main hall.

"No way." He shoved back. "Dying to get wild for real."

I squeezed Jonathan's hand. "What about you?"

"Only if it's less than sixty-four beats per minute."

"What?"

"You seriously don't want to dance with me, Soledad. I've got two left feet—three, if the music gets too funky." He grinned, clearly not too bothered by an open admission of ineptitude, but— he had to be kidding, right? He could march the most intricate routines while playing complex passages on an instrument, but he couldn't dance?

"Surely you exaggerate."

He didn't. To give him credit, though, he tried. For me, he tried, letting me lead him out on the floor during a relatively easy mid-tempo song. Then proceeded to stomp over my toes, cursing under his breath and muttering apologies every time he did. Which was a lot. Lucky for me, the strappy black heels that I'd brought be-cause hey, girl here—had to bring at least *one* pair of heels—had closed toes, so the damage was fairly minimal.

He dropped my hands and stepped back. "It's hopeless."

"Yeah," I sighed. Damn, I hated admitting defeat, but this was *bad*. Adorable, but bad.

He looped his arm around my waist and pulled me close as a new song—a really slow, throbbing, R & B groove—started up. *Good* DJ. Glancing over at the booth, I saw Raj standing there, flashing a thumbs-up before he returned to working his charms on the pretty DJ boy with the silver rings and guyliner.

*Good* Raj. Hands on either side of my hips, Jonathan pulled me close against him, his cheek resting against my hair.

"Listen, don't worry about me—you dance all you want."

His words vibrated against my cheek as I rubbed against his neck. You know, I was happy to stay right here. At the same time, though . . . my feet were feeling a little telltale itch, my hips shift-ing ever so restlessly. "Really?"

"Yeah, really. You go."

*Dios mío,* but I couldn't imagine my heart feeling any more full. "All the slow ones are yours."

"Definitely a deal I can live with."

As soon as the sex-on-the-floor song was over and the tempo

picked up, I sent Jonathan on his way to the food tables while I pulled Raj away from the DJ booth. Bitching every step until I reminded him, "Didn't you want to get down? Besides, hello? Side benefit of showing off for your DJ—let him see your moves. At least the ones you make on your feet."

"Nasty girl!" he yelled out over the throbbing, ass-shaking bass.

"Not yet." I spun in, the skirt of my favorite purple dress—also brought along just in case—swirling high around my thighs. My back to Raj's chest, my thighs scissored around one of his, we ground our hips together.

His hands on my thighs, he laughed. "You know, moves like this might be illegal 'round these parts."

Feeling free as a bird, I ran my hands through the length of my hair, lifting it off my neck as I rolled my head back onto Raj's shoulder and grinned up at him. "I'll take my chances."

Over and over, I took those chances, dancing with guys from our corps, from other corps, with Raj some more—shaking off the increasingly uncomfortable vibe radiating from Jonathan as he watched from the sidelines. Not that I ignored it completely. I *did* make it a point to come back to him every couple of tracks, even if it was only to share a drink and a quick kiss. But now that the dancer had been set free, the lure of the floor was just *too* powerful. I moved on to dancing with some of the locals, including a sweet deputy who had the body of a football player but was wicked light on his feet. I shrieked as he picked me up and spun me around, praying he had a good grip but thrilling to the rush of air through my hair and the kaleidoscope of colors as the room became one big spinning blur.

Breathless at the end of that dance, I bent over, my eyes closed. Tried to regain my equilibrium as the DJ segued into a new song. A genuinely surprising song for this neck of the woods, the insistent, tropical beat shimmering and rippling across my skin and singing all the way down to my bones. Raj, again, I figured—had to be—wanting to dance again, to something that *wasn't* a tango, but was sexy as hell and completely up my alley.

"Soledad."

Opening my eyes, I sucked in a sharp breath.

Taz.

Not the Taz I knew. But one I definitely wanted to know. A Taz who had me struggling to remember that breathing was supposed to come naturally.

*Yeah . . . right. How's that work again?*

All in black, from the loafers to the sharp-creased slacks and narrow leather belt. To the dress shirt with the sleeves rolled to his elbows, a couple of buttons left undone at the collar—just enough to show off the braided black leather cord around his neck with the familiar silver medallion resting in the hollow at the base of his throat. And for the first time since I'd met him, his hair was loose, falling from a slightly messy side part and hanging straight to his shoulders, that silver streak fully exposed, shining against the black of the rest of his hair, the diamond studs in his ears just barely glinting through the strands.

*Still not pretty.*

*Nope. But dead sexy is a whole different beast,* m'ija.

And without his saying a word, just a subtle lift of one eyebrow, there I was, moving into his arms like it was the most natural thing in the world and there wasn't a damned thing I would've done to stop it. And none of this dancing with a couple feet between us stuff—no way. The music wouldn't allow it, the demanding rhythms insisting that we really dance. Linger over the movements and savor each beat like they were bites from a juicy, sweet mango on the hottest day of the summer.

And *madre santísima*, did Taz *really* know how to dance to music like this. One hand holding mine, the other warm on the bare skin of my back, not so much distance between us that it was formal, but definitely close enough to be . . . dangerous. With each step, his breath brushed against my cheek, his chest skimming mine as he spun me out, then back in, bringing me *maybe* just a little closer. Close enough so a hint of spicy-sweet cologne wrapped around me, the way it had the day he loaned me his jacket.

This was so new. So different. With danseurs, or even with Raj, I followed my partners because it's how I'd been taught. With Taz, however—it was natural, following that smooth, confident lead. Responding to his smile, matching him step for step, my hand sliding across his chest and hooking around his neck. Two parts coming together into beautiful, organic movement. Everything sensual and arousing and heart-stopping about *really* dancing with another human being.

And with every turn, I moved in even closer; with each beat, my body swayed more seductively, learning the contours of his body, inviting him to learn mine. Realizing with the tiny part of my brain that was still operational that one of his hands was splayed across the middle of my back, the other tangled in my hair, the tips of his fingers brushing my neck while both of my arms rested on his shoulders. *Pull away,* that tiny part whispered, but I couldn't. Not as long as I could feel the subtle bunch and shift of muscle beneath cotton warmed by his body's heat—could keep playing my fingertips through the ends of his hair. *So* soft, enticing my fingers to explore more, to shape themselves to the curve of his skull as his head lowered, his eyes closing, thick, ink-dark eyelashes spiky just above broad, high cheekbones. My own eyes closed, feeling the heat of his skin, closer . . .

"Taz, *no*—"

*God, no . . . What am I doing?*

"No." Pushing him away, as I shook my head. "Oh, God, I can't."

"I know."

We faced each other—no more touching, some actual breathing room between our bodies as the song wound down and another started in its place. And still, all we did was stare at each other, me breathing hard, closing my eyes, but when I opened them again, he was still there.

"Then *why*, Taz?"

"Because it was our last chance." He reached out and twisted a lock of my hair around his finger, then slowly let it slide free. "I should say I'm sorry," he added softly. "But I can't." The tips of his fingers brushed across my lips, stayed there for a moment as he said, "We're leaving tomorrow," and I knew he meant I wouldn't see him again. Touching his fingers to his lips, he lifted them and disappeared into the crowd.

Dazed, I turned and nearly plowed into Raj, pale and shell-shocked behind me. "I didn't even know he was here. I was gonna dance with you, but then he got to you first, and maybe I should've cut in or something, I don't know. . . . God, I'm so sorry, Soledad, I'm so damned sorry—"

My heart clawed its way into my throat with every word, each breath coming shorter and faster and leaving me swaying. "Where's Jonathan?"

His mouth opened and closed, like he was trying to figure out how to say what I already knew.

"Raj, please, where *is* he?"

His eyes closed as he sighed, "Gone."

# wild horses

"Jonathan!"

He was walking fast, head down, hands shoved in his pockets. From this distance, in the dark, it could've been anyone, except it wasn't. I knew that body—the straight, tense line of the shoulders way too well.

"Jonathan, wait, *please!*"

He walked faster, long legs burning up the sidewalk, but I was running barefoot—having ditched my shoes—and desperate.

*"Jonathan—"* Just as he made it to the iron fence ringing our host school's campus, I caught up, reaching out to grab his arm, skin slipping against skin. Lunged, grabbed again, and slipped harder, this time because my palms were so slippery with sweat, losing my balance. . . . Heard the sickening rip of fabric as I bodyslammed onto the brick walkway.

"Please," I cried, my knees and palms stinging, looking up to where he stood a few feet away, finally having stopped. "It was just a dance, Jonathan."

"You were practically fucking him on the floor."

The words were low and bitter and full of as much hurt as I'd ever heard from him. His head dropped and he started to walk away again.

"Jonathan, I'm *sorry*. . . ." He stopped, his head turned slightly to the side. "I can't—" I took a deep, shuddering breath, not wanting to say it, not wanting to admit that maybe it had been more than a little harmless flirting—or could've been. But I couldn't lie to him either. "I can't deny there's something there, some sort of . . . of attraction, I guess, but other than that one dance, I have never once acted on it, Jonathan. *I swear.*"

And this was the last fair we had a show at. We were headed toward Indianapolis and Finals after tomorrow night, and Taz . . . was gone. He'd promised.

"I'm never going to see him again."

"Do you want to?"

"No." My response was immediate—the single syllable sharp and panicked and leaving a bitter aftertaste on my tongue. It wasn't completely true. But it *had* to be. Right now, it had to be. I rolled to a sitting position, rubbing at my forehead. "No."

"But he wants you."

"He can't *have* me, Jonathan. And he knows that." I finally made it to my feet, knees burning like fire, and limped the few steps between us. Reached out to touch him, flinching as he jerked back. Took a step away. He'd never *not* let me touch him before.

"Please."

Everything hurt. Not just my knees and hands and the bottoms of my feet from running barefoot more than six blocks, but everything—inside and out. My lungs burned as I took a deep breath, fighting the urge to fall back to the ground in a sobbing mess.

"Please don't leave."

And everyone said "I love you" were the three hardest words in the world to say.

Not in my world.

"Jonathan, please—don't. Don't do this."

"Don't do what? Go off and act like a whore?" he ground out, sounding eerily like his father. "Make a fool of the person who loves you most?" His voice broke, bringing tears to my eyes. "Tell me, Soledad, why shouldn't I leave?"

"Because you're not like them." Every word felt like a Band-Aid being ripped off, not fast and easy, but inch by inch and hurting all the more for it. "My mother, my father, my grandfather, all of these people who've left." My fists clenched, fingernails digging into my raw, aching palms, using the physical hurt to anchor myself as I forced out, "I screwed up. I know I did, and I'm so sorry, and I'll do anything to make it up to you, but please, don't leave. My whole life, I've been so careful to *never* put myself in a position to be left. But I let *you* in, Jonathan. So let me have the chance to fix this. *Please.*"

He shook his head, took another step back, this one bringing him beneath the mellow glow from one of those old-fashioned lights, and now I could see the damp trails on his cheeks.— "I *can't*. Don't you understand what you've done to me, Soledad? To us?"

As he turned and started walking, then running, I stood there, my feet feeling like lead weights, like I was going to throw up, like my head was about to explode—letting loose with a completely unexpected laugh, because I was really hoping that Marty McFly and his DeLorean would show up. I could go back and never have danced with Taz—never have kept his jacket or even turned to talk to him, reacting to his impossibly cheesy Spanish commentary.

Then . . . the longer I stood there, all those thoughts running through my head like some Greek tragedy, I started, believe it or not, getting pissed. Really, more than pissed. I . . . I . . .

I hadn't done *anything*. It had been close tonight, yeah, but I had stopped. Had made the conscious choice to pull away when the alternative could've been so easy. I could've kissed Taz. Could've done a whole lot more if I'd wanted, because in those few seconds when we *hadn't* kissed, just staring at each other, I'd seen in that dark gaze that all I had to do was step forward, into his arms again, and it could've been the beginning of anything I wanted.

And I hadn't done it.

I'd chosen Jonathan.

Each one of those thoughts let something loose, and I took one step, then another, then another, until I was running again, around the side of the building and toward the gym, because we were going to figure this out. Because maybe we were only eighteen, but if we were even going to *try* to be together, for the next year or next fifty years or whatever, he was going to have to get that we might run into this again. Next time it might be *him*, attracted to another girl, and would he be able to back off—to make that choice?

If we couldn't figure this out, then we *were* over.

"Haven't you done enough?"

I jerked to a stop just shy of the gym doors, grimacing at the sharp pain shooting from my knees, and squinted into the shadows.

Oh, I couldn't deal—no . . . "With all due respect, Dr. Crandall—" I took a deep breath, pissed at how my voice was shaking, wiped at my face, feeling grit and dirt scratch my skin, my palms stinging with a whole new fire. "This is none of your business."

He stepped forward under the security light, his eyes an unholy pale blue. "You've ruined everything—I took the solo, he could care less. Told me he's not going to bother to compete in individuals at Finals. What's next? Dropping the corps altogether? School? Become some kind of vagabond gypsy wandering the country in search of jobs like you?"

*Ay madre santísima*—there's no way he could know. Nothing had been decided for sure, not yet. And there's no way Jonathan would have told him anything anyhow—would he? I lurched back as he took another step forward and *hated* myself for it.

"Are you that selfish? That intent on killing his entire *future*?"

"Back off, Marc. You're overreacting." Gray appeared from around the corner of the building. "And she's right—it's none of your business. You got issues with Jonathan's future, that's between you and him. Maybe."

"You've done nothing but protect her all summer," Dr. Crandall snapped.

"No more so than I would for any of my kids." Gray's tone was as mild as ever, but with some definite steel running below the drawl. "Now you—" He leveled a stare at me. "Let's get you cleaned up."

The way he looked at me—he already knew. That something had gone down. "Bad enough you're probably going to be stiff tomorrow, you don't need infection setting in."

Right—taking the cue and going in, away from Dr. Crandall and all his rage. Let Gray help me clean up and then I'd try to find Jonathan. And if I couldn't find him—couldn't make this right—curling up in my blanket and wanting to shrivel away into nothingness sounded like a pretty decent alternative, because no matter how unreasonable I thought Jonathan was being, truth of the matter was, this whole fucked-up situation was my fault.

*It was only a dance. He's overreacting.*

"It was more than that."

I was so tired of lying.

"More than what, darlin'?"

I looked down into Gray's face as he knelt in front of me, carefully swabbing out the scrapes that ran deeper than I'd thought.

"It's just . . . It's . . . nothing." I sighed and shifted on the bench, bunching my torn skirt in my fists and blinking away tears. The antiseptic was a great excuse for those.

"Sit still, baby girl. Besides—" The glaring overheads reflected off his bright blue eyes, making it difficult to read them. "He's not here. Blew in and out like a bat out of hell."

More tears and I couldn't even blame it on the antiseptic. "Oh."

My knees bandaged, he moved onto my palms, which weren't as torn up. "I'm worried about you, darlin'."

"Don't worry, Gray. I'll be good for the show."

He flashed a half-grin that didn't quite make it to his eyes. "Not the show. I'm worried about *you*. Both of you."

I wouldn't cry. Not anymore. But I did let him hug me and rub my back while I didn't cry. Afterwards, I let him wipe my face and get me a bottle of water and some painkillers, and let him tell me to get some rest, even though we both knew I wouldn't.

I wanted to fix it. Now.

*Look, you've already gone after him. You told him how you feel—he knows you want to fix it. Next move has to be his.*

Yeah. It did. But if I didn't do *something*—I couldn't just continue to do the agitated pacing thing, and look where dancing had gotten me tonight. I poked around in my backpack . . . my duffel . . . my suitcase . . . Where was it? I repeated the search, even retracing my steps back into the ladies' locker room, making sure I hadn't left it behind, but I *never* left it behind. Since that one time, I'd been so careful.

"Where *is* it?"

My words bounced off the shiny, tiled surfaces, a mocking echo. Standing in the middle of the brightly lit locker room, I turned in circles, like maybe I expected it to just . . . appear out of thin air. Maybe if I clicked my heels three times?

Choking down a half-laugh, half-sob, I ran back into the thankfully still-deserted gym, riffling through everything I owned, *knowing* I couldn't have just left my journal lying around anywhere, but it . . . wasn't . . . here.

I froze, my hands twisted in a mass of dance gear. The bus. That had to be it. I wasn't religious about zipping my backpack closed, so it had to have fallen out of my backpack and it was sitting in the overhead compartment above our seats, the bus safely locked for the night.

Slowly, I let the camisoles and tights slip from my fingers as I sank back onto my mattress, pulling my blanket around myself. Turning my back to the room, I curled up in as small a ball as I possibly could.

Staring down at the bright keypad of the phone I'd kept close by like a talisman, I finally hit one digit, silently counting the customary three rings before she picked up.

"*¿Qué pasa, angelita?*"

I made a noise, low in my throat, that I knew I'd never made before, that I kept making as her voice crossed over all the miles separating us, wrapping itself around me more securely than my blanket. "Shhhh, *mi ángel,* it's going to be fine. It is all going to work out. *No llores* . . . don't. There's no need to cry."

252

"He . . . oh, Mamacita—" I sucked in huge gulping breaths, trying to say it. "He left."

*"Ay mi vida."*

"Tell me he'll come back." She could do tarot, throw bones, read our charts, whatever, but I *had* to know. "Please," I begged.

"Yes. He'll come back." Her voice was so calm and steady and sure, and I latched onto every word. "He has no choice. He doesn't know what to do without you."

# when the stars go blue

*Choices are such weird things. We make them every day—big things, small things. Funny how it's the small choices—like just saying yes to a dinner . . . or a dance—that wind up having the biggest impact.*

"Oh, no . . . oh . . . *God . . . no.*"

The thing I'd come back to, over and over again, was that it hadn't been my best performance. Not my worst, either, but not my best, not technically. What it had been, was my strongest.

That's what I kept coming back to.

He hadn't come back. Not during that long horrible night. But I clung to Mamacita's words. He'd come back. He *had* to. Then finally, right before rehearsal, he'd shown, having changed into shorts and a T-shirt, but unshaved and with dark circles beneath his eyes that told me his night hadn't been any better than mine. Taking his place without a word to me—or anyone. And we'd rehearsed and done run-throughs and had lunch and dinner, passing by each other like we were freakin' ghosts, unable to connect. But he had to make the first move. If there was anything I was going to stick to, it was that.

It wasn't until we were released to get ready for the show, though, that he finally approached me, cornering me in the ladies' locker room. And by then, I was beyond pissed. Gritting my teeth, I forced the hand holding the eyeliner to stop shaking. "What do you want?"

Without a word, he took the pencil from my hand and pulled me up, his hands tight around my arms, growing tighter as I shoved my hands into his chest, trying to break free.

"Stop it." As I fisted my hands in his T-shirt, he shook me slightly. "Just . . . stop. I was wrong, okay? I was wrong to walk away." The words came out ragged and hoarse, like he'd been railing out loud the way I had been in my head, all these hours. "I swear, I'll never do that again. I'll never leave and I'll *always* take care of you." Despite how tight his hold was on my arms, I could still feel how his hands trembled. "Always, Soledad. I swear. I'll do everything in my power to prove it. You're *everything* to me."

Slowly, I lifted my hands until I held his face in my palms, staring into his eyes, trying to look past the urgency and desperation. Trying to steel myself against the pity and tenderness that twisted my insides over the circles beneath those haunted eyes that had deepened into fragile bruises. Trying to see if he really meant it.

"Do you believe me?"

"Yeah—I do."

But I was still furious. He'd left after all, and I wasn't sure how easy that would be to forgive. I was really thinking I was going to need some time—and space—to work on forgiving him. But he'd also come back. Which was a first in my world.

"Don't you understand how much I love you, Jonathan?"

"I didn't." He turned his head away, his lips grazing the inside of my wrist, the caress a live-wire charge up my arm.

And along my cheek, a velvet touch, a rich, intoxicating perfume—

I took the lavender rose from him and held it to my nose, breathing deep.

He smiled, his fingers caressing my cheek along the same path as the rose. "I'll do anything to show I love you as much as you love me."

So we marched onto the field for our last show before Finals Week, ready to crank it up another notch. I knew, going in, that it wasn't likely to be a great show for me—I was exhausted, my knees were stiff and achy with their scrapes and bruises—but I wasn't about to take it easy, no way. Tonight was about pushing through the physical pain and giving it everything I had and then, digging deep and giving just that little bit more.

I was moving, dancing, flirting with Raj and the rest of the corps and the crowd like never before, enjoying every damned moment of being on that big, huge field that had become my stage—my home—this summer. Savoring the roar of the crowd as I tossed my rose at Don José and received his adoring glance in return. Swaying and seducing through the tango, then beginning my final solo with as haughty, mocking, downright *seductive* a smile as I'd ever delivered.

And I was turning and turning and turning, as "El Tango" grew toward its intense, passionate climax, turning in the glorious *fouetté en tournant,* my head whipping around as I spotted each turn, gaining strength with each rotation, feeling as if I could go on forever. I was balanced so perfectly, held such command over my body, it felt as if the world around me had come to a standstill as I turned and turned, like a ballerina in a music box.

Then, suddenly, piercing my perfect bubble—tumbling in a long, graceful arc as if in slow motion, even though I knew it had to have only taken a fraction of an instant—a rose.

A rose?

No. . . . We'd already done the rose trick—I threw it, Raj caught it. There should be no more roses. And not thrown *at* me. *No.*

But there it was, skidding along the polished surface of my makeshift dance floor, trapped beneath the smooth sole of my shoe just at the same . . . exact . . . moment Don José lunged at me for the fatal stab, but it wasn't right, the timing was off, my arms flailing as I tried to regain my balance enough to get out of the way and instead lurched right into him. A horrible tearing sensation sheared through my leg, then . . .

Nothing.

Just . . . numb.

"Oh, no . . . oh . . . *God . . . no.*"

I couldn't breathe . . . couldn't see anything, fueling the panic and terror, until I realized it was Raj, sprawled on top of me, pinning me down. Then—blessed relief as he rolled off, saying it over and over . . .

"Oh, no . . . oh . . . *God . . . no.*"

Finally, I could breathe again . . . could see the stadium lights above and the surreal angle of the uniformed legs marching past, because you know, the show *always* went on and we were so near the end anyhow—

We'd even rehearsed what would happen, if for some reason there was an accident, since that final lunge had always carried such a huge element of risk.

My hands clawed at the wood of the makeshift dance floor, trying to find something to hold on to against the searing fire shooting down my right leg, finally finding the weighted stem of the rose that wasn't red. Wasn't silk, but real, the deep lavender petals crushed and already falling off, their sweet fragrance overwhelming and *God*, kind of sickening.

Then my eyes met his—what would normally be our secret moment. Our private exchange of glances as I lay there pretending to be close to death.

But as I lay there, feeling very real pain and fear and bewilderment, he gazed down at me and I saw something in those pale gray eyes—the desperation from earlier finally stripped away to reveal something horrified and triumphant and, bizarre as it sounds, *loving*.

I'd already known. The second I'd seen the color, felt the scent wrap around me, like a beautiful memory. But it was in that moment when our eyes met that I really *knew*, without a single doubt, not just where it had come from, but that where it landed hadn't been any kind of an accident.

"Soledad, *no!*"

Raj tried. He really did.

He shouldn't have bothered.

"*Why?*" Fresh pain shot through my leg as I rolled and lunged, just snagging the hem of his uniform pants, the wool so smooth and fluid beneath my fingers, like quicksilver, almost slipping away, more pain shooting up my arms as I hung on, determined to not . . . let . . . go. I needed answers. I needed to know— "Why, damn you, *why?*" Pulling, pure fury overriding blinding agony, then—Jonathan pitching forward, no time to catch himself. His horn hitting the ground, bell first, then his mouth—that talented, beautiful mouth—smashing into the mouthpiece a split second later.

I rolled to my back, gasping, fighting not to scream, my eyes stinging, as I stared up at the sky. The final chords of *Carmen*—

those lone, echoing chimes that evoked church bells—rang mournfully into the silent summer night.

The smell of the fresh-cut grass was so thick around me—heavy and rich and . . . and . . . Could a smell be compared to a color? Because it smelled so amazingly, completely green and alive as I lay there, staring up at the blue-black night sky, feeling like a part of me had just died.

A harsh, choking sound had me turning my head, meeting his gaze, trying not to gag at the sight of his bloodied face, and trying not to gag again as I realized *I'd* done that. And closed my eyes against the sick, incomprehensible sight of him smiling—or trying to.

"I love you."

# the pieces don't
# fit anymore

It was *such* an eerie silence. Not like the kind of silence where I was so far into my own head that the rest of the world didn't exist. No . . . As the last chime faded into the night, nothing but heavy, overwhelming silence, the crowd understanding—this was *not* part of the show. Followed by a hum that got louder and more in-sistent as they understood that whatever it was, it was bad.

Then the hum broken by shouts calling to get the corps off the field, *now,* where the hell were the paramedics, the ambulances—a flurry of movement as Gray appeared beside me. I was *trying* not to look, but at the very edges of my vision, I could see another instructor kneeling beside Jonathan, holding a towel to his mouth, Mrs. Crandall running onto the field and dropping to her knees, easing his head into her lap.

"Keep still, don't move." Gray's hands held my shoulders. "We're getting a cart—I don't want to take any chances."

"I didn't mean to hurt him so bad, Gray, but he threw the rose

and then it hurt and oh . . . *madre santísima,* it hurts so much—"
I fought against his hold, trying to sit up, to get to my leg, to see
what I could feel was so wrong. "It *hurts.*"

"Dammit, I said stay *down*—" Gray moved his body more completely over mine, blocking my view even as I still struggled against
his hold. "And I know, darlin'—I saw it all. I know it hurts. I
know . . ." Crooning in that soft, deep rumble as I collapsed back to
the ground. Releasing my shoulders, he brushed my hair back off
my face, looking over at Raj sitting beside me, clutching one of my
hands. "You okay?"

He shook his head hard, his fingers tight around mine. "My
ankle hurts like a sonuvabitch—but, God . . ." He closed his eyes,
swallowed hard, then turned away, his back heaving and jerking
even though he never let my hand go. A few seconds later he
straightened, wiping at his mouth with his uniform sleeve. "Jesus,
Gray, where the fuck is that cart?"

"It's coming right now."

"What about him?"

Raj's narrow stare was focused across me, but I was done looking. I couldn't . . .

"He can walk." Gray's voice was as cold as Raj's stare. "They're
taking him right to another ambulance."

"Oh, good," I sighed.

Then I passed out.


I came to, still staring up at Gray and Raj. Only thing different
was the location—no more green field and stadium lights with
their fuzzy silver-white halos piercing the night sky. Instead, tight,
narrow walls, lots of technical-looking equipment, a squawking
radio, and a guy in a blue shirt hovering behind my head, flashing

some stupid light in my eyes. I ignored him and his questions that sounded like so much noise—like the teachers in the *Peanuts* cartoons, all *wah wah wah*—instead focusing on Gray.

"It really happened?" But even before I finished the sentence, I had my answer, my leg feeling tight and rigid and when I tried to bend it—

"Why can't I move my leg? Gray—why isn't it moving? *Why* isn't it—"

"Shhh . . . relax, darlin'" Gray's hands on my shoulders did a lot more to settle the panic than the paramedic who was barking shit in my ear. "You're in a brace. We don't want you hurting your knee any more."

"My knee?"

"At least. We'll know more after we get to the hospital."

"My knee." I tried not to whimper—to not sound so damned scared—but no matter how hard I tried to keep them back, a few tears still managed to escape.

"Don't, Soledad—not until we know more." Gray wiped away the tears, the sweat, but no matter how gentle he was, he couldn't wipe away the terror. My knee. How could I dance without a knee that worked?

As I reached up to swipe at fresh tears, my hand brushed against the front of my costume—against the tiny rose pin I'd never once performed without. My piece of Jonathan, always with me on the field. Curling my fingers around it, I yanked hard, the fragile material tearing. My arm falling to the side, my fingers uncurling, I let the pin roll out of my palm, the sound of it hitting the ambulance floor lost amid the radio and sirens and questions. So many questions that I didn't have answers for.

Luckily, the hospital wasn't that far, and once we were there, things were pretty cut-and-dried. If it'd been Miami, I'd have been shuttled into some hot, overcrowded waiting room, hanging out with the junkies jonesin' for their "medicinal" fix, and probably still waiting five hours later. Here, though—I didn't have to wait, seen immediately by the ER doctor, an older lady, a little gray around the edges, who gently probed and poked, making note of my reactions, writing out orders for a high-tech immobilizer for my knee, and—may all the saints and idols and goddesses and everyone rain blessings down on the woman—she ordered drugs. Pain-numbing, make-me-stupid-in-a-hurry drugs.

Unfortunately, they didn't kick in fast enough.

"Nerve damage?"

Sharp and biting, the voice cut through the whole ER, not that it was that big a space. And with my cubicle's curtain open, I had a clear view, too. The back of Dr. Crandall's head—the tense line of his shoulders— My fingers twisted in the blanket.

"It's possible, sir. It'll take time before we know for sure—however, in the meantime we do have an excellent plastic surgeon who's coming in to stitch him up. Really, he got off exceptionally lucky—his teeth went clean through his lip, but he only just chipped and loosened a couple of them. Nothing else as far as we could tell other than a nasty sprain to his wrist."

"The mouth—how long?"

"It's difficult to put a timetable—"

He whirled, an accusing finger pointed at Jonathan. "You stupid little bastard."

"Sir—" The doctor held his hand up, like he meant to block Dr. Crandall from the bed. "I understand you're upset—"

"You . . . kept saying . . . she'd . . . leave." Each word slow and difficult, but understandable. "Said . . . I should . . . should leave before she . . . betrayed me."

Gray muttered, "Jesus God . . . ," as I reached out and grabbed his hand, holding on tighter at the sharp laugh that bounced around the room. The laugh that sounded way too dark and edgy and just . . . *wrong,* to be ringing through such a bright, clean room.

Another laugh—sharper—that made me flinch, gritting my teeth against the pain caused by even that small movement. "You were . . . wrong. She didn't . . . leave. Didn't do . . . anything—just danced. . . ." His voice faded into a cough, then he went quiet for a minute.

"He was like . . . home. That's . . . what she wrote. But it's me she loves. Not him. If she loved *him* . . . she'd leave. Join the company . . . go to Europe . . . find *him*."

"You read my journal?"

My journal that I couldn't find last night. The words came out on a thin, hoarse whisper that he didn't hear, and even if he had, I don't think he could've *heard* me. He was too far gone into his own nightmare.

Just then, Dr. Crandall moved aside and I had my first clear look at Jonathan since that last terrible moment on the field. Hair flat and dark with sweat, uniform top hanging open, blood splattered across it and staining the T-shirt beneath. His mouth didn't even look like a mouth—it was so swollen and horrible, one side bigger than the other—gauze covering his chin, bright red patches seeping through. But it was his eyes that broke my heart. As translucent and beautiful as ever, but at the same time . . . so endlessly deep and lost.

"You can't—" He bent over, coughing, then sat up again, the red spots on the gauze spreading. "You can't . . ."

I knew better than to say anything. There was no possible good end to that sentence. No answer I'd want to hear. But I heard the words anyway—in my voice.

"Can't what, Jonathan?"

"You can't leave me for him." His eyes were brighter now—his voice taking on a singsong cadence. "You wondered, but you were scared. He scared you. And you didn't want to hurt me. But now you can't."

The corners of those eyes turned up and I could tell, he was smiling, as much as his ruined mouth would let him. Sitting up straight, he met my gaze directly, and even though his mouth was barely able to move, his words still managed to come out completely clear, carrying across the space between us.

"He's gone, and now you can't go. There's nothing to get in the way of us being together. I'll take care of you and I won't ever leave. I promised. Remember? Now I can prove it. We've got no choice now but to be together. Be in love forever. . . ."

My free hand twisted the edge of the thin blanket covering my legs, winding it around my fist with every soft, lilting syllable. My God, he'd read *everything*. And was so unbelievably gone.

"You stupid little fuck. You'd throw away everything and you—" Dr. Crandall spun, glared at me. "You *whore*." And if I'd thought his eyes were an unholy shade of blue before—*ay santos . . . ayúdanme*. Blue-white and almost too cold to be human.

I huddled against Gray, staring as Dr. Crandall took a step forward, fists clenched at his sides.

"You've ruined everything. Everything I worked for."

If Jonathan looked lost, Dr. Crandall looked possessed, each word coming out bitter sharp and hateful and making me lean farther into Gray, my hands moving to clutch his shirt.

"I swear to God, you'll pay—"

"Enough, Marc. Enough."

Everyone froze. Mrs. Crandall stood beside Jonathan, stroking his hair back from his face and holding his hand.

Had she been there all along?

She was pale, which made the red streaking across her cheeks look that much brighter, her gaze blazing and fierce in a way I'd never seen from this incredibly gentle woman. I wouldn't have imagined she could ever summon that kind of fierce, no matter how much she loved Jonathan. Which, *Dios mío,* she did. So much.

Staring at her, I could've *sworn* I saw Mamacita beside her, blurry and sort of shimmering, their images merging and shifting, and then it was just Mrs. Crandall, her Raiders Mom T-shirt stained with brownish-red streaks. Jonathan's blood. My gaze darted between her and Dr. Crandall, noticing that aside from some sweat stains, his staff polo was pristine.

"I lost one son to your ambition. Ambition I always felt I owed you." Her mouth thinned and she blinked hard, but her voice remained steady. "But haven't you ever wondered about Brian's accident? I know I did. He worked so hard to please you, and it was never enough. You *always* wanted more. I've often wondered if he just . . . gave up. And now—Jonathan was happier than he's ever been, and rather than take joy in it, it was killing you that you'd finally lost control with him, wasn't it? So you burden him with doubt and anger and tried to *force* him—"

She took a deep shuddering breath. "How could I let you do this to our children? Because I thought I *owed* you? Because of what you gave up? But it's what you *chose,* Marc. You chose—same as I did. And you and Brian and then Jonathan made up for anything I felt I might have given up. You were everything." Her voice cracked. "But you've never been able to say the same, have you?"

She shook her head. "No. No more. I will not lose another son. Not to what you want or your ideas of how he should live his life. Not so you can live vicariously through his achievements because you were too much of a coward to try for yourself. No. More. Do you understand?"

"You have no idea—"

"Shut up."

My heart actually hurt at how anguished she sounded—understanding there were nearly forty years of emotion bleeding through in those two short words.

"Leave, Marc. Leave now. We don't need you."

Dr. Crandall looked as if he'd been run over by a steamroller—utterly flat and like all the life and color were seeping out of him. He stood there, faded and gray, and for the first time since I'd met him looked . . . old. And maybe I was courting seriously bad karma, but I didn't feel in the least bit sorry for him.

Jonathan leaned against his mom's shoulder and stared at his father. "And you said . . . I was the one . . . who'd be . . . betrayed." And he started laughing and laughing until one of the doctors finally injected something into the IV, and he settled down almost right away, sinking into his pillows.

"Gray, I'm going to throw up."

Without a word, he reached down for a small trash can, holding it ready, and even though my stomach was churning like a mad thing and the room was spinning—even though I couldn't stop hearing that sharp, hysterical laughter ringing in my ears—I didn't lose it. Didn't even so much as heave. But a few tears did manage to escape as I watched Jonathan sleeping across the way. He'd always looked so peaceful when he slept—so vulnerable.

Slumping back against my pillows, I drifted in and out, voices sounding close, then far away, some words fast, others a slow, warm hum. At one point, I opened my eyes and found Mrs. Crandall beside my bed.

"They're taking him to a room."

I blinked up at her, trying to bring her into focus, zeroing in on the soft brown eyes that were so shiny. So bright.

"I'm not likely to have another opportunity to see you—" Her hand brushed my hair back from my face, cupped my cheek. "I'm so sorry, sweetheart, for what he did. You'll never know how sorry I am. How I wish I could have taught him how to love better."

She leaned down and kissed my cheek and I swear, her face was wet . . . I tasted vague traces of salt . . . just like when I went walking on the beach . . . and God, what I wouldn't give to be doing that right now. Just walking along the beach . . . feeling the waves splashing over my bare feet, the grittiness of the sand beneath. Tasting the salt spray.

So much gold and rose light . . . like an Atlantic sunrise.

"Soledad?"

Didn't want to open my eyes . . . that rose-gold sun would be so strong. . . . Just wanted to feel its warmth on my skin. . . .

"Darlin', I called your grandmother. She's on her way."

*Oh, Mamacita . . .*

I let myself go, sinking farther into the warmth.

*Mamacita . . . please be here when I wake up. Please explain— what happened?*

# let me fall

I could go into a whole bunch of gory, technical detail about everything that was wrong with my knee, or I could keep it short.

Short version? Fucked up.

No less technical, understand—just shorter.

I woke up in a nice, almost absurdly cheery room flooded with sunshine, away from the sterile madness that had been the ER, to find Mamacita sitting beside my bed, holding my hand. When she saw me slowly blinking she knew, like she'd always known, what I needed. As she held the plastic cup for me, I sipped from the straw, my gaze wandering around the room, pausing at the sight of Domenic, his hand resting on Mamacita's shoulder, a small, reassuring smile on his face.

"Shh . . . *mi niña, no llores.*" Taking the cup away, Mamacita came back with a damp washcloth, wiping my forehead and cheeks, dabbing at my tears, her voice calm and reassuring. "Gray went back to get some things—he'll be going with us. *Y Raj también.*"

She kept going, her voice a soft, reassuring croon— "His ankle was broken when you collided. Since he won't be able to perform in the remaining shows, he said he'd rather go home."

The cup reappeared—I glanced up at Dom, holding it for me as Mamacita continued to wipe my face and neck, the rough terry cool against my overheated skin. I sipped the water, trying to get rid of that disgusting cotton-ball feeling—the feeling that I might just throw up if I thought too hard.

"We're going home, *mi vida*. The doctors say you need to see an orthopedic specialist, but you can't see one until the swelling goes down more. *Mejor así*."

"Home," I finally managed to croak out around the tightness holding my throat hostage.

"*Y no te preocupes*—you'll be seeing the best doctors. The ones who work on all the professional athletes. Gray knows who to ask for and the corps insurance is paying for everything."

She knew, she somehow always knew. I stared up at her—dark eyes in a porcelain face, a bright red crocheted sweater thrown over an equally bright orange dress, looking like home.

My arms tight around her neck, I hung on like the scared little girl I'd been once upon a time—like the scared little girl I was now—as she rubbed my back and kept murmuring in that comforting mix of Spanish and English. *God*, but I'd missed her so much.

The next several hours will always remain fogged in a drugged-out haze. The next clear memory I would be able to recall was of waking up in another cheery hospital, but with blessedly familiar palm trees outside the wide windows, and just beyond it, a shimmering, wide, blue-green expanse of water.

Home. I was home.

At least there was that.

"You're looking good, *m'ija*." We were at twenty-four hours post-op, with Dr. Sena coming in to do her doctor thing, checking that no one was messing around with her work.

"You know, it's tremendous what surgery and modern rehab techniques can accomplish. Even with the extensive nature of this injury, it's possible you could have rehabbed enough to return to dancing."

Dr. Sena could've hid behind my charts, which were already starting to take on phone book proportions, pretending to check something as she spoke, but she wasn't that kind of doctor. She met my gaze head on, but I wasn't ready to see what was in it. Not yet.

"*Could* have? What's with the past-tense usage?" I looked from Gray, who was standing on one side of the bed, to Mamacita on the other, realizing from their expressions they already knew what I was about to hear.

"Soledad." Dr. Sena carefully sat down at the edge of my bed, the side away from my now-repaired knee, and pushed at the cuffs of the long-sleeve T-shirt she wore beneath her scrubs. "Your MRI—it raised some . . . questions. Questions that were definitively answered when I had you on the table."

"*Doctor Sena—dígale, por favor.*"

Tell you what—she *immediately* sat up straighter.

"Don't make it worse by treating her like a child." And never mind that Dr. Sena dealt with some of the biggest names in Miami sports on a regular basis—she still had the sense to look a little freaked as Mamacita nailed her with one of the patented glares. So definitely smart as well as straight up.

"*M'ija,* you have some degenerative issues going on—the cartilage in your knee is almost completely gone, and on top of that, the bones are also showing abnormal wear—degeneration that's almost unheard of in someone your age, even with the level of physical activity you've engaged in most of your life. However, given what your grandmother told us about the circumstances surrounding your birth—the fact that you mother in all likelihood abused drugs during her pregnancy and your subsequent physical weaknesses as a child . . ." She shoved a hand through short, spiky hair and glanced down at the chart she held in her lap. "Well, the best I can come up with is educated guesses. However, what I can say for sure is considering what I found while I had you on the table, the real miracle is that the injury wasn't even more severe."

I stared at my shredded knee, elevated in its space-age brace. *More* severe? Everything that could have conceivably blown or torn in my knee already had.

"So . . . what, exactly are you saying?"

"Well . . ." And even though Mamacita was glaring again, Dr. Sena took her time—obviously weighing her words. "Taking into account your physical fitness and the discipline I know it takes to be a professional-caliber dancer, perhaps you might—"

"I'm not going to dance again, am I?"

Please, *please,* let me be wrong. Let me totally be misreading what was so clearly evident in the three faces surrounding me. Let it be a figment of my imagination.

Waiting for her response, it seemed like all the air was sucked straight out of the room, like it was holding its breath right along with me, released in a long, sad sigh as she nodded, long earrings swinging like glittery, gold exclamation points.

"Tell her the rest."

Gray this time, leaning against the wall, arms crossed.

"Even if this hadn't happened now . . ." Her smile tried to be understanding and sympathetic and reassuring all rolled up in a package obviously designed to let me down as easy as possible. "Three . . . maybe five years, at most. Certainly, the degenerative issues would have progressed that much further—you would've had those additional years of sustained physical stress contributing to the wear and tear. There's no way your body could have withstood the demand."

Five years. All that turmoil and anguish over making a decision about my future and no matter what decision I made, my future would've consisted of five years. Maybe.

"Obviously, there's *never* a good time for an injury to occur, but maybe in this case—" She stood. "Frankly, it's good it happened when it did, rather than several years down the line. Again, your fitness coupled with your discipline and Gray overseeing your rehab—you stand a much better than average chance to regain complete physical strength and mobility. You might never dance professionally, but there's no reason you wouldn't be able to dance a waltz at your own wedding—take walks on the beach. Lead a full, normal life."

I'd been holding it together up to that point. Mostly because it hadn't really had a chance to register. But that last thing she said—it brought what she was saying home in a way nothing else had to that point. And man, that pissed me right off.

"Hey, Dr. Sena."

She glanced up from scribbling something on the chart.

"What if you couldn't be a surgeon anymore? Just had to be a *normal* doctor?"

Hazel eyes widened—then she nodded slowly, her earrings swinging again, gently this time, their shine even appearing toned down a couple notches. *"De verdad, lo siento, mi vida—"* And thing is, she really did look sorry as she sat on the edge of the bed again, one long, graceful hand, the tool of her trade, resting on my good leg, still strong and healthy, but with God only knows what sorts of weaknesses and secrets hiding beneath smooth skin and supple muscle.

Looking away, I stared out the window at the late-afternoon summer storm that was rolling in off the Atlantic. "I don't know how to be anything else." Blindly reached for Mamacita who was already there, already holding me close as I started crying. "I'm a dancer. I don't know if I *can* be anything else."

*Was a dancer.*

*Was.*

*How am I ever going to get used to that?*

I was crying into Mamacita's shoulder, not staring up at some endless night sky, blanketed with stars like a million tiny spotlights.

I was lying in a hospital room, the pain dulled by drugs, not sprawled out on a football field, agony slicing through my leg.

Jonathan was gone—he'd never hurt me again, and I was surrounded by people who loved me. People who would help me heal.

Everything was different.

But the end of the story was the same.

Because right then, a part of me died.

Again.

# many the miles

I slept, stared out the window, slept some more. The drugs had me all messed up, making me drift in and out and losing all track of time. Maybe I was asleep for a few minutes, maybe longer. Once upon a time, that kind of lack of control would've bugged the shit out of me. Now? Not so much. I was kind of welcoming the lack of control, actually. I was glad to not be expected to do anything or make any decisions. So I just lay there, not quite with it and trying not to think at all—about anything.

The cousins had cruised in and made "duuuuude" noises over the brace, and the *tías* had visited and clucked and left all manner of soups and homemade goodies and a stack of scratch-off lottery tickets, because really, had to plan for the future now. Raj had barged in earlier for his daily visit bearing this enormous floral arrangement that went beyond gaudy and straight into God-awful, with giant fern leaves and clumps of baby's breath and carnations dyed colors *not* found in nature. It even had these fiber-optic sticks, waving in the slight breeze from the air conditioner, like little glow-in-the-dark sea anemones.

It was genuinely hideous and yeah, it made me laugh. At least, as long as he was here. Had taken a lot of energy to pretend things were going to be okay—telling him about Dr. Sena's five-year prediction, like she was the medical equivalent of a Walter Mercado–style clairvoyant, just with better hair and makeup, and repeating the "It's a good thing it happened now, huh?"

Yeah, he didn't buy it either.

Vaguely, I remembered Mamacita whispering that she was going to run home, check on things. Gray reassuring me he'd be back in a few days. He was flying to Indy to be with the corps for what was left of Finals.

At the knock, I didn't bother answering or even looking toward the door. Just too tired and besides, who was left? When it came again, I closed my eyes.

"Look, please don't give me grief. I wasn't hungry, and I really hate lime Jell-O, so you know, take my temperature, my blood pressure, do whatever you need to do, but please, don't make me eat this swill."

"*Yo no conozco esa palabra. . . .* What is 'swill'?"

You know, the drugs had been doing some freaky stuff to my brain, but hallucinations were a new one. Slowly, I opened my eyes, still staring at the window, figuring if what I was hearing was real . . . I'd see the evidence there and if it wasn't . . . well, then, I could just ease into going crazy, right?

Wasn't the dark angel of that final night . . . which was good. He just looked like a nice, regular guy, standing there in shorts and a short-sleeve buttondown open over a T-shirt, his hair pulled back like usual, and even in the window's reflection I could see that distinctive silver streak.

"What . . . ? How . . . ?"

"I went to Indianapolis."

He did *what*?

"*Pero . . . ¿por qué?*"

I watched his reflection shift from side to side—like he wished he had a ball between his feet that he could be fidgeting with. "We had a break and I wanted to see you. I had thought maybe to fight for you. Let you know—" His fists briefly clenched before he opened them, turned outward, palms up, like he was surrendering. "It was a bad idea. You had made your choice. So I was just going to watch you perform one last time. I wasn't going to talk to you or bother you. I didn't want to create any more problems. I just . . . I wanted to see you again. Take a final memory of you home."

There was a long silence as I watched his reflection shift some more, then I quietly said, "You didn't create the problems. They were just . . . there." Like the boogeyman—waiting to jump out from the shadows and catch me by surprise.

He was staring at my bandaged and braced leg, and give the boy credit—he didn't look disgusted or horrified. Just a little freaked. Like he couldn't connect that Frankenleg was actually part of me.

"I did not help, though."

"No," I agreed. "You didn't." Then I shrugged. "Then again, neither did I." And sighed. "And obviously, neither did he."

Finally, I turned my head on the pillow—looked directly into his eyes, dark as ever. "So why are you here now, Taz?"

He glanced toward the nearby armchair and waited for me to nod before easing down to sit on the edge, setting a backpack down by his feet.

"When I didn't see you in Indianapolis . . . or your dance partner, or boyfriend—" He stumbled a little over the last word before going on. "I had this sick feeling. I knew, in here—" He tapped his chest. "That something was very wrong." One corner of his mouth turned up and a faint blush streaked across his cheeks beneath his dark bronze tan. "My *mamá,* she says I should listen to those feelings more often, but you know how they are."

*Now where have you heard that before?*

"Oh, shut up," I muttered.

*"¿Qué?"*

"It's the drugs," I said really fast, feeling my cheeks heating up. "They sometimes make me say stupid things."

At least he seemed to buy it, nodding and saying, *"Ah,* okay," with another concerned glance down at Frankenleg.

"Why are you here, Taz?" I repeated, starting to feel antsy as his gaze stayed fixed on me, steady and dark.

"It was very easy to find out what happened. Everyone was talking— About what you did. What *he* did." I watched his fingers curl around the chair's armrests, his knuckles going white. "After I learned you had come home, one of the American *futboleros* helped me call information here in Miami and I got your home phone number and talked to your *abuela.* I told her we had met this summer and had become friends. She told me what hospital you were at."

Mamacita had a big mouth. And we so needed to get an unlisted phone number.

Another one of those long silences, then I finally sighed. "We're not friends, Taz."

"No. We are not." Then he was standing beside the bed and somehow, from this angle, with me lying down and unable to move and feeling so damned helpless, he seemed so overwhelming. Healthy and strong and larger than life.

It was so unfair I could scream.

"We were never meant to be just friends." And while the words had a surety to them, his voice held a tentative note of hope that left my head spinning, and for once it wasn't the drugs.

"Why are you here?" I repeated yet *again,* hating how weak even my voice sounded. Hating the pain. Hating that I couldn't even sit up straighter or pace or just drop to my knees and scream.

He took one of my hands and laid it over his so we were palm to palm, his fingers gently curled around my wrist. Loose enough so I could pull free if I wanted. When I didn't move, he lifted his free hand to tap his chest. "I am just listening to my feelings."

My fingers tried to curl into a fist again, my nails digging into his wrist.

"Your feelings are *wrong,* Taz. And you're crazy and honestly, I've had enough crazy for one lifetime. You don't belong here. And you sure as hell don't belong with *me.* You have soccer and a career and . . . and a normal *life* waiting for you." I looked him over again, top to bottom, not seeing a single scar marring that smooth tan skin—not like me, with my hideously destroyed knee and whatever else lurked beneath the surface. And maybe it was just my mind playing more tricks on me, but he even *smelled* healthy, warm and with a hint of that spicy cologne that was only his as far as I was concerned. Nothing cold or antiseptic or medicinal about him. "*Why* would you even want to be with me?"

While I did my raving-lunatic thing, he just held my hand and gazed down at me, and when I finally ran out of steam, all he did was lift our joined hands to his chest, where I could feel, just beneath his T-shirt, the subtle outline of the medallion he always wore. And the beating of his heart—a fast, rapid tattoo which made my eyes go wide. He was an athlete. His heart shouldn't be beating like that at rest.

And in a voice that was so soft it was like the faintest sea breeze playing over my skin, he said, "You know why."

*So* not fair. Admittedly, I was cooked on drugs, but not so far gone that I didn't know what he was doing, the *cabrón*. He was making it my call. He'd said his piece and instead of being all Latin guy and barreling forward with all sorts of chest-thumping proclamations over how we belonged together, something I could easily say "Oh, hell no" to, he was leaving it up to me.

Didn't he understand I didn't *want* to be making any big life-altering decisions right now? My life had just been turned completely ass-up, altered beyond recognition. I didn't *need* anything else, dammit. Didn't want it.

Not to mention, he still hadn't answered my question . . . Why would he want to be with me—now? Or ever, for that matter? After all of this, what made him think I'd want to be with him? Ever?

"Why, Taz? Why me?"

"I have been asking myself the same question since the moment I stepped on a pretty girl's cloak." His fingers curled around mine as his gaze shifted to the window. I turned my head, following his stare, studying the shifting blues and greens of the water outside. "There are many answers," he finally said. "The only thing I know for certain is that I couldn't let that girl go. I don't know why, but I couldn't. As for the rest—I don't know. But I know discovering the answers requires time."

"I can't, Taz." I looked from the window to my leg and back up at him, feeling unbearably trapped and hating it with every molecule in my body. I stared at him, seeing him not just standing beside my bed, but how I'd seen him so many times before, running effortlessly, fluid and graceful, his body bending to his will. And here I was, stuck in this stupid bed—hadn't even taken a step yet. Couldn't even begin to imagine what kind of effort it would take— that first step. It was too scary to go there. To think about it. And forget about thinking what would come after. Add that to knowing he was right *there,* healthy and mobile and strong and everything I wasn't right now? No.

*No.*

"I don't have that kind of time to give to you right now."

Wonder if he got it?

Our gazes stayed locked together for the longest time, his eyes going kind of shiny and bright until finally, he looked away. Releasing my hand, he reached down for his backpack and carefully placed it on the bed, taking care not to jostle my leg.

"I did not imagine you would want flowers."

Now it was my heart beating a little faster, because yeah—Raj's gaudy, not-found-in-nature arrangement aside—flowers weren't real high up on my happy list. I watched as he put this enormous tin on the bedside table.

"These are *Valor.* Remember? My favorite chocolates from home. But I found them here. In Miami. *Qué cosa*—a store with things from home, right here." Shaking his head and smiling that smile that showed off his straight white teeth and the dimple at the corner of his mouth. "This is a tremendous city."

I nodded, but didn't say anything, simply watching as he pulled something else from the pack—his . . . oh, *God,* his sketch pad.

His smile faded as he shifted from side to side again. "You asked me that night what I was drawing and I said *una bobería.* I lied." He set the pad on my lap, but as I edged a finger under the cover, he put his hand over mine, shaking his head. "*Espera.* Wait until I am gone. Having you look at these with me here—" His hand shook a bit on top of mine and he looked surprisingly young and unsure of himself. "I think it would feel like standing naked on a busy street, *¿tú sabes?*"

My hand turned over beneath his, closing in a tight hold, all of a sudden desperately uncertain. "Taz—"

"No—*nada más*. Don't say anything else." His free hand rose and traced slow lines around my face, his fingertips barely brushing my skin in a breathtakingly gentle sketch. One of his fingers caught the tear that spilled down my cheek, matching the lone tear leaving a damp trail along his.

Leaning down, he kissed one cheek, then the other, but instead of pulling back right away, he stayed with his mouth against my skin. Kissing my cheek one more time, he whispered, *"Hasta la próxima vez, Soledad."*

Until the next time. Not good-bye. He'd never once said good-bye. Always so certain there would be a next time.

Foolish boy.

But—then again—I couldn't bring myself to say good-bye either.

# everybody hurts

I was *such* a total wuss.

Sure, I'd been ready to look through his sketch pad while he was standing right there, but once he was gone, it might as well have been a cobra. But something about Taz saying that my looking through his sketch pad would feel like standing naked on a busy street—made me think of how I'd feel about letting anyone read my journal. How I'd *felt* when Jonathan declared he'd read my journal. So yeah, it scared me, what I might find behind that stiff cardboard cover.

So after he left, I set it on top of the tin of chocolates and went back to that drifting-in-and-out-of-consciousness thing that I'd gotten so good at. Let Mamacita pack it into a bag with a silent, questioning glance I couldn't bring myself to answer when I was finally sprung from the hospital a couple days later. Let it sit in said bag for the next week while I learned how to get around with a stupid walker and tried like hell not to scream every time I accidentally bumped my knee, sending hot bolts of pain through the stiff, braced length of my leg.

A week later, and there I was, sitting on Mamacita's sofa, because even though our house was small, it was easier on her if she didn't have to trot halfway through just to check on me. And as she'd scolded when I tried to insist she really didn't need to be checking on me all that often, it was better for me to not be left alone in my own head.

Sighing, I plunked the bowl of Tía Gracy's latest cooking disaster on the table beside me.

*Wonder if the neighborhood cats might eat it.*

*Even they've got standards.*

"*Oye,* Mamacita, does Domenic work tonight?"

She glanced up from preparing her worktable for the next customer. "*No, mi vida.*" She glanced at the still full bowl and rolled her eyes. She didn't like Tía Gracy's cooking any more than I did, but we both knew she was trying her best to help, so it's not like we could say no to the chemistry experiments. "*Dame un momento* and I'll at least get you some toast before this next customer."

Shuddering, I draped my napkin over the bowl. "Don't worry about it—I'm not that hungry anyway. I can wait 'til Dom gets home." Because God love him, Mamacita's boy toy could cook stuff from the Old Country like no one's business.

Shifting on the sofa, I tried to get interested in the drama playing out on the TV, some crazy Spanish-language talk show where the host had bodyguards standing on either side of the stage because her guests were *those* kinds of whack jobs and she received death threats on a regular basis.

"Why don't you just watch Oprah?"

Mamacita glanced over her shoulder at the chair-throwing, hair-pulling chaos taking place between two big-haired, big-boobed chicks. Over a priest, apparently, who was watching the craziness from the safety of the green room.

"Too earnest. *Esta es picante.*"

"Huh—I'm not sure spicy's the word I'd use."

But Mamacita's mani/pedi customers lived for this stuff, so there was no changing the channel. For that reason, I tended to like the tarot customers better—flaky, maybe, but at least they were more about the soothing music. My gaze wandered away from the television and around the familiar room, looking for something else to grab my attention, feeling all the conflicting emotions beginning to churn away inside of me. Happy that I was home. Totally pissed off that I *had* to be here. That I'd be here for the foreseeable future, because at the minimum twelve weeks before I'd even be allowed to stand without using the walker.

Trapped.

My gaze landed on the tote bag sitting on the floor. Leaning, I was able to stretch just far enough to snag the handle of the bag, pulling it up beside me and rummaging through all the bits and pieces we'd dragged home from the hospital. Looking for some specific bits and pieces. Pulled the tin of chocolates out first, still wrapped tight, then reached in for the sketch pad, putting both on my lap and staring down at them. Wasn't sure if I was ready to deal with this just yet, but you know, it was one thing to feel helpless and trapped, but I'd be *damned* if I'd slide right into major pity party with a side of gutless wonder. Taking a deep breath, I lifted the cover and folded it back.

The first few sketches were familiar—the pictures of cartoon characters like Taz, of course, and Bugs, dressed as Carmen Miranda, and a funny-as-hell image of Pepé Le Pew as Romeo, trying to romance that poor cat huddled up on a balcony, clinging to the curtains.

Farther in, there were sketches of landscapes, different places—mountains, mesas, endless rolling fields with rows of wooden poles holding power lines disappearing off into the horizon. A huge, empty stadium, drawn from the highest row so the deserted vastness of the field and the sprawling, crowded city the stadium overlooked were equally visible. Even without the dates scrawled in the corner beneath the flamboyant "Taz" signature I would've known that these were drawings he'd done this summer as the teams traveled. The different places he'd been, so far from his home. I leafed through them again, feeling a tightness in my chest at how he was able to capture so much with so little—moody and distant at the same time that they felt incredibly intimate.

But that's not what he'd wanted me to see. I mean, maybe he did, but it wasn't what had had him putting his hand over mine and asking me to *please* wait. Because it would be too hard for him. About halfway through the book, after a couple of blank pages, I got to the first one. Then the next. And then one more.

Just three sketches. Of me. And I guess somehow, once he placed that sketch pad on my lap and told me to wait to look, I'd known. But you know, I'd also assumed they would be sketches of me dancing—in motion, doing what I'd once been so good at which was one reason I'd waited to look. Wasn't sure I was ready to see what I'd been. What had drawn him to me in the first place.

I was so unbelievably *wrong*. God, it would've been laughable if I didn't feel so much like crying.

One sketch was of me leaning against a bus, my hair twisted around one hand. Oh my God, *how*—? After all, we'd literally only just met. A fleeting exchange after he'd saved me from falling. Yet . . . there it was, incredibly vivid and so real. He'd even drawn the faintest rivulet of sweat rolling along my collarbone, immediately recapturing the heat and humidity—the exhaustion and adrenaline rush from that first performance.

The second one was a profile sketch, sitting on a bench, looking up at a mountain vista. Again, something he had to have done strictly from memory, because I recognized the closed-in feel of those mountains and how much I'd been missing the ocean. Remembered how we'd talked, the cocky soccer jock giving way to the boy who'd confessed he loved walking on the beach. Recognized the jacket I wore, the one that lay hidden at the bottom of a drawer.

But it was the third one that really hit me—hard and down low to where I doubled over. I must have made some noise, because through the roaring in my ears I heard, "*M'ijita,* are you all right?"

I grabbed the glass of cream soda I'd been working on and took a long drink. "I'm okay. Just . . . swallowed the wrong way."

Yeah. So not buying it. But she only pursed her lips and glanced down at the closed pad on my lap as she passed by on her way to the kitchen, taking the glass from my hand. *"Te traigo más."*

Giving me that moment alone she knew I needed. For once, I didn't question how she knew—was just grateful for it.

Slowly, I lifted the cover and found the page again. It was of me at the show in Missouri. The first time he'd seen me perform, "for real," as he'd put it. The only time. The drawing blurred momentarily, then cleared as I blinked. There I was, in my beautiful costume, the tiny rhinestones scattered across the bodice, the beaded rose winding its way down my arm, and captured in a few light, graceful lines, my tiny rose pin. But like in the other sketches, I wasn't moving. I was simply standing on the sidelines, eyes closed, and the way he'd drawn me—it was . . . indefinable.

With a few strong lines, he'd captured nothing but . . . me.

It was the last drawing in the book, but not the final thing. On the following page, a couple of scrawled lines:

*Con la sombra en la cintura ella sueña en su baranda. . . .*
—*García Lorca/Romance sonámbulo*

*With the shade around her waist she dreams on her balcony. . . .* Carefully, I closed the pad and slipped it into the bag I had attached to the front of my walker for carrying stuff around the house. Later on, when I hobbled back to my room, I'd hide it at the bottom of the drawer beneath the never-used-in-Florida sweaters, along with the jacket that still carried memories of mountains and shared confidences wrapped in the faintest hint of spicy cologne.

The chocolate, on the other hand?

I grabbed a corner of the plastic wrap and pulled. Hard.

# love is a losing game

Meds and chocolate could only do so much. Even good meds and even better chocolate. Yeah, they'd numb the pain for a while, but you always had to come down. And the pain always came back. I seriously got a genuine insight into how people wound up total junkies—continually scoring so they never *had* to come down. Never had to think all that much. If I hadn't been held captive there in Mamacita's workroom, dependent on her or Dom controlling my fixes—who knows what might've happened.

Day after day, propped on the sofa, pretending to be interested in a book or staring at the television with its mindless, never-ending chatter. Mustering up polite smiles and thank-yous for the well-meaning clients who'd bring me *pastelitos* and little gift baskets and saints' medals on plastic chains, never mind that I couldn't tell you who half of them were—and honestly didn't care.

Suffering through the clients who brought nothing more than

overly solicitous commentary with a really annoying overtone of criticism. A particular specialty of Latin American women of a certain age, shit like, "There, there, *m'ija*, things will look much brighter when you start moving around more," as if I was sitting there like a lump because I *wanted* to. Or, "So what are your plans now?" because God forbid I shouldn't be figuring out what to do with the rest of my life two seconds after it had fallen apart.

And my personal favorite, a couple of weeks after the surgery:

"Well, it's not as if you *really* expected to be a dancer forever, *verdad*? You would have met someone and that would've been it. You'll see—now you'll meet someone sooner, then once you have babies, trust me, *m'ija*, you won't have time to miss the dancing." Said with, *te lo juro*, this little *laugh*, like it was some hobby I'd been using to kill time until I started breeding. And I *had* met someone and . . . and . . .

Then, when the old battle-axe noticed me strangling a throw pillow, trying like crazy not to say anything, she actually had the nerve to lean down toward Mamacita, who was scrubbing her heels with a pumice, and say in a pseudo-whisper, "*Pero* she's a little high-strung, no? She'll have to work on that if she actually expects to find a *novio* who will put up with"—nodding at my leg—"the *other*."

Yet another reason to completely love my grandmother—she did at least take the time to dry off the woman's feet and cram her sequined flip-flops back on before she kicked her ass out the door and told her not to bother coming back.

And those were just my days. Bad as those were, there were at least . . . distractions—the sights and noises of day-to-day living acting like heavy theater curtains, muting what was going on in my head. The nights, though . . . . *God*. At night, the monsters felt free to come out to play, the dark and silence magnifying them to terrifying proportions.

I didn't know what I was going to do. I'd never thought about my life without dance—whatever form it took.

And more and more this summer, I hadn't been able to imagine my life without Jonathan. Even with all the questions and doubts, he'd become such a huge part of me, in such a short amount of time. But now he was gone. One minute I was grateful he was out of my life, the next missing him so much I felt like I was shriveling up into myself.

Then, as if I didn't have enough—there was the might-have-been named Taz. Just *thinking* of him pissed me off beyond all reason, and I couldn't figure out why I was so pissed off, which pissed me off even more. How *dare* he leave me with that sketch pad and nothing else? Just disappear, even if it's what I had wanted? Who knew what I wanted? Not like *my* judgment could be trusted—and you know, I just didn't have room for all of these damned "might haves" and "should haves" and "once upon a times."

I couldn't deal with lost promise and possibilities. With memories.

I had to get rid or them . . . had to start over—

Throwing back the covers, I hopped on my good leg over to my closet and grabbed my dance bag, stuffing it full of my shoes and as much dance gear as I could cram in there—the leotards and tights and cardigans and dance pants. Grabbed a nylon laundry sack for what wouldn't fit in the bag. Good thing I couldn't ever afford to be a diva—less to get rid of. Had room to add the programs and pictures and medals and the little gold shooting-star necklace. The battered copy of *Heartbreak Hotel* with its story of a girl defying expectations. Becoming more.

None of it—didn't want any of it. It wasn't me anymore. It would *never* be me.

Tying the straps of the bags to my walker, I started making my way, step by agonizing step, down the hall and out the front, trying my best to be quiet so Mamacita wouldn't hear. Sweat sliding down my back and stinging my eyes with each step across the porch and down the driveway, mixing with the tears, because it hurt . . . it all hurt . . . and I just . . . I couldn't. I *couldn't.*

The garbage cans were sitting at the end of the driveway but I was so tired, I couldn't even wrestle the lid open and keep my balance at the same time. The last straw. Me, who'd always had control of her body, didn't have the strength and coordination to open a stupid garbage can. Untying the knots holding the bags, I let them drop to the ground beside the cans, the dance bag falling on its side, shoes spilling out of the unzipped top. My sweaty hands slipping on the walker, I slid to the ground, Frankenleg extended out in front of me, looking like just another piece of mangled shit under the streetlight. I laughed into the dark humid night— laughed again when I got an answering bark from the neighbor's dog. Maybe they'd take me, too, when they came by to get all the rest of the trash in the morning.

Maybe it would've just been easier to cart it out to the concrete-block barbecue pit in the backyard and burn it. Just douse the mess of it in lighter fluid and torch the shit out of it. With my luck though, that's when we'd finally get a concerned citizen in the neighborhood, someone who'd smell the smoke and call 911. Hey, then I could add crazy arsonist to useless former dancer with no viable future to my list of accomplishments, right?

Dropping my head to my upraised knee, I laughed and hiccupped and cried until snot ran from my nose, joining the drool pooling in the corners of my mouth because I couldn't breathe anymore. And the thought that I was sitting there, *drooling*, of all things, made me laugh more until I started choking, pounding my fists on the sidewalk, the stinging hurt not even beginning to compete with what was going on inside of me.

That *fuck*, Jonathan—

Why?

*Why?*

"Soledad, what are you doing?"

I laughed again. "Putting out the trash, of course." I glanced up at Dom's blurry watery outline as he crouched beside me, holding a handkerchief to my face, his bike parked behind him. Hadn't even heard it approach. Had totally forgotten he was closing tonight, so of course he'd be cruising home at four in the morning, in time to catch me doing my best bag lady imitation. Just what he wanted to see after a long night of dealing with SoBe crazies, I'm sure.

He straightened my dance bag, tucked the shoes that had fallen out back inside. "I see that."

I watched him, the raging hurt and fury settling into a dull ache. "Doesn't matter, Dom." That ache even echoed in my words.

"Of course it does."

"*No*, it doesn't." And would he just leave it alone? Leave *me* alone?

"It will."

Of course he wouldn't. Italian was just another flavor of Latin. Whatever. It didn't matter as long as I didn't have to look at the evidence of my former life anymore.

I ground the heels of my palms against my eyes, feeling the burn and grittiness. "I'm just so damned tired, Dom."

His arms slid under my legs and around my shoulders. "I know, *cara bella*." He lifted me and I let my head fall to his shoulder.

Okay, so maybe sometimes these Latin take-charge types weren't all bad. Especially with the driveway looking like an endless journey from here. As he carried me up into the house, he kept murmuring in Italian. At first I thought it was just soothing stuff, trying to calm me down, since I was still hiccupping and sniffling into the handkerchief he'd shoved in my hand, but as I caught the occasional word that was close enough to Spanish for me to understand, I realized he was going on about the misery of first love.

"You, too?"

He nodded as he edged into my room, taking care to maneuver through the doorway so that my leg didn't hit anything.

"It sucks."

"It does," he agreed. "And I know you don't want to hear anything about how it will get better with time or how you'll know better when the real thing comes along. Truth is, sometimes it doesn't, and besides, who is to say that it wasn't the real thing?"

Setting me down on my bed, he disappeared for a minute, then returned with a small bowl of lemon gelato that he handed me along with a pain pill I gratefully swallowed. My little driveway field trip had left me with some hellacious throbbing action going on. I was going to be paying, and paying hard, for the next couple of days.

"But it got better for you."

"Yes. And no." He retreated to the doorway, leaning against the jamb.

"Thing is, Soledad, every time, it's different. The real thing—it evolves. Takes different forms. Sometimes you don't even recognize it when it comes back around because you're so busy looking out for what once was."

I leaned back against my pillows, seeing this guy in a whole new light. Beginning to be really grateful he was around, beyond the obvious fact that he made Mamacita happier than I'd ever seen her.

"When you feel things passionately, all the way down to the marrow of your bones, the memory of it still lives in you—like an echo—even if the original passion itself is dead. And just because you're young, it doesn't mean the passion is any less valid or intense. It might even be more so, because you're so much more open to the experience—haven't yet had opportunity to become a cynic." Crossing his arms, he half-smiled. "I won't lie—it makes for some long nights and shitty moments."

"Great," I sighed. "So much to look forward to."

"Ah, but you do have much to look forward to. When you experience it again, it's such a beautiful feeling, familiar yet new."

"I don't even know if I want it."

"Forgive me for sounding like your grandmother, but it's not like you have a choice, *cara*." He lifted a shoulder. "Love's really a bitch. It just has a way of finding you, whether you want it to or not."

# october

# the last goodbye

                                                                  October 25

Dear Soledad,

I know. A letter. Yeah, I finally understand what this letter stuff is about. How you have to think about what you want to say. I don't know if you noticed the return address (or if you even care), but I'm in Utah—at a clinic that Mom found for me to go . . . I don't know, I suppose you could say get better. Definitely a good place to figure out how everything got so unbelievably fucked up. I was inpatient for a while, when things were really bad, but they eventually cut me loose—sort of. I'm still being treated as an outpatient, but at least I don't feel so . . . trapped. At least, not physically.

If you haven't guessed by now, that is, if you haven't tossed this without reading, I'm writing as part of this getting better gig. In a way, recovering from a mental breakdown is a lot like breaking down a musical score—it's not just about melody, but *about countermelodies and rhythms and chord structure and key changes and God, I'm being a total wimp, stalling and talking about shit that isn't important.*

*We'll start with the basic stuff—answers to the easy questions. Mom's divorcing Dad. When she got going, she didn't screw around. She's here, too, doing her own version of getting better. Things between us aren't what you'd call great, lot of stuff to work through, but you know, when it finally counted, she came to bat for me—saved me, I guess, even if in the beginning I was more pissed at her for doing that, than grateful. Anyhow, it's somewhere to start. She knows I might not ever be able to completely forgive her for being such a doormat my entire life— but she's not looking for forgiveness. And there comes a point where I've got to take responsibility for myself and the choices I made. I guess what it comes down to in the end is trying to figure out how to go forward. Learn who we are as individuals and figure out how to be a mother and son without Marc Crandall being the thing that defines us.*

*Definitely a work in progress.*

*As for just me, well—no nerve damage, not that it matters. I'm not going to play again. I'll always love music, but it's not going to be about being a professional ever again. Thank God, actually. I think it'll be a relief to just enjoy music for itself, and damn, I'm rambling again, right?*

*All right—here goes.*

*I'm sorry, Soledad. I'm sorry I let my shit with my father get so far in my head that I <u>ever</u> doubted you. I'm sorry I didn't talk more to you—really talk. That I didn't trust myself or you—or us.*

*I'm sorry for what those stupid doubts and being so afraid I'd lose you drove me to do. That I got so fucked up I thought hurting you was the only way to keep you and God, I'm so damned* sorry we were in each other's lives this summer. That I wasn't any better than my father—pushing for what I wanted, no matter what—because you know, what I've been figuring out is it wasn't our time.

Don't get me wrong, I don't regret being with you. That's something I'll never regret. But as much as I once wished that we could've been each other's firsts, now, I just wish we could've loved other people first and come into each other's lives later. You could've been that beautiful girl I would have always carried a "what might have been" torch for and at some point, after ~~we'd~~ I'd done some growing up, I could have looked you up. Gotten to know you and let you get to know me. Like normal people. I like to think we still would've been perfect for each other—even more so, with some life experiences behind us, because honestly? I don't know if I'm ever going to find anyone I'll ever feel like is so perfect for me as you were.

Look, don't worry, I'm not going to turn into some bizarre creepy stalker guy, hovering around the edges of your life. Actually, I don't have a damn clue what I'm going to do after I leave Utah (we haven't gotten to that point on the therapy road, yet), but I promise, bugging you won't be part of it. I guess I could go to college and be a regular student, or maybe I'll just travel. Get a job. Be on my own, do more of that figuring out who I am stuff. That's my gig, though—not yours.

And yeah, I know I'll probably even find someone to love and make a life with at some point in the future. Maybe. Eventually. At least, that's what everyone keeps telling me and I don't know, I guess I can see that. Not like you only ever have one person you love in your life. But no matter what—you'll always be . . . the one, you know?.

At least for me.

*Unless I hear from you, this'll be the last time you hear from me. I promise.*

*Love,*

*Jonathan*

*P.S. I already know I probably won't hear from you, but—*

*~~God, I miss you so much~~*

# looking forward

"Should I not have given it to you?"

That was a new one from Mamacita—uncertainty. I glanced up from the single sheet full of small, neat handwriting—almost too neat, like he'd been so careful. Glanced down again at that last line, which wasn't so neat. More scrawled and sloping down at an angle, like it'd been written in a hurry, before he could lose his nerve, then scratched out even faster, because he'd lost his nerve.

"That's never been your style." I sighed and carefully folded the letter along the creases and slipped it back in the envelope. "Even when I was little, you played it completely straight with me about my mother and *abuelo* and, well . . . everything."

I fidgeted in my chair and rubbed my knee. It was always sore after a session with Gray, but much as he pushed and urged and worked me until I wanted to whimper like a little girl, I couldn't deny results were happening. I'd stood without a walker or crutches at seven weeks post-surgery instead of twelve and was down to wearing a flexible neoprene brace instead of the big technological monster. No more Frankenleg. Not unless you counted the scar that remained raised and angry-looking, even now. And even that would eventually fade.

"Any more mail?"

"In the workroom."

Given the post-workout wobblies, I didn't feel like taking chances, so before hauling myself to my feet, I grabbed the carved-wood walking stick Raj had given me the day after I stood on my own. He'd stuck with me this whole way, the crazy boy, insisting on joining me for every single workout session, because he *did* need to rehab that nasty broken ankle and we might as well suffer together. Such an unexpected gift he'd turned out to be.

"The mail is on the table by the sofa."

I eased myself onto the leather beast, but rather than look through the pile of catalogs and sales fliers, I unfolded Jonathan's letter. Read it again. Remembering. That "us against the world" feeling when the two of us were together and the tremendous sense of strength I'd once drawn from it. The power that came with knowing how much he cared.

"*Ese niño lindo* . . . he was so lost." Mamacita's fingertips brushed across the letter resting on my lap. "Don't you understand? It's why he reached out and grabbed on to you with both hands. You were *so* strong in who you were and what you wanted. He loved that—almost as much as he feared it. Feared that ultimately, you'd leave him behind."

With a deep sigh, I folded the letter once more and slipped it back into the envelope. "He maybe wasn't wrong about that. At least, to a certain degree."

That was beyond difficult to confess. But I couldn't deny that the offer from Señor Márquez—the pictures of my flamenco number from the senior showcase—had haunted me more than I wanted to admit. And I'd been so close to making the choice. To risk what Jonathan and I had on the dream of a lifetime. If we were meant to be together, we would've lasted. I honestly believed that. But it would have never lasted. Because he'd never given us a chance.

"But Jonathan took away my ability to choose." I stared out the window at the steadily falling rain. "How am I supposed to forgive that?"

"*No seas boba, nena,*" she snapped. "He's not asking you to forgive, is he?" she added, tapping an impatient finger on the envelope.

"No—I never said the boy was stupid. He knows that's impossible." Just like he knew we'd never be together again. No matter what he wished.

"And maybe he took away your ability to choose where you and he were concerned. But no matter what you think, he did not—and has not—taken away the ability to choose where *you* are concerned."

She reached past me to the table while I rolled my eyes. "*Oye, Mamacita—*"

"*Tranquílate.*"

Instead of handing me the deck she simply turned it over and began thumbing through the cards, obviously looking for something. When she found it, she pulled it out, holding it up.

"*¿Te acuerdas?*"

I nodded and shivered, looking at the Death card. Generally not a card one could easily forget—especially in this deck, the one with the lovers that she'd used so many months back. In this case, it was actually an incredibly beautiful, haunting card, depicting Pluto, god of the underworld, with Persephone. Now, you want to talk dysfunctional—

"It's the truest interpretation of this card, I think," she mused as she studied the image. "This myth of love and transformation and rebirth. Of what can happen when one resists change."

She set the card down on top of Jonathan's letter and went back to skimming through the deck. "After you went to bed that night, I pulled one more card."

I stared at the card she was holding up. *Desire?* Tristan and Isolde? And *their* tragic, ill-fated, crazy-making love affair? "Isn't that a little . . ." I chose my next word carefully, aware of the possibility of getting smacked upside the head. "Convenient?"

"In this deck, some of the cards go by different names. Traditionally, this card is known as the Chariot."

At my shrug, she looked heavenward with a long-suffering sigh. "Movement. Fate. Transition."

"And again, I repeat, *convenient?*"

*Now* I got the Evil Eye. "I'm just telling you what I saw, *m'ija.* Whether or not you choose to believe or what you do with the knowledge, that's up to you. Remember—"

"It's just a guide," I finished with her. "For what, though?"

"That's up to you, too."


A couple days later, I was perched on the Corolla's hood, swiping damp sand off my feet with a towel. First thing I'd done, once I'd been cleared to get back behind the wheel, had been to go straight to the beach and walk. Not far, but for just those few minutes— salty air and gritty sand and cool water—I felt more . . . *normal* than I had in months. And with Gray's blessing, I was able to go more and more often, increasing both time and distance.

You'd think I would spend all those long walks thinking, right?

Actually . . . no. Thinking was the *last* thing I did. The beach—it was a vacation from the normal noisiness inside my head. Replacing it with the sounds of perpetual construction and the incoming surf and seagulls squawking as they fought over scraps.

Normally I'd end my walks ready to go home and collapse, but today, though . . . today I was restless. "Sign I'm getting better, I guess," I muttered to myself as I slid behind the wheel. "Even as the talking to myself is a clear sign I'm losing it." I sighed, looking into the rearview mirror and brushing away the grains of sand that somehow always wound up around my hairline. Restless or not, I needed a shower. And who knows? Maybe that would be the thing to settle me down.

So explain to me why an hour and a half later, I was still driving around aimlessly? In and out of the parking lot of one of the big bookstores. Then the mall. And the movie theater. Until finally I pulled into a strip mall, slightly ratty around the edges, kind of like me at the moment.

Parking directly in front of one of the storefronts, I crossed my arms on the steering wheel and stared through the windshield.

*So. You gonna just sit there,* m'ija?

Pushing open that door was like stepping through a time portal. No, it wasn't fry-an-egg-hot outside, but the inside was still cool and damp, the smells wrapping around me still those of powdery rosin and warm, stale sweat, and still tickled the insides of my nose until I was rubbing at it. And as I slowly made my way across the small, carpeted lobby, that beautiful, long expanse of floor *still* called to me. Still looked as if it would go on forever and I knew, if I touched it, would still feel smooth and rich and alive.

I closed my eyes, feeling the tears stinging the corners of my eyes. I'd missed this—*so* much. As much as I knew I needed to be moving forward, I couldn't. At least, not without saying good-bye.

"It's about time, *chérie.*"

My head snapped up to find not only Madame, but a room full of little girls, maybe seven or eight years old, all lined up at the barre, staring at me skulking in the doorway. Madame was in standard dance drag: black leotard and pink tights, gray-streaked hair in a regulation bun. The little girls, in their own version of the same outfit, some of the leotards so faded they were shades of gray and brown, which let me know they were from Madame's stash of hand-me-downs. Same for some of the pink slippers, battered, with only the elastic across the tops of the feet looking new, because they'd been replaced more than once as they got stretched out. My throat tight, I saw myself at that age, staring back from each of those curious faces.

"Excuse me, Madame. I didn't mean to intrude."

*"Pah."* She waved her hand and sniffed. "I need your assistance. You know I do not normally take such large classes, but it was difficult to say *non.*"

"Uh . . ."

Her lean dancer's back already to me, she waved again. "I have slippers in my office. Get them."

I got them. You just didn't say *non* to Madame. Although what she thought I could do . . . She knew the extent of the injuries— had been one of my first visitors in the hospital and according to Raj, had terrorized the doctors every bit as much as Gray and Mamacita. Had called every couple of weeks, just to chat and see how I was feeling, but hadn't ever asked for me to return.

I thought maybe she didn't want me. But in her face, in that split second when our gazes had met, I'd seen just how stupid I was. How could I have *ever* thought that? It's just she understood— better than I had—this was something I had to come to on my own.

Going into her office, I opened the door to the closet where she kept spare dance gear and somehow wasn't at all surprised by what I found. There, on the top shelf—a familiar bag with a nylon laundry sack beside it. If I had to guess, I'd say Dom must have rescued them from the trash and asked Mamacita what to do. Of course Mamacita would opt to bring it all here. Reaching up, I pulled the bags down and poked around, unearthing a pair of soft slippers. And as I turned to leave the room, I saw, hanging from the small bronze Degas dancer posing on her desk, a delicate gold chain with a shooting-star pendant. Carefully, I lifted it off and slipped it around my neck, rubbing the tiny star as I returned to the studio and took a place at the end of the barre.

Realistically speaking, I was going to have to be extremely careful—but it was a beginner class, everything going slow, with Madame moving down the line, taking her time to correct the position of a foot or an arm. When she came to me, she knelt and with her familiar, gentle touch smoothed her hands down my legs, skimming over the brace to my feet, arranged in a modified first position—as far as I could go without strain.

"That's it, *ma petite*. Feel what your body can do—listen to it. Trust in it, and it will learn to listen to you once again. And you'll be as beautiful as you ever were."

march

# my heart was home again

*Turning, soaring, feeling the hum of the strings like a caress along my skin, the notes from the brass and woodwinds swirling around my body like a cape. The percussion throbbing beneath my feet, urging me to turn faster, leap higher and farther, to push my body to its absolute limits—to reach for the heavens.*

*The beautiful movements set to music—swathed in graceful tulle and flowing satin, the stories played out on the stage for an audience held under a spell.*

*No better feeling in the world.*

*At least, that's what I used to believe.*

I read the final passage over, tried to reach past the emotion and tension so I could be objective and critical about it. Right. Like I could ever be objective about this—and the assignment had been to compose something that spoke to a very personal experience.

This was personal. So maybe the last sentence was sort of ambiguous, but it was a creative writing exercise. I figured we had a little leeway with ambiguous. I printed a copy and put it in my notebook, ready for tomorrow's class. And please, God, don't let Mr. Delgado ask us to read out loud.

Now, for part two of the homework assignment.

You know, when I'd read over the Freshman English class outline and seen there was a fair amount of creative writing involved, I was actually pretty jazzed. That was, until I realized part of the creative writing process was journaling, and I nearly turned tail and ran. Because God's honest truth was I hadn't had the nerve to crack my journal since last summer. Was terrified to get sucked into that world, reliving every moment. Was afraid I'd find myself analyzing every word and phrase and obsessing over what, exactly, might have set Jonathan off.

And writing in a new journal? Equally nerve-wracking. I mean, who knew *what* might come out if I let my subconscious free to play?

Okay, yeah . . . total coward. But I could do this. I had to.

I pulled the wrapping from around a pristine new book, inhaling the distinctive smells of leather and fresh paper. Folding back the cover, I wrote my name on the inside, then stopped, the blank expanse of the first page reminding me of an empty stage.

Slowly, I lowered my pen to the paper and started writing.

And writing.

And writing some more . . .

"*Soledad, presta atención, m'ija, por favor—*"

The pen skidded off the page, leaving a purple trail before landing under my desk. Leaning over, I fished it out, then straightened to find Mamacita glaring at me from the open doorway.

"Pay attention to what?"

"I have been calling you and calling you—did you not hear me?"

Guess my face was acceptably blank, since she just sighed and looked toward the heavens.

"The phone? It was ringing—with a call—for you." Her gaze ranged around the room, ending at the handset sitting on the night table. Hadn't heard a thing, I *swear*.

"I was busy?"

"Ah." Exasperation turned to an understanding smile. "You know, you did not study this hard even for your favorite classes in high school."

"I know. Weird, huh? But I guess I feel like there's more on the line now." I stroked the smooth, dark brown leather cover of my journal, stretching my cramped fingers at the same time. Lot to write about. Hadn't even realized how much until I got going.

"So . . . the phone?"

"Oh, that." She waved her hand. "I told him you would call back."

"Who him? Gray, Raj?"

"No." She shook her head and came all the way into the room. *"Pero un muchacho chévere."* And with a smile that could only be called mysterious . . . wait, no, *enigmatic*—she handed me a piece of paper, then turned and left the room, gently closing the door behind herself.

"Wait—who? What?" But the door was already closed and there was no getting her back in here, and what was up with the "good guy" comment? I hadn't heard her use that word since—

*Oh, no . . . please, God, don't let it be . . .*

*Come on, be real. There's no way Mamacita would've copped that look if it was Jonathan.*

Okay, then. Okay. Right. No need to panic. I glanced down at the piece of paper.

### *Rafael Fernández*

Um, who?

I didn't know any Rafael Fernández. At least I didn't think I did, and I know I didn't recognize this number, although it was local digits.

*What* was she up to? I hoped to God it wasn't a blind date. Talk about the last thing I needed.

*She'll hound you until you call, so you might as well just get it over with.*

*Argh.*

I grabbed the receiver and punched in the numbers, muttering, "She must be out of her mind. No matter how much *she* says I need to get out and experience life and grow as a person—"

"*¿Hola?*"

I pulled the phone away from my ear and stared at it, then brought it up again in time to hear, "Hello . . . Soledad?"

"Taz?"

"I hope I am not interrupting. Your *abuela* said you might be busy and that she would have you call me back."

"Taz?"

"Yes, it is me. I promise." He laughed, just a little cocky, and with that laugh I could *see* him, plain as day—standing there, big smile with the white teeth and the tiny little dimple that hid in the corner of his mouth. How he'd looked, staring down at me, holding my hand against his chest, those dark eyes shiny as he let me see what was in his heart.

But I hadn't been ready and he'd known it and he'd walked away—and God, he was so incredibly brave.

"Taz . . ." I sniffled, and of *course* I wouldn't have any Kleenex handy. Yanking open my bedroom door, I crossed the hall to the bathroom and pulled toilet paper off the roll, wadding it up and swiping it under my nose.

"*No, Soledad, por favor, no . . .*" His voice was super soft and made me feel even more like he was right there, right next to me. "Please do not cry."

"I'm not crying," I wailed, sinking down to sit on the edge of the bathtub. "And who's Rafael Fernández and . . . and . . . *how . . .*" And this was *so* not how I wanted to play this. I'd thought if, by some miracle, the "next time" he'd promised back at the hospital ever actually happened, the first thing I'd do was apologize. For resenting him for not being hurt, when I was falling apart. For sending him away. Tell him how I'd wished, so many times, I hadn't had to send him away, but hopefully he'd understand why I'd felt I needed to—even if it meant I might not ever see him again.

And I had really, really wanted to see him again.

*So tell him, genius. Instead of going all mental, tell him.*

But he beat me to the punch.

"I have moved to the United States," he said in Spanish. His voice was still soft, like he was trying not to scare me. "I'm going to school here now. Starting in May, actually, but I came over early in order to get settled in. Learn the city and—"

"You're in Miami?" My head was spinning and I couldn't even blame it on high altitudes.

"*Sí.*"

"Going to school?"

"*Sí*—at Florida International University. The architecture program. A useful way for me to put my drawing skills to use, *verdad*?"

"But . . . soccer?"

"My time with the team was over—" He sounded casual, like, no big. "I turned twenty-one in November."

"But . . . weren't you going to go pro?" Raj *swore* there would be contracts waiting for him, and the way he'd played—it was like art. Why wouldn't he—

"There were a few offers, but they did not interest me."

"*Why?*"

"Did I never tell you what my *papi* always said to me?"

"Uh . . . no. We never got past your *mamá* and trusting your feelings."

"My *papi* always told me to have a backup plan in place because *Dios sabe cómo la vida se puede cambiar*," he intoned in a dad-like voice. "And I saw for myself how quickly life could change—in a moment."

With me, I was guessing. "But—you're *such* a good player."

"You really are not that familiar with the sport, are you?" He laughed, the sound of it rich and warm, yet it had me shivering. In a good way. "I am good, yes, but there are a hundred other players in Spain alone who are as good as I am, or better. I could have turned professional, but I would have been a mid-level player, at best. Besides, I promised my parents that even if I went professional, I would also get my university degree." His voice was a quiet hum over the connection. "It was an easy promise to make. I never wanted my entire life to revolve around one thing. I always wanted more. So I visited schools in almost every city to which we traveled. Including Miami."

"Why? But I mean . . ." I tried to organize my jumbled thoughts into something that made sense. "Why the U.S.? Why not a school at home?" And could I be playing any more twenty questions?

"Here, I can have the best of both worlds. In America, I'm a *very* good player—good enough to have schools fighting to give me . . . *¿cómo se dice?* A full ride? Just for playing *fútbol.*"

I hugged my free arm around my midsection, remembering Jonathan and that full ride that had been anything but.

"Yeah," I said. "Full ride. And you chose FIU?"

"It is a good team. They had an architecture program I liked. Miami is a comfortable fit for me. And you were here, Soledad. At least, I hoped you would still be here."

Every muscle in my body was going so wobbly, I could barely keep my balance on the edge of the tub as I tried to piece together everything he was telling me. "So . . . who's Rafael Fernández and why did you use his name?"

"Actually . . . that is me."

*"What?"* I slid off the edge of the tub and landed on the floor, my ass stinging as it made contact with the tiles.

"Baltazar Rafael Fernández—" I could hear the deep breath he took, even over the phone. His voice went even softer as he admitted, "I was afraid if I said Taz—if you knew it was me—you would not call back."

Letting me see inside again. Letting me know just what it meant to him.

"I would have called back." Time for some admitting of my own. "I almost e-mailed your team in Spain a couple of times. To try to find you."

"You did?"

I rolled my eyes a little because just like that, it was back—that sound in his voice that reminded me of a peacock. He just couldn't help himself, and it *was* cute. In small doses.

"Yeah, I did." And I would tell him all the reasons why I'd wanted to, and the reasons why I'd chickened out. I'd tell him all of it. Eventually. But at the same time, you know, I really wanted *eventually* to start as soon as possible.

"Where *are* you?"

Another one of those soft, warm laughs. "I thought we already went through this—in Miami."

"No, *cabrón,* I mean, where are you *now*? When can I see you?" And glared at the phone as he kept laughing. Forget *cabrón*— *pendejo* was maybe the better term. Or just smart-ass.

Finally, he quit laughing enough to say, "Come outside."

Good thing I was still on the floor. Wasn't sure my ass could take another meeting with those tiles. "What?"

Nothing.

"Taz? What do you mean come outside? *Taz*?"

The phone went dark, a teasing wink.

He couldn't possibly mean . . . could he? No way. We needed time to work up to this. Or *I* needed time. At least to make sure my hair was brushed.

Screw it. I didn't even bother checking in the mirror to see what I looked like. Just left the bathroom and walked down the hall to the living room, past Dom and Mamacita cuddled on the sofa with their evening wine and cheese. As I blew past, she smiled and said, "*Muchacho chévere,* right?"

And something about that smile and how she said the words stopped me dead in my tracks. Flashing back to pulling the cards and having her tell me he was *un muchacho chévere.* Saying there had been a reason she'd been compelled to choose the deck with the beautiful illustrations of lovers throughout the ages. Of course, I'd thought she meant Jonathan, because I was so full of him that night. It'd been the night he first proposed my becoming

Carmen—starting this wild, twisting, painful, and—yes—even beautiful journey. That night, I couldn't have possibly imagined it being anyone else.

But it hadn't been Jonathan. Standing there, in the middle of my living room, one simple realization smacked me upside the head with this brilliant clarity, like one of those vintage neon signs plastered on the deco hotels in South Beach: Jonathan really had been a decent guy. He certainly hadn't been *bad*—not at heart. But maybe because of his impossible situation, everything he'd ever done—even when it was supposed to be for me—had really been, if I was completely honest, for him.

But Taz . . . Everything he'd done where I was concerned really was for me. Even if on the surface it was all about him. Coming to the United States on a full soccer scholarship and choosing, out of all the schools that wanted him, one in Miami. No doubt he'd weighed all his options and of course he was probably going to be a total Big Man on Campus, or at least on the soccer team, the way he played, and he'd love the attention, but he'd told me, he'd made his choice with me—with *us*—in mind.

And giving me his sketch pad—allowing me into that most private corner of his soul. Opening himself so I could understand how he saw me. What he saw in me.

Taz might be full of surface flash, but underneath . . . his heart and soul were real and true . . . and good.

*Chévere.*

*God, I'm clueless. It's a miracle I can walk upright.*

"I don't care how you knew—" I glared and pointed at my grandmother. "There is *no* way you could have possibly known."

And all she did was lift one delicate shoulder. "Rafael. He's the patron saint of love, you know."

"No . . . travelers," I replied, recalling Taz playing with the medal on his chain. Explaining his mother had given it to him as protection.

She waved off my correction. "Rafael's an archangel, *mi vida*. A bit of a multitasker. So yes, travelers, but also young people, happy meetings . . . love—" Then she smiled that blasted enigmatic smile that I only caught a flash of because, forget it—she could school me on patron saints and angels and what*ever* later. I needed to get outside. Needed to see, and oh—catch my breath because . . .

There he was. Across the street, leaning against a shiny sports car, *of course*. Wearing faded jeans and a T-shirt, and smiling, and you know, it was just the best thing I'd ever seen, especially the closer I got. Close enough to see that tiny, curved dimple and those dark eyes that brought to mind laughter. And chocolate.

"You cut your hair."

He ducked his head, the curve of his neck looking strong but kind of vulnerable at the same time, and ran both hands through his hair, making the short strands stick up, wild and spiky. The distinctive streak was gone, replaced by a patch of silver, right at his hairline, with random silver strands scattered throughout the jet-black.

"It was time for change."

"Big change."

He nodded, knowing I meant more than the hair, then asked, "And you? Your *abuela* said you were probably doing homework."

"Yeah, I'm going to college, too," I said quietly, breathing in something that hadn't changed—that warm-spice cologne that was totally his. "Maybe you'll think I'm crazy, but I decided I wanted to learn how to run a not-for-profit. Something with the arts—for kids. So I'm getting a business degree." I laughed. "And an English degree, too. That's just for me. And because clearly, I *am* crazy."

"I think that is wonderful." His smile just lit up his whole face, like he was as jazzed by the crazy notion as I'd been, when it first occurred to me a few months back, during a long, "time to consider your future," kick-in-the-ass talk with Gray. "Not crazy at all."

"You might want to hold back on thinking that." I took a deep breath. "I'm also back with the corps again, Taz. Gray offered me a job and it's good hands-on experience—learning how to run that kind of organization."

This was kind of a big step to be taking right now. A confession that could potentially backfire. But it had to be done. I'd decided, in that short walk from my bathroom to where I stood in front of him—no secrets, no holding back. If there was anything I'd learned, it was that.

"And what about—" He shifted slightly, side to side, that endearingly familiar, nervous habit.

"He's gone, Taz. Far away from here. I doubt he'll ever come back."

Releasing a deep breath, he reached out, taking my hands, his hold loose but still warm and comforting. "It would not matter if he did."

Not a question. Just a statement of fact. And it sent the most amazing sense of calm combined with anticipation rushing through me. Like nothing I'd ever felt before.

"No." I tilted my head back slightly—just enough so I could look up into his eyes and smile. "It really wouldn't."

After one of those wonderful moments—sharing an entire conversation in a single glance—he pulled away just far enough to lean through the open window of the car. A second later, music. . . . Slow, romantic piano. Some strings. Weaving together in a sweet, heart-tugging melody that drifted from the speakers, gradually filling my body like it was sinking in straight through my pores and waking something up deep inside. That piece of my soul I'd been so sure had died, that was all about letting someone in. But I guess it had just been dormant. Waiting for the right moment to come back to life, all hot-pins-and-needles sensation just beneath my skin.

Waiting for the right person.

I swallowed hard. "You know, it's really stupid to leave your keys in the ignition in Miami."

He lifted my hands to his shoulders, leaving them there as his fingertips trailed down my arms, goose bumps rising in their wake. "You can teach me all the customs." And oh . . . the palms of his hands were *so* warm against my cheeks. "Later."

"Later?" One of my hands wandered over to his neck, exploring the exposed length of it and making him arch into it, like he wanted more.

"We have so much time, Soledad."

His lips brushed against mine, as soft as his breath on my skin. "But for right now—" One hand took mine while the other dropped to my waist, drawing me close.

And we danced.